By ANA RAINE

ANIMA
Hidden Wings
Captive Wings

Published by DREAMSPINNER PRESS
www.dreamspinnerpress.com

Captive Wings

ANA RAINE

DREAMSPINNER
PRESS

Published by
DREAMSPINNER PRESS

5032 Capital Circle SW, Suite 2, PMB# 279, Tallahassee, FL 32305-7886 USA
www.dreamspinnerpress.com

This is a work of fiction. Names, characters, places, and incidents either are the product of author imagination or are used fictitiously, and any resemblance to actual persons, living or dead, business establishments, events, or locales is entirely coincidental.

Captive Wings
© 2018 Ana Raine.

Cover Art
© 2018 Blake Dorner.
blakealexanderart@gmail.com
Cover content is for illustrative purposes only and any person depicted on the cover is a model.

Trade Paperback ISBN: 978-1-64080-263-6
Digital ISBN: 978-1-64080-264-3
Library of Congress Control Number: 2017919798
Trade Paperback published May 2018
v. 1.0

Printed in the United States of America
∞
This paper meets the requirements of
ANSI/NISO Z39.48-1992 (Permanence of Paper).

Thank you to everyone at Dreamspinner
for their patience and dedication,
but also to Thomas for letting me bounce off ideas
until headaches ensue.

CHAPTER ONE

THE TREES within the parameters of the Pasky Nature Reserve used to breathe, a crescendo of sounds so vivid and colorful there was no denying they were as alive as the unsuspecting humans who lived in the surrounding Canadian wilderness.

A single month had passed since the Sidhee demons had come from their world to ours. Their campaign to take over the Dryma fairies and subdue the Kuro swans had ended with lives lost on all sides. A single month and yet... the forest looked like there had never been an inkling of life.

The Dryma souls were contained within individual trees, so when the Dryma and Kuro had been taken back into the demons' world to serve as slaves, the magic in the woods ceased to exist. Which was exactly why the Kuro had been made into their slaves and forced to protect the twisted bark and winding branches.

For so long, I had believed the Dryma needed the trees, but it had never occurred to me how desperately the trees may have needed them.

I removed my glove, exposing my pale hand to the chill December air, and pressed my hand to the trunk of a tree. Because I was the Prince of the Kuro, I'd been expected to keep detailed maps of which tree belonged to whom and make sure they were protected at all times by one of the few members of my dying tribe. Those who had gotten away were finally able to feel the tear of their skin as their inky wings jutted between their shoulder blades. But most of my kind had been taken prisoner.

Sighing, I counted to ten, begging internally to feel the faintest of thumps from the tree. The faintest trace of life I could hold on to.

I refused to believe in the finality of what the Sidhee demons had done.

Giving in to the unmistakable truth, I let my arm fall to my side and accepted the fate of the empty carcass rooted in front of me.

"Kanji? Where are you?"

I tried to project my thoughts to Seth's mind, but because he wasn't a Kuro, the words never reached him. "Over here."

I saw his short reddish-brown hair darting between what was left of the swooping branches before Seth appeared. He was wearing the tight blue jacket and black pants he had worn as part of his Dryma guard uniform, but I knew he was just trying to keep his sanity by pretending he was still in control. The empty look on his tanned face already gave me an answer.

"You couldn't find Joel?"

"No."

There had been a time when Seth had been one of the many dutiful guards who served under Christophe, a red-haired Dryma who had refused to release me. The fight was still a blur in my mind because my only concern had been for my mate, Prince Tristan.

Thinking of his flaxen hair spun like gold and round emerald eyes nearly brought me to my knees with longing. I'd been away from him for too long already in our attempt to find other Dryma or Kuro who might've escaped.

"We can come back tomorrow," Seth said before carefully stepping over the dark roots as though they still could feel.

"This is our second time this week," I replied, feeling the ache in my throat where the cold was seeping into my lungs. "It would be too risky to come again so soon."

Seth's expression told me he would come back regardless. "How can you be so spineless? Joel stayed and fought and was taken prisoner."

"And unless we can find a way into the Sidhee world, we have no way of reaching him or the others."

Seth narrowed his eyes and if I hadn't been the mate of his beloved prince, he might've tried to kill me. "You are a Kuro, and now you have your wings back. Can't you just fly there like you used to?"

"When we served the Sidhee, we only left and entered their world with one of the demons." My heart constricted, reminding me to return to my comatose mate's side. "I'm sorry, Seth. Joel is my friend too, you know?"

The main reason I let Seth berate me was because he was right. While I'd saved my mate and a few of the Kuro who were now in hiding, most of my kind was gone. The elders, who could no longer fly, including my aunt Catherine, had been sent down south in an attempt to heal their dying bodies. Those who had fought were the same as me, sinewy pale creatures stretched over china-white bone.

Whenever I saw Tristan's chest rise and fall, the only indication he was still living, I felt justified in my actions. But there was no denying I was selfish and cruel, not worthy of being a Kuro prince.

"I wonder what Joel would think of you abandoning him."

Although Seth and Joel were lovers, they were not mates according to our ancient rites. Only Kuro could be mates to each other, which was something I should've realized when mating to Tristan. The blood he'd gotten from his Kuro mother was what kept him alive.

"Joel chose to stay with the children he cares for," I whispered, feeling the dead crunch of frosted leaves beneath my feet. They snapped like tiny bones. "Including Chiaki, our healer."

Seth made a strangled noise in the back of his throat, but stomped past me in an effort to get to the river where we could fly. Chiaki and his mate, Aiden, had only been sixteen, but finding them was my best chance at saving Tristan.

"Where are you going?" Seth demanded. I could hear impatience dripping from his voice and knew why. He didn't have to take orders from me and could leave when he wanted to, but he was as trapped as I was.

"You know where," I replied, scraping the mud from beneath my boots as I headed to the most sacred spot in the forest. "The same place I always go."

"There's no point...." Seth let his voice trail away and for a moment, I thought he would abandon me. But then there was the clunky sound of his boots as he followed.

Positioned on the edge of a cliff overlooking the tumultuous lake was a single tree. The branches were entwined, dripping with hues of gold and amber, refusing to submit to winter and concede their color. My heart hammered against my ribs, my slight, lanky body swaying from the force.

So many trees had been reduced to chalky, starving skeletons. The Dryma were fierce warriors, but the weakest among them were dismissed so easily.

Standing as proof to the strength of their kind was the willowy tree refusing to die. Out of respect, I pressed only my fingertips to the ashy bark. Softly, like a quiet whisper of a dying relative, came the sound of the faint beating, a sound I would know even if I had been in the deepest of comas.

My mate's heart still beat, even though he had tried to sacrifice himself after revealing he was half Kuro. Our wings had been contained within him and even though I could feel the stretch of dark feathers between my shoulder blades, the loss of Tristan at my side was much worse than any enslavement.

"I know you don't talk about what happened that day, not even to your kind." Seth didn't understand the respect needed for this tree and barreled onto the cliffside like he was claiming a road. "But tell me. Tell me how you managed to save my brother after he stabbed his tree."

I allowed my eyes to close, the reprieve just enough to let me breathe. My black hair was silky and slipped through the hair tie I'd used, the strands slapping against the skin of my neck like a violent whip.

"The flowers."

"What?"

I turned to look at Seth, who had a dumbfounded expression across his face. "The flowers Tristan had been working on in order to save your kind. I transferred his life into it."

"If that is the answer, why aren't we collecting these flowers?"

"Tristan was half Kuro…. I think the only reason the flower was enough was because only half of him needs to be connected to the earth."

My hand fell away from the tree, as heavy as a river stone.

"The others will be expecting us," I whispered.

My toes dangled over the edge of the cliff, and I wondered what would happen if I just kept falling. If my wings would refuse to aid me because they could sense how much of a traitor I was. Time was limited, but I had to find a way to save both my mate and our kind. As if to confirm the coward I was, before my body could slam into the rocky waves, my wings protruded and lifted me away from what remained of our home.

CHAPTER TWO

FOR YEARS, the Dryma had grown weary of having to be protected by my kind, but because they could not detach themselves from the trees, the leaders had decided to join the Sidhee on equal terms. Perhaps that plan would've succeeded had I not interfered and gone to Tristan's side dressed as the Sidhee prince.

There was no taking back what I had done, but the long, cold flight back to where we were hiding gave me time to reflect on what I could've done differently. Tristan had been willing to marry Prince Calhoun of the Sidhee, a deformed monster with eyes the color of blood.

It had been me who stopped him.

Yet another reason my shame was overwhelming.

Before the Sidhee attack, my kind had lived just outside the Pasky Nature Reserve in a decaying mobile community. If the paper-thin walls weren't enough of a prison, being trapped within our own bodies and incapable of flight certainly was.

Now we had sought refuge in a cluster of abandoned cabins near a river meant for canoeing and tubing. On one side of a dirt road were the six cabins Seth had claimed for his kind, all empty. On the other side, the remaining six cabins were lined up in a jagged row on the deteriorating hill.

Set farthest away from the other log cabins was the one Tomas and Zain had chosen for Tristan and me. All in all, there were just over twenty of us, mostly males who had escaped the fight. I offered to let them sleep in my cabin, but Zain refused to budge on the matter.

It was like being in our mobile home all over again. Even if there was nothing to hold on to, my position as prince was always honored.

"You're back. It's about time," Tomas grumbled as he tossed the hot dog buns he was in the process of opening onto a frosted picnic table. "I was starting to think he finally betrayed you."

Without a backward glance, Seth kept his shoulders proudly raised and marched to the cabins on the other side of the campground. It wasn't until his rigid back was out of view that Zain appeared in the doorway, his hands full of uncooked meat.

We'd retreated with what money we had, but Zain had just gotten creative in his use of hair dye. His short hair always had a few strands of color no matter what the occasion. He raised his hand in salute, the dark red of his mitten matching the single strand of color standing out like a beacon.

"Quit berating him," Zain ordered gruffly.

Kuro swans are naturally thin and tall with dark hair and blue eyes. Because we had still been unable to fly to warmer climates, our skin was like bleached paper. Tomas had always pretended to be human and usually bleached his hair white so he looked like an albino. But with our funds lacking, he had impossibly dark roots.

After setting the meat down on the table, Zain went to his battered yellow Jeep and pulled out a heavy quilt. "It's been getting colder, Kanji. Take this."

"What about the others?"

Zain narrowed his eyes but didn't respond. "Your mate needs this."

Although Zain understood how important Tristan was to me and would never challenge his right to be my mate, he never referred to him as anything other than "your mate." As though saying his name would finalize his place in the tribe.

"Kanji, you're back."

At fifteen, Micky was one of the younger Kuro who had been forced to serve the Dryma. His hair was tangled around his face, and his boots were caked in mud. In his arms were bundles of wood that he set down next to the fire pit. "Did you find anyone?"

Micky always asked the same question, but I knew he just wanted to know if I'd found Joel. After his parents had died, Joel had offered Micky a place in his home. The house had been small, but several kids were eternally grateful to Joel.

"No luck," I admitted.

Tomas brushed stray twigs from the wooden bench of the picnic table, but instead of sitting, he offered the seat to me. Reluctantly, I glanced at the lone cabin concealed within the towering landscape of trees before collapsing.

As if sensing my anguish, Micky said, "Before I went to get wood, I was sitting with him. And now Shinji is."

"Any change?" The words felt like thick bark twisting around my vocal cords.

"No," Zain responded. "We would've called you."

Micky's hand was resting on the bench beside mine, a small pale hand caked in so much dirt he looked like a porcelain doll that had been thrown away. The way his clothes hung from his body certainly didn't help.

"Your aunt called," Zain mentioned casually as though he were talking about seeing a frog by the creek. "She says the elders can no longer phase. They tried, really, they did, but they are human now."

I felt my stomach sink to the rocky ground. "Even though our wings have been freed?"

"Too much time passed."

"We should've killed the Dryma when we had the chance," Tomas said angrily as he threw a hot dog onto the metal grill laid over the fire pit. He threw the meat with too much force and it bounced off the hot iron and landed in what was left of the grass.

"Have some respect," Zain howled, standing up so quickly the food slid from his lap. If the meat hadn't been covered in plastic, we would've been eating rice for dinner again. "Our prince's mate is a Dryma."

"Guys, stop fighting," Micky pleaded quietly.

Curious faces had started to poke out from the cabins and from the surrounding woods where they had been on patrol. I could see the gaunt shape of their faces and the hollows of their eyes like I was looking at a scene the grim reaper himself had painted.

I was only twenty-six, but those older than me obeyed my command.

I choked on my own breath, the taste bitter and deformed in the crevices of my mouth.

"He's also a Kuro," Tomas argued. "And isn't that what matters?"

"For all we know, he's also one of the only Dryma princes left."

I could hear their thoughts swarming in my mind, a mix of tense fury and fear. If I didn't stop their words, things would be said. Things I wasn't strong enough to hear.

My feet were taking me away from the picnic bench before I had time to grasp my bearings. My only thought was to get to Tristan. I knew how loyal my kind were to me, especially Zain and Tomas, but there was a biting fear locked within my heart that told me what they were truly capable of.

In the time I'd been gone, what if their words had turned lethal? Leaning heavily against the wooden door to my cabin, I wiped sweat from the back of my neck and twisted my hair into a knot at the base of my skull.

I was sure I smelled of death and decay, but I couldn't shower until I was inside. The cabin was filled with candles, the kind Chiaki always made. But without his healing touch, they only offered natural light.

"How is he?" I whispered, pulling my boots from my feet so I wouldn't drag the grime of the world in with me.

Shinji was the same age as Micky, but he had seen so much less, and his wide-eyed look gave him away. Standing abruptly, he knocked over a plastic cup that had been teetering on the arm of the couch in the small living area.

With alarm in his eyes, he glanced at the dark curtain separating the bedroom from the rest of the cabin. Tristan didn't make a sound apart from his heavy, regulated breathing.

"He got cold earlier, so I gave him an extra blanket," Shinji said, nervously shuffling from foot to foot.

It had been so long since the Kuro had their wings, but even longer since their prince had had a true mate. No wonder Shinji appeared panicked. Having to care for the second-most important member of the tribe couldn't be easy.

"Tomas started some food." I sighed, shrugging from my jacket and hanging it on the hook beside the door. "Go and tell him I said you and Micky can eat first."

He pulled a knit cap over his short hair. "Are you sure?"

"Yes."

"I'll bring you something. What would you like?"

If it were even possible, I was thinner than before the Sidhee attacks. I could already imagine what Tristan would say when he saw how malnourished I was. "Just a burger."

Without another word, Shinji disappeared, almost forgetting his coat in the process.

The bathroom was too tiny to accommodate a mirror, so the only looking glass was hung above the sink in the kitchenette. I caught a glimpse of myself. I'd only been wearing a coat so I would be able to fly without ripping a shirt, so I could see the harsh outline of my shoulder blades and the definition of my spine. Tristan deserved more than a skeleton to hold when he woke up.

On second thought, I should've asked Shinji to bring me as much food as he could carry.

I vigorously washed my hands before brushing the curtain away and entering the dimly lit room where Tristan was sleeping. Originally, there had been a set of bunk beds in the corner, but Zain and Tomas had helped me move them to another cabin so every Kuro could have a place to sleep. All that remained was the queen bed pressed against the right wall and then an empty space on the left where I'd been keeping our clothes.

"Hey, Tristan," I whispered.

Even in his sleep, Tristan was an image from fairy tales. When humans imagined fairies, I knew he was what they were seeing. His long dark lashes rested on the top of his cheeks, his mouth slightly parted as he drew breath. His defined jaw was absent of facial hair, but he didn't look like a child.

Only slightly taller than me, he had broader shoulders, and his hands could cover my chest effortlessly. But his most striking feature was his emerald eyes, a color I longed to see again.

I brushed his golden strands from his face and pressed my palm to his forehead. The cabin wasn't meant for winter use, so the only source of heat was an old space heater we'd found.

Perched delicately on the small nightstand was Tristan's flower, silently hovering above a small bowl of lake water taken from Pasky Nature Reserve. Despite my many efforts to adjust the flower's position, Tristan refused to wake up.

When there was nothing waiting for him apart from me, I couldn't really blame him.

But the anguish was enough to kill me.

"Please, please come back," I begged quietly, resting my head on the stale sheets. The linen was cool to the touch but couldn't compare to the icy fist wrapped around my heart.

His hand was heavy and limp on the top of my head, but at least it was something tangible.

WHEN I awoke, the cabin was dark. Apart from the few lingering candles flickering in the living area, there was only the color of night to keep me company. There was a hamburger on a paper plate next to me, so I assumed it was Shinji who had blown out the other candles.

After stretching, I rummaged through my bags until I found a heavy turtleneck and pulled it over my head before grabbing my coat. My teeth rattled like bones and my limbs felt as stiff as glue. Checking Tristan's pulse, I let out a breath after confirming it was normal.

The burger tasted like sulfur, but I still downed the meal. My intention had been to throw the garbage out into the dumpster located behind the cabins, but I couldn't stop my legs from carrying me toward the lake.

Cool air assaulted my lungs, suffocating me. I was only wearing my turtleneck, pants, and boots, so the wind pierced my skin like thousands of needles, but I couldn't stop.

Just down the dirt path was where campers could bring their RVs, back when there had been a campground. Nestled in a tiny alcove was the mouth of the river, surrounded by woods and tiny pebbles scattered like glass marbles.

There was enough light from the stars for me to clearly see the way the leaves spun in the water, creating circular ripples that went on and on. Tristan was part of the earth and even his skin carried the lingering scent of flowers. In my attempt to bring nature to him, I'd been gathering rocks and setting them along the window in our bedroom.

"You shouldn't be out here by yourself," Zain said, startling me. He was wearing a heavy coat and narrowed his eyes when he saw me. "Especially being near water isn't a good idea."

I rubbed my arms. "The Sidhee can only access our world through the lakes at Pasky."

Zain cleared his throat and stepped up beside me, his boots crunching the tiny pebbles. "For all we know, that was another lie we were fed. It doesn't hurt to be safe."

With one arm, he nudged me away from the water relentlessly until I was at a satisfactory distance.

"Zain." My voice was heavy and I was shocked the words were able to come out. "Am I wrong to do this?"

"Do what?"

"Hold on."

"I don't—"

"What if he never wakes up?" To actually say the words made something burst deep inside of me. It took everything I had to not crumple to the ground like used tissue.

"He's your mate. The only course of action you can take is the one you chose." There wasn't bitterness in Zain's voice, just resignation.

His acceptance was another reason he always seemed to take me by surprise.

"I'm not as smart as him…. There's something I'm missing."

"From what you tell me…." Zain shoved his hands into his pockets and stared up at the looming sky. "He's quite a genius. Studied genetics and botany in an attempt to fuse them with Dryma magic. Not something I would've thought of."

Or something I thought would work.

I'd been working on not invading the thoughts of Kuro because I knew there would be sorrow, but as the prince of the tribe, sometimes words slipped through my carefully guarded wall. Zain's thoughts made me realize how few had believed in the magic of the flowers.

Really, I couldn't blame them. Not when the only relative success had left my mate comatose in his bed.

I should get back to Tristan. Saying his name was so much easier in my mind. There was a painful tightening in my chest, a sensation so familiar it was like saying hello to an old friend.

"I sent Shinji to watch him when I saw you leave."

"You didn't have to do that," I told Zain, kicking a pebble with the toe of my boot. "Poor kid should get some sleep."

"We are all obligated to protect your mate, Kanji." Zain sighed, once again pushing me away from the water as though the Loch Ness Monster was lurking in two-feet deep water. "But Shinji and Micky are better about it."

I was silent. The rhythm of water was almost soothing as it slapped viciously against the rocks one moment and then swayed gently the next as though apologizing.

Sometimes I felt like the water was more alive than we realized. Just like the trees were living entities with heartbeats more intense than those of humans.

The trees across the river, resting on the raised bank, swayed gently as the branches took in the last of the light they would see until morning. The wind was bitter and tore through my sweater like a swarm of wasps.

When I realized Zain wasn't going to leave me alone beside the riverbank, I turned to head back to the cottage. A gust of air like a whisper caught my attention and rooted my feet firmly to the ground.

Zain was right about not knowing for certain what bodies of water Sidhee could use as portals to our world, but the life coursing through the water was anything but demonic.

I quickly tore my boots off, the jagged pebbles digging into the tender flesh of my bare feet.

"Kanji, what are you—"

Before he could realize my intention, I ran forward into the river, ignoring the pressure beneath my feet. The uneven rock bed did everything in its power to push me back to the shore, but I ignored the shooting pain racing up my legs. Now I was in the water, I couldn't just hear the life beating nearby, I could feel it.

Long ago, when Dryma and Kuro co-lived with humans, there had been other creatures. My acute sense of smell and hearing had returned with my wings, but the life I was tracing didn't belong to a common herring.

"What are you doing?"

The water swarmed around my waist, transforming my jeans into a second skin. The pulse of life thumped around me in time with my racing heartbeat.

For so long, we'd been slaves to the Dryma, and we still weren't free. What was more, our fear of the Sidhee dictated our every move and even limited our time beside the water.

I wasn't sure if it was my hatred or fear that propelled me forward, but I filled my lungs with air and dove headfirst into the murky water.

I felt something else, an ancient kind of creature who belonged in my world. There was little moonlight, so I could barely make out anything farther than my arm's length.

Kanji, dammit. Are you okay?

Zain's thoughts were frantic and I knew the only reason he wasn't flailing around behind me was because he was worried he'd knock me out with his strong arms.

There's something down here.

Yeah? Rocks?

No… something more.

There were many human things about me, but once a Kuro had filled their lungs with air, they could hold their breath for long lengths of time.

But I'd been submerged for too long. I could feel my lungs stretching painfully, like twisting rope deep inside of me. Dejectedly, I was about to return to the surface and admit defeat when I saw what I'd been searching for.

Lying on the river floor was a pale-haired boy no older than ten. If his eyes hadn't been open, I wouldn't have seen the watery film over the pupil enabling him to see.

He was naked, with his arms floating at his sides as though he didn't know about shame and therefore couldn't feel embarrassment. Reaching for his arm, I expected him to lash out, but he surprised me by wrapping a small slimy hand around my wrist.

Breaking the surface, I inhaled sharply. The boy's hand slipped from my arm, but before he could drift back beneath the water, I cradled him against my body.

In the moonlight, I could see that his pale skin made me look like a bronzed statue. If there hadn't been a bluish glow covering his skin, he would've appeared white as chalk. His fair hair was the color of water lilies, draping around him like a silk curtain.

"Jesus," Zain cried. He wrestled with his shirt and managed to lift it over his head without crashing into the water. "Here."

I carefully treaded to where he was standing and took the shirt. The hem was soaked but at least the boy was covered.

"He's not dead, is he?"

"No," I murmured, pulling a loose strand of hair away from the boy's face so I could make out the shape of his upturned nose. "He's not human."

Zain tugged at the red in his hair.

If this boy was part of my world, there was only one thing he could be. *Asrai.*

"Impossible," Zain exclaimed. "He can't be an Asrai. Water fairies all died a long time ago."

"Then what do you think he is?" I asked quietly, nudging the boy's cheek with my hand. He stirred but didn't open his eyes. "Just because we haven't seen an Asrai doesn't mean they're extinct."

"No, but aren't they supposed to be hot chicks or something?"

"Asrai aren't mermaids," I pointed out, shaking my legs like a dog when I finally hit the shore. "Most of the time they're women, but sometimes boys are born too."

Zain eyed the small figure in my arms. His hand twitched at his side and even though duty told him to relieve me of the boy, he was frightened to. "And when they're born boys?"

I closed my eyes, willing back memories that seemed like another lifetime. "My father told me they killed males."

Warily, Zain stared at the water, once again still after my intrusion. "Maybe we should put him back."

I was surprised at the hostility coursing through me at the suggestion. My word came out as a growl. "No."

Zain looked as taken aback as I felt. He pulled at his crimson hair. "We are already running from the Sidhee, who want your mate and probably our lives. Do you think we should be running from mermaids too?"

But he didn't feel what I did. The vulnerability. The despair. The hopelessness.

"He was cast out of his own home," I whispered as I awkwardly slipped back into my shoes. "Imagine what that feels like."

Zain spit on the ground. "As if I already don't know."

"At least you weren't alone."

With a heavy sigh, he held out his arms. "Fine."

I stared. "Fine what?"

"Give him here. I'll take him back to my cabin."

My hold only tightened. "Your cabin is already cramped. You guys all have to take turns on who gets to sleep in a bed."

"Then take him to one of Seth's cabins. He's as beautiful as a Dryma."

"Seth won't like that."

Zain gritted his teeth. "I'll make him."

"I'll take him back to my cabin."

"The hell you will." Zain stepped in front of me, his face a mask of impatience. "You are already taking care of your mate. You don't need to take care of some kid too. And we don't know anything about him."

"So your plan is to let him near other members of our tribe."

Zain sighed. "If that's what it takes to keep you and... your mate safe."

I didn't budge.

"If it makes you feel better, Micky or Shinji can sleep in your cabin. They come over all the time anyway," Zain added, clearly trying to reach a compromise. "Then there will be room for this kid in mine."

I want him with me. I didn't make a habit of reading the minds of my kind, but this one time, I wanted to know what had Zain so flustered. Reading through his worries, I saw how desperately he clung to both my reign as king and my friendship. One more blow and he worried he wouldn't recover.

"You think of me as your king?" My eyes widened at the admission.

He rolled his eyes, "Well, yeah, duh. You're the only king we have, and I don't want someone slitting your throat while you sleep."

And I got that, I really did. "I trust him."

Zain crunched snow beneath his boot. "You don't know him."

I touched his shoulder reassuringly. "Trust me, Zain, please."

Whatever he wanted was overruled by his instinct to obey my command. His eyes were the picture of defiance, but he moved away, falling into step beside me.

"If this kid kills you, I swear to God...," he muttered, kicking every spare rock he came into contact with.

I felt guilty not providing a reasonable response to why I held this Asrai child so close, so I couldn't begin to tell Zain something he would accept. All I recognized was the need for protection I had felt as a child combined with the beauty I saw in Tristan. If I could just save this child, maybe I wouldn't be damned as a failure.

CHAPTER THREE

SHINJI HAD fallen asleep on the floor beside Tristan's bed, one arm outstretched as though willing to share what little life he had left. I laid the Asrai boy down on the couch and removed my coat, gently laying the garment over his small body. The warmth wasn't much, but at least it was something.

Turning the space heater dial as far as it would go, I held my hands against the small grates until I started to feel my fingers again. My clothes were soaked from my expedition, so I hastily removed them and grabbed the warmest sweater and pajama pants I could find. After checking on Tristan, counting the small rises and falls of his chest, I went back to the living room.

Maybe Zain was right about my behavior being foolish.

The small kid didn't have any obvious injuries, apart from being waterlogged. I knew little about the Asrai and even less about how they disposed of their male offspring. Had his watery bed really been a grave?

My cabin felt like a desolate cemetery, one without the gratification of rest. Apart from Shinji, I had no way of knowing who would awaken.

The soft sigh of breath was like a chill tearing through my soul.

Running a hand through my tangled hair, I attempted to pull apart the long strands so I had some semblance of humanity. I pressed my back to the door so anyone wanting to come in was going to have to come through me.

My attempt at protection gave me small comfort, enough to rest my eyes.

"PRINCE KANJI." Shinji's voice was soft as he urged me awake. As he rubbed sleep from his eyes, his pupils darkened as he took in the deflated figure on the couch. "You found a Dryma after all?"

With such long fair hair, high cheekbones, and delicate eyelashes, I wasn't surprised Shinji mistook him for a Dryma.

"An Asrai." I cleared my throat, pulling myself to my feet. My back was frozen from resting against the rickety door. "Zain and I found him in the lake."

"An Asrai," Shinji repeated, the word strange on his lips. He looked like he was working out a math problem he'd never solve. "What's that?"

"Kind of like a mermaid."

I didn't think it was possible for someone to jump as high as Shinji did. "Mermaid, are you sure?"

Eyeing him, he lowered his gaze.

"I didn't mean to be disrespectful," he apologized, his voice sincere. "I'm just surprised."

"Don't worry. I was surprised too," I said comfortingly, annoyed at myself for upsetting him. "I remember very little of the legends my father told me, but I can tell you."

Eager wasn't strong enough a word to describe his expression. "Yes, please."

"Back before fairies lived in the human world, they all lived as one race. The Sidhee, the Dryma, and the Asrai."

"They were the same?"

"Yes." I rubbed the back of my neck, straining my mind to remember the legends. "The first wave of fairies to come here later became the Dryma. They loved this world so much, they never wanted to return to the icy cold, and became tied to the earth. The second wave was the Sidhee, but they refused to not be able to return to the world that they had called their home. But they couldn't return, not without a sacrifice."

Shinji swallowed. "Did they use humans?"

"No, they coaxed the third race of fairies to this world. Many of them escaped the slaughter, turning to the sea for refuge. They became the Asrai."

"Why didn't they destroy the Dryma?"

"I can only assume the Sidhee see something in the Dryma they long for. Destroying them completely isn't really what they're after. That's how I know they are being kept prisoner. As barbaric as the Sidhee are, they wouldn't really destroy a race they envy. The Asrai… they were already different before the Dryma brought them here.

Aloof, isolated, protected. It makes sense the Asrai would become who they did."

"So where are the Asrai now?"

"If only I knew," I admitted, surveying Shinji. "That's enough questions for now. I've told you all I can remember."

He sighed but quickly hid his displeasure.

Zain and Tomas were the only ones who treated me somewhat normally. Most of the Kuro were as deferent and humble as Shinji. I almost looked forward to the days I spent with Seth. Despite his constant stream of complaints, at least he was straightforward.

"So what are you going to do with him?" Since the moment Shinji had seen the Asrai boy, he'd been unable to look away. I wasn't sure if he was held captive in awe or fear.

I mulled over an answer I never got to because Zain burst into the cabin, followed by Tomas, who looked like he'd been in a bar fight. His white hair was plastered to his face and his right eye was swollen.

"What happened?" I demanded.

Zain took a single glance at the sleeping boy and the open curtain revealing Tristan's figure before jabbing his finger to the door.

Ushering Shinji outside first, I savored what I could of the warmth before I was thrust back into the frozen air. I took a few steps away from the cabin, just in case there was shouting, and crossed my arms. Tomas and Seth were less than a foot apart, their body language suggesting they were near destroying each other. "Well?"

"This… traitor," Tomas spit as he indicated Seth, "has been going back to Pasky without you."

"I don't take orders from a Kuro," Seth said defiantly. His eyes were the color of his short reddish hair as he swayed on his feet. For all of his attempts at intimidation, I knew it was just a show; he was as exhausted as the rest of us. "I can do as I please."

"If you stay here—" Zain struggled to keep his voice even, shielding me with his body before continuing, "then you listen to our prince. And his orders were to not leave without telling him."

"What a lovely sentiment," Seth mocked, spinning around so he could glare at the crowd of Kuro around him. "All of you might be content rolling over and taking defeat, but I am not. Hide here all you like, but I will continue to search for survivors."

"We are searching," I said patiently. "But leaving every day draws too much attention."

"Spoken like a true Kuro." Seth's voice had a deadly edge. "I shouldn't expect much from you submissive creatures. Without a master, you run."

Tomas flew over the picnic table, his wings a clash of black and blue as he toppled Seth to the ground. There was indistinct shouting as a few of the other Kuro tried to pry them apart. But the fight had already left the ground. Dark wings sprouted from Tomas's back, Seth's gossamer in comparison.

"Kanji," Zain warned. "Stop them."

"Tomas."

No matter how consumed he was by hatred, Tomas instantly stopped upon hearing me call his name. Hitting the ground hard, he tucked his wings away and clenched his fists. At least now I had my answer as to why he had a black eye.

"Tell him the truth." Tomas could hardly speak without screaming. "Or I will."

"I've been enlisting help from other Kuro to help me search." Seth spoke like he couldn't have cared less. "Since you won't."

I blinked. "You have been taking other Kuro with you to Pasky?"

"Yes."

"Without telling me?"

"Yes."

"Who?"

Micky's guilt was scrawled across his thin face. "I'm so sorry, Kanji. I just… I just wanted to help find Joel."

My need to keep my tribe sane overruled my anger.

"You'll be punished later," Zain assured him before I could speak. "No one acts without speaking to Kanji. If you don't want to answer to him, then leave."

The words hovered like thick smoke. Micky's eyes were so wide I thought they would burst out of his skull.

"No." He shook his head violently. "No, I don't want to leave. It won't happen again."

"Zain." I touched my friend's shoulder. "Enough. There's more you have to tell me, isn't there?"

"You know me so well. Seth found something you have to see."

"At Pasky?"

Zain simply nodded.

"Tomorrow we can—"

"No." Tomas growled fiercely. "You have to see it now."

I was taken aback. Out of my friends, he was the least submissive to my will, but he was never this defiant.

I glanced longingly to my lonely cabin set apart from the others. Two beautiful figures lay in dreamless sleep, and I was less than thrilled to abandon them. Shinji wasn't outside so I'd assumed he'd gone back in to keep watch.

"Fine," I agreed, shrugging out of my sweater as I prepared for travel. "Micky and Zain, come with me."

Tomas took a step forward. "I'm coming too."

"No, I need you to stay here and watch my mate."

"My place is with you," he insisted.

"I need someone here who I can trust." Micky squirmed beneath my gaze, but I was too anxious to care about his needs. Seeing Tomas in such a state had me worried. "Please."

He groaned and kicked a log that had fallen from the fire pit, but I knew he would stay. "You can count on me."

Then without any further instruction, he sauntered to my cabin.

"I already told him about the kid." Zain must have noticed my startled expression. "Let's go."

On the surface, every detail down to who would watch Tristan had been covered. Without a reason to delay my departure, Zain and Micky waited for me to make the first move. With shaking hands, I closed my eyes as a gust of air warmer than fire caressed my skin. The stretching of my skin to allow for my wings was both painful and tantalizing. After so much time, I was unused to the extrusion, but I didn't desire the freedom any less.

Spiraling into the air, sweater in hand, I felt the whoosh of air beside me as Zain and a timid Micky flanked me. The kid wouldn't meet my eyes, clearly ashamed of his betrayal. In my mind, his shame was considerably less than my own.

Once we had gained height, our wings produced a soft shimmer of power meant to conceal our identity from humans below. Rather than see three humans with large dark wings, they would simply see three jet-black swans.

Sometimes I wondered if I ceased to be Kanji when I left. Tristan was my only humanity.

MY QUESTIONS were silenced by the raging wind. We had barely left the campground before we arrived at Pasky, the six-hour drive shortened to a mere forty-five minutes of flying. My pulse thumped as I attempted to cover my chest.

Zain sighed and grabbed my sweater, stuffing my bony body into it before retrieving his own. "Remind me to stop and get some food on the way home."

"Why?"

"Because you need to eat more."

"We have food at the campground." I sniffed. "We don't have any money anyway."

A quick jingle from Zain's pocket told me otherwise. "Shut up and let me feed you."

Micky watched our exchange silently, not daring to interject. The flight had freed his mind but I knew he still felt guilt creeping on him like a spider.

If Seth had been listening to our conversation, he didn't show a grain of interest. "This way."

"Where are we going?" I took note of my surroundings, finding the area strange.

Distinct perimeters had been set around Pasky, each tree meticulously documented to the Dryma it correlated to. Technically we were in the nature reserve, but we were on the far north side where there weren't any special trees.

Seth stopped his heavy tread long enough to meet my gaze. The shame, sadness, and absolute hatred I saw in his eyes was a bitter reminder of my former servitude. Without a word of explanation, Seth continued on his invisible path.

For the first time since the Sidhee had attacked, I realized I didn't know what to expect. If we managed to free the Dryma, what would our lives look like?

I would never go back to being a slave.

Not unless I could exclusively protect Tristan's tree.

"I don't know how I could've missed this before. Stupid!"

Seth's sudden exclamation made Micky jump as he darted behind Zain for protection.

"Missed what?" After being dragged away from my mate, my patience with Seth was wearing thin.

"Graves."

My heart slid into my throat as I took a timid step toward Seth. His feet were dangerously close to the edge of the cliff, the rush of the wind urging him to fall. Hills and even small cliffs weren't anything out of the ordinary, but I realized this was more of a basin.

With a burst of courage, I covered the last of the ground and peered below. The sight that greeted me was enough to turn my blood cold.

What was once so strong had been reduced to delicate fragments of bleached bone and fractured skin. A patchwork of bodies lay across one another, over and over until there were only specks of earth visible beneath them.

Micky retched behind me and I caught the awful stench of what little remained in his stomach as Zain pulled him away, cursing.

"There aren't any Kuro," Seth whispered, his voice defeated. "If that's what you were wondering."

"I never wanted this," I assured him. "I swear."

Aging was difficult to explain because Dryma and Kuro retained their youth for much, much longer than humans. Combined with the fresh wash of snow over their faces, it was impossible to tell how old the Dryma were, but the crinkle of skin in the corners of their eyes told me they were at least double my age.

"How many?" Zain managed to ask, his face pale.

"Five. I think they had already been evacuated."

"Evacuated?" I echoed.

"Yes, before the war."

Many of Tristan's brothers had gone into hiding, as had the elders. "Why are they here, then?"

"How can you even recognize them?" Zain asked quietly. "I don't."

"Look around you," Seth screamed as he shook his fists at the barren landscape. "What do you see?"

"Death," I replied.

"Exactly. It wasn't enough to kidnap my kind. Those damned Sidhee had to destroy any chance of them coming back."

I gave him a puzzled expression. "What are you—"

"Kanji, don't be an idiot," Seth shouted.

"Don't you dare insult him," Zain thundered, stepping between Seth's shaking frame and mine. "Or I'm seriously going to get mad."

"Zain." I touched his shoulder. "Enough."

Seth took a shaky breath that made him seem as vulnerable as Micky. "When the Sidhee took away the Dryma, they destroyed most of the forest. My kind can't come back without worrying their tree was one of the ones that didn't make it. If they do…." He gave one last sickened look at the grave of bones before storming away. "If they do this is the fate awaiting them."

"There are still elders down south," I told him.

"Yes, and they have become as human as your kind have." Seth turned his back on what remained of his people. "No matter what happens, the elders can't return to who they were."

I stumbled for answers. "But you and… Tristan are alive," I argued. "And we don't know the trees won't come back to life when more Dryma return."

Seth gave me a tired glance. "Tristan and I are at least within the same province. But the elders went down south and the rest of our kind went to another world. Trees are alive and they feel abandoned."

The pain in his conclusion was heartbreaking. "The Sidhee did something," I whispered. "Something worse than using sacrifices. By hurting the trees, they've destroyed any chances of life being restored for the Dryma."

"When they do," Seth corrected angrily, "the rest of my kind will return and whether they die or fall into a coma like Tristan, I'm going to find out why so I can stop it."

I considered him for a moment. "I know you will and I promise, I will make it a priority to find out why too."

"A Kuro caring about my kind," Seth scoffed. "Such bullshit."

"I care about Tristan," I said as I stopped Zain from charging forward. "And what he cares about."

Satisfied for the moment, we turned our attention back to the elders.

It was possible the Sidhee had destroyed the elders in order to punish them for trying to escape, but there was something sickly about their bones. About the way their closed eyes were sunken in the frame of their skulls.

"They were sent back here purposely so the Sidhee could see if they could die?" I breathed.

Seth's face was blank. "Yes. Somehow, they must've known their trees were too weak to be restored."

"Where are you going, Kanji?" Micky asked quietly. He had risen from his knees, but his mouth was wet and he was very careful to not catch sight of the shallow grave.

"To find a shovel," I whispered, ignoring Seth's sharp intake of breath. "No one deserves to be discarded like that."

Zain and Micky followed at my heels, their loyalty unwavering even in the face of death. Seth lingered behind, his eyes sharply trained like a hawk's upon his kind.

"They'll pay," he vowed, fists clenched at his sides. "And Joel...."

There was the real reason he came day after day, sifting through ash and heavy comforters of snow. He claimed Kuro were worthless, less than the Dryma, but there was a double meaning to every word he uttered.

The truth was he would keep coming back until he found his lover.

He and I were the same. Seth just didn't see it yet.

"Kanji." Seth stopped me with a silent plea in his eyes.

"Yes?"

"You asked me why I am fine, even though my tree was collateral damage."

I released the air in my lungs. "Yes?"

"Do... do you really wish to know?"

His expression was anything but certain, which was unusual for someone so strong and callous as Seth. I could only nod.

"My tree was damaged but not to the point it could not be healed. The reason I came back so often after the battle wasn't just because I was looking for others...." His face flushed with shame. "But because I held on to my tree. Every time I left, I felt near death. Until finally, I felt whole."

"Tristan—"

"Tristan's state has nothing to do with his tree."

"But so many of the trees were killed," I pointed out. "Could they all revive?"

He sighed heavily. "For the most part, they die in the winter, but the damage the Sidhee caused…. I just don't know. I need more time."

That, at the very least, we could agree on.

ON THE flight back to the campground, a weight was lifted from my chest. The farther I flew, the more I could see the faces of those who had died. My skin was caked in dark hard mud, and my fingers were numb.

Zain let out a groan beside me, spots of dirt smeared across his face. The one lonely red strand of hair fluttered in the wind and even though there was absolutely nothing to feel grateful for, I was happier than I'd been in weeks.

Apparently, Zain saw my elated expression.

"What the hell is his problem?" Seth asked gruffly, sweeping his dark hood over his short hair. He looked like he was ready to punch me.

"Kanji, man, are you okay?" Zain was beside me, but I could only grin like an idiot.

"I'm fine." More than fine, but explanations evaded me.

Micky caught up to us, his face slightly green. "Are we almost there?"

"Are you going to be sick again?"

He gave a curt nod and mumbled, "Sorry."

"Can you hold out for a few more minutes?" Zain scoured the scene below us.

We just started flying, I told him. *What are you planning?*

I said I was getting you food. And it works out because then the kid can rest.

Was there really a point in arguing?

"I'm going to go on ahead." Seth's eyes were vacant. "I need some time alone."

Zain shrugged, unbothered. He had never liked the fairy, not even if Seth had been Joel's lover. The bad blood between Dryma and Kuro made me wonder if we would ever truly be united.

We had already passed the major towns so we were once again surrounded by wilderness, which made it easier to conceal our true forms as we descended. I tucked in my wings and slid into sweater the moment my feet collided with the pavement. Luckily, the diner parking lot was pretty empty so Micky instantly doubled over and retched. The dumpster concealed most of the scent, considering there was very little left in his stomach.

"I felt sick," Micky confessed. "Even before we got there."

"Don't feel ashamed, kid." Zain clapped him on the back. "It was pretty gruesome. But food will do you wonders."

Micky gave a slight smile before straightening his jacket. "I'd kill for some fries."

Of course he would. Living on burgers, hot dogs, and cold soup was a definite spirit killer. The scent of warm rolls and greasy food greeted me. After we were led to a quiet table in the corner, I ordered my fill of fries, rolls, and steak.

When I saw Micky's smile at the heap of food, I couldn't have cared less.

Just as we were about to devour a third order of buttery rolls, Zain's phone rang. He looked reluctantly at his eggs and answered.

"Tomas," he mouthed before breathing into the phone, "Hey, what's up?"

Zain was silent for a moment as he listened, and then his eyes went wide. Instantly, he was staring like he'd never seen me before.

"Are you sure?"

"Zain, what's going on?" I pressed, uncomfortable with his abrupt behavior change.

"We're leaving right now." Zain stood up and signaled for the check, his plate of food forgotten as he spoke into the phone. "Give him anything he wants. See you soon."

He dug in his pocket for some money, which he hastily threw on the table before practically dragging me from my seat. I started to argue that I should pay, but we were already preparing for flight.

"I wanted to make sure we weren't in public when I told you," Zain said.

The cryptic way he was speaking made me gasp. "Tristan?"

"He's awake."

CHAPTER FOUR

KURO CLEARED a path for me, their faces masks of surprise and apprehension. In my desperation for information, I had entered the minds of every Kuro I crossed paths with. Shinji had been dutifully watching my mate, but when the Asrai boy had awoken and headed to Tristan's room, he had screamed for help. By the time Tomas and Lyon had arrived at the cabin, Tristan was already awake.

"Where is he now?"

Up until Tristan's awakening, the thoughts were detailed. But afterward, everyone had scrambled to alert me and to determine what had happened.

"Your mate's waiting for you inside." Tomas indicated the cabin. "Shinji brought him some food and water, but all he wanted was to know where you were."

My head felt like it was underwater. "And the Asrai?"

"Passed out again. I took him to my cabin."

"Did he really...? Is he really the one who woke Tristan up?" My lower lip trembled.

Tomas bowed his head against the wind. "Looks like it."

"Go ahead," Zain said comfortingly, using his body as a way to shield me from wandering eyes. "I know how long you've been waiting."

Tomas nodded in agreement. "Take as much time as you want. I'll watch the boy."

My heart pounded with excitement, but I had one final question. "Does Seth know?"

"He's not back yet."

I gnawed at the inside of my cheek, my steps heavy as I entered the cabin and shut away the outside world. The scent of my mate was everywhere. There was the lingering smell of flowers and wood in the bathroom, detailed footprints dusted with snow across the floor, and breathing I would recognize anywhere.

I kicked off my boots and started on my sweater, but stopped. So much time had passed since I'd last seen my mate, since I'd felt his touch upon my skin. Was that the reason I was nervous enough to hesitate?

The floor was hard beneath my knees as I dropped beside the bed. Tristan had his face turned away as though he were sleeping, and I had a terrible sense of dread he'd gone back under.

"Tristan." My voice came out as a whimper. "Tristan, please, I'm here."

"Kanji."

A heavy hand was in my hair, tangling my long dark strands around his fingers. Even though he had been in a coma, Tristan still felt as strong as he had before, as if his deep sleep had merely been a passing dream.

His fingers twitched as he gently caressed the base of my skull. His other hand lay limply on the bed, so I pressed my face against his palm. Just inhaling his scent would've been enough to bring me to my knees if I hadn't been already.

"Kanji," he repeated, his voice thick with emotion. His body shuddered as he touched my hair, my neck, my shoulder... everywhere he wanted. "You saved me."

I released a breath I hadn't realized I was holding. Cold tears burst from my eyes, but I was powerless to stop them.

"Baby, why are you crying?" He sounded alarmed.

"I've missed you," I admitted, keeping my hands firmly on my jeaned thighs. The urge to touch him was overwhelming, and just his little circles on my neck filled my cock. "It wasn't me."

"What do you mean?"

"It wasn't me who saved you."

There was a silence as heavy as the coats we had to wear to stay warm. "How can you say that?"

"Zain and I found an Asrai boy. He's the one who saved you."

Tristan's laughter was like music I wanted to covet for the rest of my life. "Maybe he woke me up, but he didn't save me. I assure you, that was all you."

I tried to bury my face deeper against his hand, just in an attempt to get closer to him. "I failed."

"Kanji, look at me."

I groaned. "Do I have to?"

"Look at me, love."

I would do anything for him, so slowly, I peeked up through the curtain of my hair and into the eyes of my mate. For days, I'd been staring at his beautiful face, but now that he was awake, my knees were weakened at the sight of him.

His bright emerald eyes were shining with life and his blond hair I had washed so many times gleamed in the moonlight streaming through the small cabin windows. He was naked from the waist up, his golden skin pulled taut over hard, lean muscles.

"What happened?"

"I couldn't save everyone. So many Dryma and Kuro were taken."

"We weren't?"

"No."

"And you were able to save some?"

"Yes."

Tristan tightened his hand in my hair, forcing me to look up into his gorgeous face. "Then you didn't fail."

"But—"

"You never gave up on me," he whispered as he traced my lips with the tip of his finger. "And you haven't given up on your kind."

"Never," I said fiercely. "Not on them. Or on you."

"Then"—he adjusted himself so he was sitting up—"don't give up on yourself either."

How could he so easily break me down? Everything I had thought of myself seemed to be put into a different perspective. He didn't command me to feel a certain way, just guided me toward an understanding of who I already was.

"You still know me so well," I admitted, lifting his hand so I could press kisses to his wrist. "Do you need anything? Water? Food?"

Tristan shook his head as he stared out the window at the glowing light. He may have been a Kuro swan, but he was a Dryma at heart. His body and mind were forever connected to the earth. "My flower worked for me, didn't it?"

I nodded to the bedside table behind me. "Yes. There wasn't time to try with the others."

He pressed his lips together. "It seems I may have failed my own kind."

"You didn't have time either," I assured him. "Don't sell yourself short. You're brilliant."

"Must be why you're with me."

"You're intelligent." I released his hand and gently climbed onto the bed, my knees between his long muscular legs. "And beautiful. Breathtaking. And above all, you're kind."

Tristan leaned his head back against the headboard, and I enjoyed just watching his chest rise and fall softly. It didn't escape my notice that his eyes slid to the bulge in my jeans. "You asked me if I wanted anything."

"Yes."

"I want you."

His words made my body go up in flames. I thought of denying him for the sake of his health, but any protest died on my tongue when he leaned forward and took possession of my mouth. His kiss was hot and needy, his hand wrapping around my neck securely so he could make sure I stayed exactly where he wanted me.

Frantically, I pushed away the blankets and dipped my hand beneath the elastic of his briefs. Tristan moaned into my mouth as I stroked his hardened length, feeling the pearly beads of precum gathered at the tip.

"Why are you still wearing clothes?" Tristan demanded, breaking our kiss so he could suck the junction between my shoulder and neck. Swatting my hand away from his thick, long shaft, he placed my arms behind my back so I was at his mercy. "I want, no, I need to see your skin. I feel like I was asleep for years."

"You can do whatever you like to me," I gasped.

He pulled my sweater over my head, and then his hands were at my belt buckle as he loosened it and eased my jeans and briefs down over my hips.

My breath hitched as he took my nipple into his mouth, rolling the nub between his teeth. He hadn't told me to move my arms, so I kept them placed behind my back, but I wanted to touch him so badly I knew I would beg if necessary.

Releasing my nipple, he traced the contour of my chest and my abdomen. "Have you been eating properly?"

I sighed. "I know. I'm not very pretty—"

"You are always beautiful," Tristan promised. "But I'm going to have to make you eat a lot more."

He wrapped his hand around my leaking cock and stroked while looking deep into my eyes.

"I'll eat."

"And your dark feathery wings, I want to see you fly." His other hand traced my shoulder blades, fingering the sensitive spot in between. "And I want you to help me cultivate my flowers."

"I'll fly and I'll help," I cried breathlessly. "I'll do whatever you want."

"Why?"

"Because you are my mate, my lover, and my prince."

He sucked on his fingers until they dripped with saliva. I moaned in pleasure when he inserted a finger into my deep channel. Bucking into his hand, I thought my body might give out before he even had a chance to enter me. Another finger was added, a burning sensation quickly melting into unbelievable heat.

"How do you want me to take you?" Tristan asked as he inserted a third finger, rubbing against the tight bundle of muscles. "I want to please you. Desperately."

The fact he even questioned whether or not he could was absurd. Everything my mate did to me was earth-shattering.

"However you want. My body is here for your pleasure." I leaned forward and kissed his neck, licking his strong jawline. Placing my mouth next to his ear, I whispered, "If you want me to take you into my mouth, I will."

I was giving him an out, an easy way for him to receive pleasure. He had just woken up and even though he looked like a stunning prince from a fairy tale, I was the last thing he needed to worry about.

"What kind of lover would I be if I didn't take you into account?"

And that was exactly why he was so kind.

Another Dryma would've sought to use me as a slave, disregarding my feelings completely. But Tristan... in his eyes I could only see absolute love and need.

He needed to bring me to my knees.

"I want you to fuck me hard."

Tristan raised a perfectly arched, golden eyebrow. "Do you have lubricant?"

"Use this." I reached over and gently grazed his flower bowl in my attempt to get the unscented oil I sometimes rubbed on his body.

He eyed the oil. "I don't want to hurt you."

"You won't."

In one motion, he had me pinned beneath him on the bed. He coated his shaft with the oil and hooked my knees over his shoulders. Without ever breaking eye contact, he slowly slid his cock into my slippery heat.

"Don't close your eyes, Kanji. I want to see what I do to you."

Biting my lower lip to keep from screaming, I did as my mate requested and kept my eyes locked on his.

"How can someone be so beautiful?" he murmured as he eased out of me before slamming back in.

I couldn't hold back my scream as he continued to thrust into me. With each determined movement, he was erasing my pain. "That's my line."

"You're the beautiful one, love," Tristan promised me as he pressed my hand to his chest.

The steady thump-thump of his heart beneath my palm almost had me in tears again. "I thought I'd never see you again," I confessed breathlessly.

Tristan stilled his movements and gave me a pained look. "There was a time when I thought I could live without you. A time I used to think I had to die in order for you to be free."

I was practically holding my breath. "And now?"

"Now I won't ever be parted from you again." Tristan thrust back into me with such force my body lifted up from the bed. "Now I will never let you go. You belong to me, Kanji."

"Yes, God, yes."

When he once again fisted my cock, I was pushed over the edge. Feeling him buried deep within me while his hand grazed my sensitized flesh was too much. Throwing my head back, I screamed as wave after wave of pleasure assaulted my senses. Tristan increased his pressure around my shaft as he moaned in unison.

He called my name as he found his own release, my body milking his orgasm from him until I thought he might collapse from the sheer strength of it.

Finding my mouth, he kissed me deeply, holding me tightly as I rode out the aftershock of my staggering orgasm.

"Kanji," he murmured, kissing my cheek, my ear, any part of me he could readily reach. "I love you."

For one moment, the chaos around us was reduced to nothing. The lives we had yet to save and the decisions we had yet to make seemed too far away to be real. In this tiny cabin in the middle of nowhere, there was only Tristan and me.

And the way the moonlight bathed his stunning body was enough to make me bury my face in his shoulder and wish this was how our lives could always be.

CHAPTER FIVE

"How long was I unconscious?"

After allowing my mate to ravage me, I had welcomed the darkness like an old friend. I'd woken up with the intention of preparing a shower for Tristan and hunting him down something decent to eat, but he had other plans.

Crushed to his chest, my head resting on his shoulder, I was held captive within his embrace. Struggling wouldn't have done any good, not that I wanted to be anywhere else.

"Almost six weeks." I shifted in his arms so I could stare into his handsome face.

The last time we'd made love, he had been fast and merciless, determined to imprint his memory into me. So lying casually together felt like something out of a dream.

He entwined our hands, my fingers bending to his will.

"What are you thinking about?" he murmured, adjusting himself so his other arm was draped over my chest.

"How pale my fingers look in comparison to yours."

Tristan chuckled. "What else?"

Bringing his hand to my lips, I kissed his callused palm until his breathing hitched and I could hear his irregular heartbeat.

"Kanji," he whispered. Moving so I was on top of him, my knees on either side of his body, I kissed each of his fingertips, relishing in the sweet scent.

"Whatever you want," I vowed, going back to worshipping his palm. "I'll give it to you."

Tristan was amused; I could see it in the way his eyes widened and his thick lips parted as he breathed deeply. Amused and... aroused.

"Oh, I know you will, love."

"I wish we didn't have to get out of bed," I groaned, bending so my forehead was pressed to his bare chest. The scant blond curls between his well-formed pectorals tickled my cheek as I pressed kisses to the hollow of his throat.

"We have right now." Tristan was ever the kind optimist. "Even if only for a minute."

Our minute was short-lived as a quiet tap against the door broke our illusion.

"Must be Shinji." I shifted away from my mate and pulled on my clothes. I felt Tristan's eyes lingering on my skin before he threw off the blankets in an attempt to follow me.

"Here." I offered him the blanket as he was only wearing a pair of pants. "Stay warm. I'll be right back."

Tristan rolled his eyes, swatting away the offering. "Don't tell me you honestly thought I'd stay here?"

I shrugged. "Worth a shot."

Expecting Tristan to falter, I was prepared to help him, but he surprised me. He moved with such grace, my mouth dropped as I watched him navigate through the cabin to the front door. Now I was the one stumbling to catch up.

Upon seeing who greeted him, Shinji's eyes grew large. Stuttering, he looked away as though he wasn't sure whether to run away or fall to his knees.

"Are you looking for Kanji?" Tristan asked.

Even after Tristan stepped to the side, Shinji hesitated. Considering he had been a slave to the Dryma for most of his life, I could hardly blame his reluctance.

"Shinji, what is it?"

"Zain sent me to find you." He stared at his hands, tiny red things cracked and bloody from the wind. "The Asrai boy woke up and took off running."

"Where did he go?" I was already pulling on my boots, Tristan following suit. I had kept several of his clothes, waiting for the moment he would awaken.

"Into the woods. Zain and Tomas went after him, but they didn't want to go too far from camp."

"Good thinking," Tristan added. "He could be working with the Sidhee."

"Is that likely?"

"Possibly. Asrai live in the water. Sometimes I'd catch sight of them when Calhoun came to visit."

"Coincidence?"

"The Sidhee were desperate for a way to enter our world more easily, the way they used to when they had enslaved the Kuro," Tristan wondered aloud. "So I wouldn't put it past them to enlist their help."

The betrayal was stinging. "But he saved your life."

Tristan reached for the second pair of gloves, meant for him, and offered them to Shinji, who was so silent I had forgotten his presence. "Take these."

Adamantly refusing, Shinji took a step back until his back was pinned to the wall. "N-no, I couldn't. You'll be cold."

Tristan's eyes softened when he caught sight of Shinji's shaking frame. My heart surged with love because I knew he'd seen Shinji's wounded hands. Instead of acting like the prized Dryma prince, he was as humble as ever.

Damn, I loved him so much.

The gesture itself wasn't grand, but I knew just how much more caring he could be. The thought made me want to drop to my knees and let him do what he pleased. Tristan took advantage of Shinji's compromised position and stuffed the gloves into his hands. Then he raised his handsome face, blond curls the color of honey falling into his face, and signaled for me to join him.

"Come here, Kanji. I've… I've been asleep for so long. I want you near me."

My hand fit perfectly in his, our lack of gloves meaning my skin could continue to touch his. We turned to leave the cabin and I didn't hesitate. If any member of my tribe didn't like seeing me at the mercy of my mate, then they were free to leave.

Our attempt to find the Asrai boy was thwarted by the menacing figure blocking our exit. Seth's arms were plastered to his sides, his chest heaving with deep breaths. When he caught sight of his prince and brother, his composure shattered. The careful walls he had built in order to stay whole collapsed, and I saw how hard he struggled to remain upright.

"Tristan," he finally said. "Thank God."

I expected Tristan to release me, but his hand only tightened around my own. "Seth, I'm glad you're okay."

Seth's eyes zoomed in on our entwined hands. Snapping his head up, he continued, "I thought you weren't going to wake up."

"I have that Asrai boy to thank, it seems," Tristan said softly, offering a slight smile. "And my mate of course."

"Kanji." Seth couldn't hide his distaste. "What has he done that warrants your gratitude?"

"Show caution with your words," Tristan warned, the dark tone in his voice reminding me how intimidating he could be. "Kanji is my mate and the one who refused to let me die."

A small crowd had gathered around our cabin, eyes eager and fists ready to fight for my honor. Zain, Micky, and Tomas were at the forefront, their pale blue eyes the color of ice.

Seth's eyes narrowed at the insinuation. "I wouldn't have let you die."

Beneath the hatred and loathing, I knew Seth had a desperate need for comfort. Tristan, as kind as he was, saw it too and conceded. "Let's not fight, Seth. Not now when love is in such short supply."

For a moment, I thought he would refuse, but letting the kindness within him take him over, Seth gave a curt nod.

"Where is the kid?" Seth asked.

The Asrai boy was small, but I would've seen his fair hair in stark contrast to the black of my tribe.

Tomas toed the ground with his boot. "Still missing. When I saw this guy"—he jabbed his finger in Seth's direction—"we came back."

"You left him in the woods?" I asked.

"You're our priority," Zain answered. There was tiredness in his voice no amount of sleep was going to change.

What he needed was a long cruise.

We all did.

"I'm going to go find him," I declared.

My movements were stopped by Tristan's hand wrapped securely around my wrist. His fingers twitched on my skin, his emerald eyes smoldering. "I'm coming with you."

Taken aback by the intensity in his eyes, I almost collapsed. His arm was strong around my body as he held me close. Leaning in, he pressed his lips to my ear. "I am not letting you out of my sight, Kanji."

I ignored Seth's blush and gave my mate a confirming nod. "Zain and Micky, search by the water. Tomas, stay here in case he comes back."

"And I do what?" Seth startled me.

I blinked. "You are free to do what you like."

I ignored his scoff as he stomped away. Whether he was going back to his cabin or to help search, I didn't care.

"I'm sorry," Tristan said. "Seth can be such an ass."

"Glad you can admit it," Zain agreed, pointing to one side of the path. "Micky and I will go this way."

"Got it." I hugged my jacket to my chest. "He's right about some things, though."

"Like?" Tristan's eyes hardened.

"I should've done more."

Tristan roughly shoved me against the base of a towering tree, the tight knots of the trunk digging into my lower back. "Tristan—"

His lips were scorching, his tongue separating my lips and silencing any argument. Tristan's hands were gentle but insistent as he took my wrists and held them above my head. Separating my legs with his knee, he pinned me completely to the tree. With his other hand, he freed my hair from the rubber band and buried his face in the crook of my neck.

My long dark strands were like ribbons.

"Enough."

Trailing a line of kisses from my jaw to my collarbone, he nipped at the flesh. Not enough to draw blood, but enough to leave a mark.

"No more, love." He released my jaw and undid my belt. "No more talking about how you failed or what you could've done or how you are worthless. I won't stand for it."

How could Tristan disarm me so easily? As his fingers slipped into my briefs, teasing my already hardened flesh, I moaned deeply.

"The way you react to my touch," Tristan murmured, the pupils of his eyes dark and alive. "You drive me mad with desire. I just can't keep my hands off of you."

He sounded almost angry he couldn't get closer.

"Me too," I panted, uncaring of the freezing wind or light dusting of snow. Beneath his touch, my body was on fire. "I want to touch you too."

Tristan chuckled, cupping me through my jeans. "Is that so?"

"Yes." I sighed.

With a resigned glance, he stared into the empty woods and shook his head. "Later. As much as I want to push you face-first into this tree so I can have my way with you, we have more pressing matters. I will take care of you later."

My mouth was dry at his promise.

Most of the campground was surrounded by water, which made sense considering the main attraction was canoeing. But because we were looking for an Asrai, having so much water did nothing to limit our search area.

"What's his name?" Tristan asked as he crouched down and peered into the mouth of a tree. The space was narrow but as slight as the boy was, I wouldn't have put it past him to squeeze inside.

"I don't know."

"Did he say anything to you?"

"No."

"Did he tell you he knew how to wake me up?"

I shook my head. "He said nothing."

Tristan's look was thoughtful as he stroked his jaw. "I hope he didn't get hurt. Being born male in the Asrai world is very unfortunate."

I peeled away a discarded tarp. The canoes beneath were covered in a layer of ice as thin and glistening as sweat. "His own kind would try to kill him?"

"If he wasn't a chosen."

I wiped my grimy hand on my pants. "Chosen?"

"Asrai females need males when it comes to having children. They don't have the ability to impregnate themselves, after all."

"So how does it work, then? If they kill all the males, do they just repopulate with human men?"

"I imagine sometimes they do." Tristan seemed to notice the amount of space that had accumulated between us because he crossed the distance until his shoulder touched mine. His intense gaze forced me to avert my eyes. "Sometimes they release Asrai boys and wait until they are old enough to procreate."

"Why would they come back to someone who tried to kill them?" I blanched.

"Compulsion?" There was a vague excitement in his voice he couldn't hide. I imagined being as intelligent as he was caused awkward social situations. "Asrai are fascinating creatures. What little is known about them is very exciting."

I couldn't contain my laugh.

"What?"

"You always surprise me," I admitted. "Your love for nature and biology… it goes further than just flowers."

He narrowed his eyes, "I don't follow—"

"Life, Tristan." I pressed my lips to his. "You're full of life."

"And this is a good thing?"

"The best."

I allowed myself to linger for one more moment before reluctantly pulling away. Whenever I was near him, the air permeating my lungs grew thick and logic evaded me.

Chuckling to himself, Tristan followed my lead and continued down our narrow makeshift path farther into the woods.

"A little late to be asking now," Tristan mused, pocketing his exposed hands, "but what made you take him in?"

"A feeling."

"You are always surprising me as well, Kanji."

After another hour, I was ready to give in. Tristan would never back down, but if his fingers felt anything like mine, they were frozen. And my toes were an entirely different story.

Find anything?

The harsh wind was my reply, and then faintly Micky's voice. *No, sorry, Kanji.*

Not a damn thing out here. Not even animals are sticking around for this cold, Zain remarked.

I squinted against the wind and gave a curt nod, even knowing they couldn't see me. *Go back and get warm.*

You coming back too, right? Zain was as persistent as ever.

Yes. Tristan and I both.

His thoughts raced but they weren't for my mind. I tried to block them out, but it was hard when he was so focused. Zain must've sensed I was listening because he thought a hasty goodbye and was gone. The last thing I saw was an image of a giant burger he wished he could get his hands on.

I opened my mouth to ask Tristan if he was done when a muffled cry caught my attention. My mate was instantly at my side, his arm extended in front of my body so anything coming at me was going to have to go through him first. The comfort of having him there was replaced with worry when I saw the small figure making the wounded animal noise.

"It's him." I ducked past Tristan, and my boots pounded the frosted ground until I was close enough to see the Asrai boy.

He was crouched so low to the ground, he could have been mistaken for an intricate-looking rock. His pale hair had lost some of its sheen, and his skin was less translucent.

"Hey," I whispered, gently pushing back a strand of long hair. Without the added effect of the water, I saw his hair barely grazed his shoulders. "Don't cry. I'm not going to hurt you."

I wondered if he could speak English, looking up at Tristan for help. His eyes were kind as he crouched down on the kid's other side. If the Asrai made a run for it, he was in for a hell of a struggle.

"Thank you for waking me up." Tristan's smile was radiant. "I wonder how you were able to do such a thing. You must be very powerful."

My mouth dropped as the boy wiped his eyes and focused on Tristan. He was still crouched, but he looked less like a cornered cat.

"You must be scared," Tristan continued, his voice like silk. Effortlessly, he was talking to the child as though he were his own. The thought sent a thrum of pain through my chest. "Why don't we start with some introductions? I'm Tristan, and this is my mate, Kanji."

The Asrai boy didn't speak, but at least he didn't run away.

"And you might be?" Tristan continued.

Blue lips slowly moved, but the sound that escaped was a gargled version of any language I'd ever heard. Ducking his head in what looked like embarrassment, the Asrai put both his hands on his mouth as if he could keep the warmth from fleeing his lungs.

"I'm sorry." Tristan touched the boy's head. "I didn't catch that."

"Ciaran."

As foreign as the sound was, the name suited him perfectly.

"Ciaran." Tristan beamed, offering a hand to the shivering boy. "Kind of similar to mine, hmm?"

Ever so slowly, Ciaran produced a hand so tiny his fingers barely reached the end of Tristan's palm.

"And how old are you, Ciaran?"

"Eleven."

Tristan and I exchanged a look, startled by Ciaran's apparent youth. When I'd first laid eyes on him, the water distorted his image so much he could've been as young as ten. Now he'd acclimated to our world, I started to notice the age within his eyes. The clear blue of his irises was rich and the smooth skin pulled taut over his face and neck gave way to wisdom hiding within his bones.

What he lacked in youth in his face, he made up for in his body. He was so slight, even if I'd lost ten more pounds, I would still look like a walrus in comparison.

"Do you think maybe you want to come back now?"

With a nod, Ciaran fluidly took his place beside Tristan. Unsure if he would take it, I reached for Ciaran's other hand. He tensed for a moment but quickly gave in. Warmth flooding through his fingers sent jolts of electricity coursing through my veins.

"What?" Tristan asked, puzzled.

"I think maybe your calling wasn't biology. It was psychology."

His answering smile was radiant.

Despite the pitter-patter of small feet between us, Tristan's eyes were so locked onto my body it was as if air itself didn't exist.

Tristan's smile was so serene and collected, he looked like Ciaran had always belonged there.

For the first time in years, I found myself clinging to a hope I thought had been destroyed.

ALL I had to do was look at the slump of Tristan's shoulders to know Seth had told him about the grave back in Pasky. He had his hands wrist-deep in the shallow water of the lake, but at my approaching footsteps, he stopped to glance back.

After choking down some beans and rice, I'd taken Ciaran to Micky's cabin. The time I'd left Tristan alone had been short, but it was enough for Seth to get him alone.

"I'm sorry." I nervously clenched the material of my coat, fumbling with the buttons. "So sorry, Tristan."

Beside him was a pile of small river stones, each and every one of them the color of honey. How he was able to pick apart nature to suit his personal taste I'd never know. Perhaps being born as both swan and fairy had given him the ability to see what others could only dream of.

"We have to go back."

"Seth and I go every couple days."

He cleared his throat. "More permanently."

"What?" I choked, nearly tripping over a rock in my haste to back away. "The Sidhee could come back at any moment."

Tristan's emerald eyes were richer than any hue in the lake as he paralyzed me with his gaze. "Kanji," he murmured, "they could come here too. Even if they have to enter a portal in Pasky, they could wreak havoc in this world until they find us."

I wasn't hearing this.

"Even if they took their time, they would have a way of tracking us."

Not now.

"And even if they couldn't," he emphasized, both hands coming out of the water, "they would wait in Pasky because they know that someday we'd return."

"Tristan," I pleaded. "I—"

"You blame yourself." Tristan nodded, one hand suspended inches from my cheek as though afraid he might crush me. "And you're afraid to live there in case the Sidhee come back. But the truth is much simpler, isn't it?"

"I don't know what you're talking about."

"You're afraid, Kanji."

"Of what?" I snapped. "The Sidhee?"

"No." His voice was soft. "Of being enslaved again."

"Why do you always break me down?" I tried to move away, but my need to be near him overcame my fear. "I won't go back."

Tristan narrowed his eyes. "I won't let you or your kind become slaves again."

I closed my eyes.

"I promise, Kanji."

"Then what do you expect to happen?" I cried, swatting his hand away before he could regain possession of my skin. The hurt on his face almost brought me to my knees. "If we are able to free the Dryma, they will need someone to protect their trees again. The trees we can even save."

Tristan captured me in his arms, my back pressed against the hard lines of his chest. "Why don't you trust me?"

I didn't want to have this conversation. "I never said I didn't trust you."

"But you're doubting me now."

I couldn't meet his gaze.

"Remember how I was willing to die for your freedom," Tristan reminded me, his voice hard. "I still would if necessary. I would do anything for you."

I felt shame so deep it was like drowning. "I know you don't want us to be enslaved. I know and yet…."

He held my jaw between his fingers, nibbling up my neck to my ear. "You think if we go back, nothing will change, but it will. Our trees aren't enough to sustain our souls. We have to explore other options of survival."

"You don't understand!"

"Then explain your worries to me." Tristan's voice was both soft and commanding. "If you aren't afraid of becoming a slave again and you aren't worried about the Sidhee, then what is wrong with returning?"

"That life is the only one I know." Admitting the truth was so much harder, even though I knew my mate wouldn't judge. "If I return, I'll fall right back into my old life."

Whatever he expected me to say, it wasn't this. Instantly, his hold loosened so he could spin me around to face him. "Your old life?" he repeated.

"If your tree needed protection, then I would stand guard forever." My breathing came hard, and I didn't trust myself not to cry. "But my decisions affect others. I chose you, Tristan, even though I could've saved others. And if I go back, my entire tribe will feel betrayed. They expect more, so much more."

Cradling my face in his hands, he pressed soft kisses along my temple. "First we have to find a way to bring the Dryma and Kuro back. Safely. Then we can figure out how to sustain life so everyone is equal. If we could do that, would your tribe be satisfied?"

On the surface, his plan sounded easy. But the inner workings were so much deeper. "I'm tied to you… forever."

Tristan's eyebrows shot up, as if he understood what I meant. "I'm sorry I didn't get it sooner," he said urgently. "I'm part of your tribe too, Kanji. If you're worried you have to choose between your tribe and me… don't. I'm never letting you go."

"So even if we left for the winter, you'd stay with me?"

"Yes, love." His soft chuckle rumbled his chest. "I'm fond of warm weather too, after all."

"What's so funny?" I mumbled into his chest.

"You're blushing so hard. Even your ears are red."

My hand at the hem of his shirt silenced his laughter. I heard him swallow hard as I dipped my fingers into the waistband of his pants. Instantly, his hold on my hair tightened. "Kanji, what are you doing?"

"I want you in my mouth."

His groan made my mouth dry. My cock strained against my pants, my body thirsting in a way only he could quench. "Come with me."

"Back to the cottage?"

I was still dazed by his kiss and the way his fingers caressed my neck and what little exposed skin he could find. He pulled my hand away and began unbuttoning my coat.

"I wanted to pleasure you," I moaned, suggestively looking up into his handsome face. "Don't you want me to?"

"Of course I do." He licked a line from my chin to the hollow of my throat, briefly sinking his teeth into tender skin as though he could mark me for the world to see. "But I have other plans for you, my beautiful Kanji."

"Do you?"

"Making you scream with pleasure comes to mind."

I looked back at the neat rows of cabins. We were far enough away no one could see our entwined bodies, but without going deeper into the woods, there was always the possibility we would be interrupted.

"Let me tell Zain," I whimpered as he reached beneath my shirt so he could roll my nipple between his forefinger and thumb. "Not to let any Kuro come over…."

"Not necessary." He undid the last of my coat buttons and lifted my shirt over my head. Rather than cast the garments to the side, he tucked them into his arm and pulled my hands away from his belt. "Fly with me."

My eyes felt so big, I wasn't sure they were still attached. "Excuse me?"

His answering grin was breathless. "You heard me, Kanji. I want you to fly with me."

"Now?" I swallowed.

"Yes." His voice was husky and urgent as he continued to touch my body with fervor. "Come with me so this time when I take you, you won't have to hold back your sweet cries."

Tugging at his blond hair, I wrapped my arms around his neck and held fast. "I'm scared."

"Of what, my sweet Kanji?"

"What you will think."

Gently disentangling us, he stepped back until he was just out of my grasp. With grace befitting a Dryma prince, he slipped from his own coat and inhaled the cold air as though it were a bouquet of flowers. Before my eyes, stiff, thick wings the color of the midnight sky jetted out on both sides of his shoulders.

The feathers looked softer than butter, each groove and ridge as delicate and unique as a snowflake. Unlike mine, his had a sparkly sheen wrapped around each feather like a hug. Kuro and Dryma couldn't have been more different, but the magic of our world was what truly bound us.

And looking at Tristan, there was no escaping the magic.

There was no denying his wings were beautiful, but they weren't why I couldn't look away. I still wasn't used to the tear of skin when my wings protruded, but his transformation was flawless. He didn't even blink as he morphed from a human to that of a fairy-tale creature.

His chest rose and fell slightly, his own clothes now bundled together with mine. With a single hand, Tristan beckoned me to his side.

"Come here, Kanji."

I felt my head move from side to side, but in the end, his will was stronger.

"Now, Kanji."

The moment my hand slipped into the safety of his, my wings grew light and the heaviness within my shoulders was erased.

"What are you smiling about?" Tristan asked with amusement, tugging on my hand to pull me closer. Our wings worked in perfect unison, so we were able to fly beside each other without becoming entangled.

"As a child, all I ever wanted was to fly. I thought it would be the best thing ever."

He frowned in confusion. "And now?"

I kissed his hand. "Being with you is the best thing ever."

"You're such a kid." He rolled his eyes, but I saw the happiness flickering behind the emerald hue.

"Am not."

"Sure, sure. Whatever you say, love."

"Tristan," I moaned as I admired his bare chest. "Please take me somewhere. Anywhere."

"The lust in your eyes is beautiful," Tristan said appreciatively. "We're almost there."

How he could possibly know where to go was beyond me, but I didn't question him. The way Tristan looked at the world was so different from my view.

I could see the beauty of the woods, the unmistakable hint of serenity within the withered leaves as they clung to life. But his eyes were always ready to find ways to utilize the earth while maintaining harmony in our world.

Tristan took a sudden dive downward, forcing me to cling tight to his hand so I wouldn't be left behind.

Where are you?

Zain's sudden interruption startled me, but I couldn't say I was surprised.

Flying with Tristan.

When will you be back?

Could be a while… depending on what he wants from me. I couldn't contain my grin.

Zain sounded a little sick. *Not something I wanted to know.*

His voice cut out as Tristan approached a small clearing hardly large enough for us to lie beside each other. But I enjoyed the closeness.

Before I could speak, Tristan had me spellbound in a searing kiss. He didn't even give me time for my feet to touch the ground before lifting me into his lap, hands feverish at my belt. My wings retreated back into my bones, my body once again returning to human form as my mate took over.

Tristan's hair beneath my fingers was damp, but his skin was aflame.

"Take me," I pleaded, my voice hoarse.

I raised my hips so he could remove my pants and briefs, leaving me exposed. His hand wrapped around my stiff cock, the sudden movement making my eyes roll back.

"Please, Tristan."

But he ignored me as he continued stroking my shaft, clearly enjoying the way I trembled and squirmed. My knees dug into the ground as I lifted my body so he could have full access to my entrance. His fingers were still dry so he didn't enter, but my insides clenched in anticipation.

The slow teasing left me breathless for more.

"Tristan," I breathed, forcing him to meet my gaze. "Touch me more."

"Not yet."

"Do you want me to beg?"

"Just wanted to make sure you really want me," he teased, releasing me so he could dig into his jeans pocket. He had a small container filled with oil from our cabin.

"You planned this," I accused.

"Yes," Tristan confessed as he generously coated his fingers and prodded my entrance. "Last night wasn't…. I'll never get enough of you, but at least I can ravage you without worrying others will hear."

Swiftly, I impaled myself on his two fingers, the stretching sending jolts of pleasure straight to my cock.

"Cry out for me, my beautiful Kuro."

I obeyed, arching my back into his movements. Expertly, he played with my body as though his needs were the ones being met.

"I wanted to please you," I whimpered. "That was the plan."

"And you think you aren't?"

"You're too kind—oh God, Tristan, there, please, right there."

My sight clouded and I screamed with pleasure as he continued to massage my prostate until I was leaking in his hand. If he didn't enter me soon, I was going to find my release before he did.

Moving in a daze, I hastily unzipped his pants and allowed him to guide me to the ground so he could remove the offending garments. His hands had fallen away from my body, but only for a moment until he could position himself. I was on my back, my head resting on our bundle of jackets.

Tristan lifted one leg and bent me so I was half lying on my side. "This way I can still see you," he started as he coated his throbbing dick. "But I can take you deep."

In a single movement, he thrust inside of me. The intrusion was so abrupt, so strong that the air was literally dragged from my lungs. Clawing the ground, I babbled incoherently as he slowly withdrew. He was teasing me so slowly I thought I'd die before he finished.

"Tristan," I begged, finding his chiseled face with my hands. "Fuck me."

But he didn't give in right away. Instead, he continued his gentle movements until I was pleading with need. When he finally relented, the pounding he delivered was merciless, and I realized why he'd positioned me only half on my knees. If I hadn't been lying down, I was sure I wouldn't have been able to take it without my legs giving out.

He once again found my cock, stroking with such insistence I felt weak. There was nothing I could do but lie there and take what he offered. And everything he gave me was so painfully delicious, I found myself pleading and yearning for more.

Tristan's hands were like fire on my cold skin, touching and eliciting responses from my body I didn't know I could have.

"You're so tight," he groaned, flexing his hold on my leg as his eyes flashed. "I can't hold out much longer."

"Then don't," I panted, forcing my eyes to stay open so I could watch my mate's eyes as he came.

With a roar, Tristan came hard, spilling his seed so deep into my channel I could hear his moans of pleasure, as though he were too far gone to even realize how deeply inside of me he was.

"Kanji, love, come for me."

All it took was his command, and I was helpless to do anything but obey. My balls drew up as my legs tightened. Moaning, I felt weightless as he continued to stroke and milk until I was shuddering and empty beneath his weight.

CHAPTER SIX

ZAIN WASN'T happy with me.

This was the case more often than not, but when he glared at me, the blue of his eyes darkened and made me cringe.

I knew he'd take care of the Asrai boy himself if no one else was willing, but with our resources running low, every Kuro was a bit testy. And I felt a connection to Ciaran I couldn't explain. Even if he preferred Tristan's company, at least he didn't shy away from me anymore.

It was amazing what a few days and food could do.

"You're seriously going to take care of this kid?" Zain asked for the hundredth time. The entire flight to Pasky had been utter hell. "I mean, since when do you want a kid?"

"Since now," I retorted. "Just drop it."

He drooped onto the bench beside me. We were keeping watch on the greenhouse outside of Tristan's family house as he gathered supplies.

"Are you sure you'll be all right?" Zain asked.

"Yes. You're the one I'm worried about."

"Don't. I can handle being alone with Seth for a short while." Zain groaned, peering past me as if a Sidhee was going to pop out from behind a tree. I couldn't contain my laughter.

"What?" He cringed.

"You just looked so serious."

"Yeah, well, we haven't exactly checked this place out yet."

Lowering my voice, I surveyed the perfect mansions positioned side by side like rows of polished teeth. Tristan had told me he needed to return to his greenhouse so he could gather his flowers and herbs. Besides being worried about the Sidhee, I'd expected to only find charred rubble.

But after giving in and arriving at the Crystal Cove gated community, I saw how needlessly I'd worried. With the thick blankets of snow and lack of inhabitants, it was obvious the community had been abandoned.

Even though humans hadn't detected the presence of fairies or swans, they would feel the emptiness lingering among them.

"I get you need to help Tristan with the herbs," Zain agreed, lowering his voice as Seth stepped out of the greenhouse. The Dryma's dark wool coat made his skin appear like gold, just like his younger brother. "But we can take the kid with us, that way you can run if a demon appears while I'm gone."

I sighed. "He'd slow you down, and I want you to be quick."

Why do I get the feeling you're worried about me? Zain's thoughts were too loud to ignore.

Because you're my best friend. A sound like broken glass made me look back, but it was only Seth stomping on what remained of a small vase.

"If you guys are done doing that weird mind thing, can we get going?"

Seth's impatience was contagious. Rolling his eyes, Zain stomped after the fairy toward the woods. They were going to do a quick surveillance, but I already knew they wouldn't find anyone.

The only presence I felt for miles was the faint hum of heat coming from the greenhouse where my mate and Ciaran were.

Although the community looked undisturbed, the same couldn't be said for the greenhouse. Vases had been smashed, water dripping on the wooden tables and benches. Flowers were missing petals, and trees carefully planted within pots had been uprooted like pieces of string.

"How can it still be hot in here?" I wondered, clinging to the heat I hadn't felt since summer. "Didn't the heater go out?"

Tristan gingerly went about setting his herbs right side up. "I made solar panels and a water filtration system so the heat could naturally be maintained."

"Oh…."

I desperately wanted to be of some use to him, but in comparison to his feathery touches and fluid movements, I felt clumsy. Seeing the light pink buds from his flowers spring back at his touch sent pride surging through my chest.

"The flowers are resilient as you," I commented.

Tristan stopped short, his fingers buried within a large pot. I could see small green sprouts, but I couldn't identify what they were.

"Is something wrong?" I took a step forward, my boot crunching over gravel.

Ciaran peeked up through his curtain of pale hair with wide eyes, but he didn't move away. In his hands, he held a small pot of dirt with a tiny sprout.

"No, just thinking."

I waited.

Instead of answering, Tristan bent to retrieve a smashed pot. The plant inside looked lifeless, the little leaves sagging against the sienna hue of the pot. "Ciaran," Tristan said suddenly, "could you help me with something?"

After setting the plant on the table, Tristan scooped fresh dirt into his big hands and tucked what was left of the plant in. He must've felt my eyes on him, because he suddenly added for my benefit, "I think I figured out how Ciaran woke me up."

I straightened. "Really?"

"When my tree was stabbed," Tristan continued, waiting patiently for Ciaran to slowly make his way over, "you managed to contain the Kuro part of me within my flower. But I couldn't wake up because there was nothing to come back to."

"I don't follow...."

"The Dryma in that..." He swallowed painfully before finishing. "...grave, they died because their trees had been destroyed."

"Right, and you didn't because you'd already connected your life force to your flower."

"Yes, but my flowers were always missing something that made it impossible for full Dryma to survive.

"But Seth is a full Dryma and managed to survive because he awoke the magic within his tree and retied it to himself. We don't have the time or the faith to hope each Dryma can find their tree and survive that way. Too many deaths could occur if I don't finish the flowers before my kind return. If my calculations are correct...." Tristan's voice was so excited; I felt bad for only partially following. The gentle way he touched the flower made me want to be a plant so bad. "Ciaran, do you mind helping me?"

The small boy gave a tiny nod, his arms like sticks in the oversized coat he wore.

"Can you make this grow?" Tristan set down the sorry excuse of a plant, the blackened leaves strangely reminiscent of a plague.

I cringed. "Isn't that plant already dead?"

"A succulent," he corrected. "And no, there is still a little bit of life left."

I held on to the tiny hope Tristan was right.

Silently, Ciaran rolled up his sleeves, exposing creamy pale skin. His fingertips grazed the brittle petals, but then he stopped and stared at Tristan as if asking for permission. With a single nod of approval, the Asrai boy dipped his fingers into a puddle of water on the table.

Then he rubbed the petals as if providing hydration and took a step back.

At first, nothing happened, but then slowly, the black of the petals morphed into brown and finally a forest green. It wasn't as lush as the surrounding trees would be come summertime, but no longer did the blossom look wilted.

"Perfect." Tristan beamed, clapping. "Water gives us life and Asrai are the keepers of water."

I tried to make sense of his words. "So the water near the flower was enough to revive it?"

"Normally, I would think not." Tristan gave Ciaran a reassuring smile before the kid scurried back into a corner so he could reclaim his pot. When he stepped closer to me, I suddenly felt much smaller than my mate. "But the way Ciaran's magic works is different. He was able to manipulate the water beneath my flower to revive me. That's why my mouth was so wet when I woke up."

"Your mouth was wet?"

"You probably didn't notice," Tristan said softly, "because I took up your attention, but the flower was gone."

My stomach did a flip. "Where did he put it?"

"I ate it," Tristan replied hesitantly.

"Ciaran thought to do that?"

"Yes."

A tiny child was the key to the Dryma's independence and my kind's freedom. "I'll never doubt big things in small packages again."

Tristan took my hand in his and opened my palm so he could deposit something small and soft. "What we need to do is simple."

"Gather tree samples?"

He beamed. "Precisely. Afterwards, we will have Ciaran manipulate the water clinging to the trees and instead pass it on to the flowers. Because I am part Kuro, eating the flower was enough. I think more effort will be required for the rest of my kind."

"Won't they still be in a coma?" I asked warily.

"Yes, but… they won't die. I'll make sure to wake them up in time."

I hated dashing his hopes, but I had to ask. "You've figured it out, but how… how do you plan to protect the flowers afterward?"

Tristan wasn't one to shy away from difficulties. "I promise, Kanji, you and the rest of the Kuro won't be imprisoned."

Even without my saying so, he knew by protecting me he also had to protect the rest of the Kuro.

"Look what I gave you."

Unfurling my fist, I saw the most beautiful flower I had ever seen.

"A camellia," Tristan told me, stroking my cheek. "Depending on the color of the flower, the meaning changes."

"So what does red mean?"

He brushed his nose against my collarbone, inhaling sharply. "You are the flame in my heart, Kanji. Now and forever."

If he hadn't reached out to steady me, I would've lost control. Lowering my voice so Ciaran wouldn't hear, I nuzzled his neck and whispered, "Why are you so irresistible?"

Tristan grinned, flashing his white teeth. "Only to you, love."

With a groan, he detached himself and took a step away.

"Zain's Jeep is outside." I struggled to catch my breath. "We can start loading everything if you want."

"Actually…." Tristan closed his eyes for a moment, long dark lashes hitting his face. "I want to inspect Seth's tree. His was set away from the others like mine, so we shouldn't have to go too deep into the woods."

I blinked. "Sure, but why?"

"To gather a sample." An overwhelming sadness clouded his eyes. "Just because he seems fine now doesn't mean anything. Maybe… maybe Christophe was on to something."

I glared. "You mean the part about him giving you to the Sidhee prince?"

"No, love. The part about our trees dying on their own. Even if most of the Dryma hadn't been carted off to the Sidhee world, I'm not entirely sure this still wouldn't have been the outcome. Eventually."

Pressing his hand to my lips, I inhaled the skin at his wrist. "I have faith in you."

He cocked his head to the side. "Because you don't want me to have to unite with the Sidhee?"

"That too," I whispered hoarsely. "You're mine. I won't let anyone harm you, my prince."

Something in his eyes shattered and before I could blink, I was once again trapped within his arms. "Damn, I love you."

"And I you."

Ciaran interrupted our relative closeness, the tiny clay pot held close to his chest. Where it had only been a small sapling, the plant had blossomed into a tall, beautiful sunflower. He grinned up at us but maintained his silence.

Just seeing what he'd created was enough to create hope in my heart.

UNLIKE TRISTAN'S tree, which was set apart on a small island, Seth's was a regal beast seated at the edge of a lake. By no means were the surrounding trees small, but next to the thick trunk and unwavering branches, they looked like frail twigs.

Reluctant as I was to venture away from Tristan, we both agreed it would be faster for me to select the elements necessary for healing while he scoured Seth's tree. Still, every step I took was less I could hear of his soft voice. And when his voice ceased, loneliness tore through my chest like the soft dirt mounds daring to trip me.

I was the last person who should be doing this, but for some reason, Tristan had complete faith in me. Actually getting a decent signal was rare, but after several attempts, Tristan had given me his phone. Even with the picture as my guide, I was having trouble locating the right plant.

"Can I help you?" Ciaran's voice was small.

He'd caught me midway picking through a bramble of weeds at the base of a tree. "Tristan?"

Ciaran pointed through a small clearing. "He said it was okay."

My concern was leaving my mate alone, even for only a few minutes. With Zain and Seth on their way back from surveying the park, I only had to wait a few more minutes.

"You can help." I smiled, moving over so he could squat beside me. "Do you know what we're looking for?"

"Snake plant."

"Ah, so that's the name."

"Yes."

Ciaran's presence was relaxing somehow. Even when his bony arms brushed mine or his hair fell over his face so he looked like a blank-faced doll, there was a sense of peace.

I cleared my throat. "What are snake plants for?"

He didn't miss a beat. "Stress."

I gave him a doubtful look. "Are there many snake plants underneath the water?"

"No." He gave a shy smile. "But I listen to everything Tristan says."

A smudge of dirt no bigger than a river stone was on Ciaran's cheek like a bruise. I had reached out to wipe away the mark before realizing. Suspended in time, Ciaran stared at me with his oversized eyes, looking more like a water fairy than ever before.

"Do you miss them?" I whispered.

He took a minute, eyes never wavering. "Who?"

"Your family."

"I didn't have one." Ciaran's response was brutal, yet he looked like he was talking about the weather. "We don't have families like you do."

No family had to be lonely, but then again, he had no one to mourn. Suddenly his reservation made sense.

"Do you want to go back?"

Ciaran shuddered. "No."

"I see." I pulled away, the offending patch of dirt cleared. Rechecking the picture, I started to pick at another cluster.

"Do you want me to go back?"

I froze. "Why would you think that?"

"I don't want to burden you."

There were so many questions on the tip of my tongue. Why had he chosen me? Why would he never go back? But the only one I could form was most important.

"Why the campground? Surely there were a lot of other portals to go to?"

Ciaran prodded a slug. "I followed you."

"From where?"

"Here. All of the portals the Sidhee use are the same ones the Asrai do when they expel boys. It took a while for me to figure out how to relocate from the lakes to get all the way to where you were, but I finally did."

This was the most the kid had talked, so it was no wonder he was panting.

Internally, I was just as frazzled. The Sidhee and the Asrai shared portals? Ciaran had no reason to lie, but his expulsion could've confused him.

When I glanced over, he'd gone back to his quiet reverie. Just as I was about to prod, I found what I was looking for.

"Here, Ciaran." I uprooted the plant as gently as I could and wrapped it into the canvas bag Tristan had given me. "Can you take this to him to make sure?"

I was sure he knew, but rather than confront me, he silently took the bag and departed. Having found the snake plant, I could return to Tristan. So consuming were my ideations, I hadn't heard approaching footsteps.

Not until a throat was softly cleared did I spin around.

The Kuro standing there was like something from a dream. I'd been looking at her heart-shaped face and wavy dark locks since I was a child. For years, she had harbored the desire we would become mates, if only to satisfy the need for a Kuro heir.

There was a time I would've run to her for friendship, but her betrayal had left a bitter taste.

"Mari," I said plainly, dusting off my pants as I pulled myself to my feet. "How?"

Her long hair was tinged gray and the dark pools that were her eyes were almost unrecognizable. I held on to the hope she had somehow escaped the Sidhee attack altogether, but her words shattered my illusions.

"I'm not bound to the demon's world," Mari said quietly. "After finding a way to their portals, it was only a matter of escaping."

"You escaped?" I repeated.

"Yes."

"What about the others? Joel? Chiaki? Are they okay?"

When she paused to glimpse behind, I knew something was wrong. Before the war, she couldn't keep her hands off me, but now she acted like a stranger. Her hands fluttered at her sides like butterflies afraid of recapture. Before my eyes, her skin began to dim from pale to translucent.

"Mari," I started cautiously, one arm outstretched. Her eyes grew darker than the deepest pit of hatred. "What's going—"

A single word escaped her lips: "Run."

Not knowing what danger she'd brought with her, I obeyed her warning. But she trembled and shook her head when I tried to take her with me. In my heart, I knew whatever she had brought lingered behind her, but I'd be damned if I was ever abandoning one of my kind.

And behind her was where Tristan and Ciaran were.

"Come with me, Mari."

Wordlessly, she shook her head.

My heart pounded madly at the thought of Tristan being captured. As much as I didn't want to leave Mari, my heart, body, and soul belonged only to Tristan. He was where my loyalties would always lie.

My attempt to reach what mattered most was wasted because I'd barely gotten three steps when I was knocked viciously to the ground.

The offending creature was covered in stone muscles. Bright eyes bored past my human appearance straight into my soul, hair the color of flame framing a handsome face. With every fiber of my being, I both feared and hated him.

"Christophe," I breathed, struggling to my feet. "No, you—"

"Came back for you." He grinned, exposing teeth as white as bone.

Wrapping a hand around my wrist, he lifted me and pressed my back into his chest. Even before losing weight, this would never have been a fair fight. "Mari was supposed to lure you to the Sidhee realm, but I knew she wouldn't be able to."

Mari turned slowly, her cheeks stained crimson as blood dripped from her eyes. Before I had time to react, her body began to deteriorate as though she were nothing more than a fabric doll being ripped apart. The lackluster hue of her hair combined with the dead stare made me think of the grave of bones.

"Why is this happening?" I sputtered. "Mari isn't a Dryma. She's a Kuro, so why?"

Any humanity I believed Christophe had was washed away by his dark chuckle in my ear. "She's my sacrifice."

"Your what?"

"Sacrifice." Christophe tightened his hold on my wrists, my arms stinging painfully from how they were being bent. "All this time we believed Sidhee were the only ones who needed a sacrifice to return to their realm. But the truth is much simpler. Once we let go of this realm, we belong to the other. The same rules that bind the Sidhee bind me now."

Mari's legs gave out, her knees hitting the ground with a sickening thud. Her lips moved rapidly, but any words she attempted to convey were lost among her unraveling.

"No!" I thrashed against his hold. "Kuro used to be able to fly between realms."

"You lost that power the moment the Dryma king bound your wings."

"Please, stop," I pleaded.

Mari had betrayed me in the worst possible way and even though she had come back with the intent to do so again, watching a fellow Kuro writhe in pain wasn't something I could accept.

"Too late." Christophe toyed with the hem of my shirt, his fingers inching up my skin like the slimy slug he was. "I've already accepted my position in the Sidhee courts. Mari, along with the rest of the Kuro slaves, have continually refused."

Pride surged throughout my body. Even when taken to a different realm where they were treated like slaves, they hadn't given in. By becoming part of the Sidhee world, they could no longer survive in the human world.

The stubbornness of my tribe would be what spared them.

Mari sank to the ground like a beaten snake, and her fingers twitched as the last of her life faded.

Watching Mari slowly come undone had made me oblivious to Christophe. With his arms like bonds around my waist and arms, he started dragging me toward the lake.

"Where are you taking me?"

"Back to the Sidhee realm."

"Why?" I asked hoarsely.

"Because that's where I belong now. And you will too."

"Tristan is going to find me."

Christophe wasn't fazed. "I'll be waiting. If you'd rather not wait, you can call out for him now."

"Never."

"Your willful nature has always been an immense turn-on for me." His hand was like a dagger as he raked his nails across the hollow of my throat, tilting my head back so I had no choice but to look into his soulless eyes.

Biting my tongue, I closed my eyes. I would never give him the satisfaction of hearing me beg for my mate, even though Tristan was all I wanted.

My heart wept as I was pulled farther from my world and mate. Mari's life was ebbing away, once again joining the earth, and I knew that even if Tristan found her, he wouldn't be able to save her.

Zain. I knew my friend was too far away, but as the water seeped into my boots, I became desperate for the smallest of comforts. *Protect Tristan.*

This wasn't the time to fight. Not when Tristan needed time to heal.

No, it was better for me to submit and wait.

This time I would locate the others and devise a plan.

I told myself over and over this was the only way. Yet I was left breathless when I could no longer feel Tristan's presence. It was worse than any torture Christophe could impose upon me.

CHAPTER SEVEN

IN MY twenty-six years of life, I had never been as cold as I was now. The chill ripped through my body like a blood transfusion, leaving a trail of ice behind. Turning to my side, I tried to conserve my heat but failed miserably.

There just wasn't any left.

And then, like a desperate wish come true, a heavy quilt was tossed over my shoulders. I was too tall for the blanket to fully cover me, but with my knees drawn up to my chest, it worked well enough.

I was just starting to feel alive when I remembered the jolting sensations of being taken from my world. If the darkness and cold were any indicators, the Sidhee realm was made up of everything I hated about my world.

My joints groaned in protest when I stretched my legs, but I had to move.

"Don't get up yet," Christophe ordered, his voice low and dark. My eyes weren't able to focus yet, but I knew he wasn't within reach. "You are still shaking."

"Yeah, from the cold." I shivered.

No matter what he did, I wasn't going to let him see my fear. That was what a Dryma like him craved.

"No need to fight me." Christophe chuckled. Fingertips ghosted along my jaw, brushing away strands of my hair. "When you realize there's nowhere to go, you'll give in."

I closed my eyes, enjoying the darkness within my own mind better than the reality.

"This world is… harsh. But once you regain your sight, I'm sure you'll become more accepting."

"So." I spoke slowly. "I'm blind?"

"No. You just need time to adjust."

That was a relief. At least I wouldn't have to walk around like a blind mole rat.

"I'm going to get you some food."

I scoffed. "As if I'd eat."

Either he was too tired to argue or he didn't care to because I heard the creaking of a door and footsteps fading away.

Angrily, I pushed the quilt away because I didn't want to accept the small comfort he'd offered. Shivering in the dark, I rubbed my eyes until I was sure they were red. Still, there was nothing.

I held out as long as I could but finally gave in and sank into what little warmth remained. Christophe was wrong about me coming to accept this place. Even if it had been warm and beautiful, my heart was always going to be cold without Tristan.

"WHY IS there a handcuff on my ankle?" I asked.

"So you don't run," Christophe stated.

Which I'd get, if there was any way I could. "Seeing as how I can't see, don't you think it's trivial?"

Whenever I spoke, he silenced his movements so I never knew which direction he would come from. The anticipation was almost more terrifying than when he finally did.

"Go back to sleep," he grumbled. But before the creak of the door signaled his departure, I felt his glove on my ankle as he removed the shackle.

At least it was a small freedom.

THE SMELL of earth and meat awoke me. I heard the clang of metal beside my head and hesitantly sat up. Where there had been nothing but darkness, there were now slight shapes, but nothing distinguishable.

"You still don't have your eyesight?" Christophe's voice was like ice upon my flesh. He brushed the side of my cheek with his finger. His touch was gentle, as though he feared he would harm me. The entire thing was comical.

"No," I replied, turning away.

But he had the advantage and held my face with his forefinger and thumb, forcing me to keep still.

"Are you ready to become part of this world?"

I licked my lips. "How would that even work?"

Christophe kissed my ear, and it took everything in me to not cringe. "By now, you must've figured out how our king imprisoned your wings."

"Uh-huh. Through Tristan."

"Long ago, Sidhee and Dryma were one race. Not until the Sidhee decided to turn nomadic and we transformed into trooping fairies was there any difference." Christophe paused for a moment and I waited, completely at his mercy. "Our lives were tied to trees. And theirs to the deep dark caverns of the earth."

"So... dirt?" I wrinkled my nose.

"Rocks more specifically." And in spite of everything, he laughed. He was happy. "They wear a rock taken from the cavern that bound them around their neck. Feel?"

The moment he took my hand, I flinched. I couldn't help my reaction, unknowing of what he expected. But his patience was running thin, and I heard the anger in his voice. "Stop running from me, Kanji. I've always told you that you would be mine."

"You don't love me," I argued. "You just feel guilty because I saved your life."

He was so quiet; I started to wonder if he was breathing. Then his hand closed tightly around my own, crushing my thin fingers. "If you're going to make light of my feelings, then remain silent."

"Yes." I sighed, closing my eyes because the shapes made me nauseous. "Whatever you say."

"So?"

"So?" I repeated.

"When are you going to join me?" Christophe's voice was urgent, and I knew better than to push him, but my pride refused to let me give in.

"Never."

The answering hiss he made was more befitting of a snake than a Dryma fairy. I had only seen the Sidhee a handful of times, but I remembered their beady red eyes and the scales across their faces.

"I always thought you were attractive," I mumbled. No matter what, I had to keep him from getting impatient. If Christophe lost his head, there was no telling what state I'd be in when Tristan found me.

My admission stopped him short. "You did?"

"Yes. You could have anyone. Why me?"

"Because you were strong enough to save me," Christophe repeated for emphasis. "There's no one else I want."

"There's no point," I whispered, a cold sense of dread inching up my back like earthworms. "I can't belong to you the way you want."

Christophe released my fingers, the ebb of blood flowing back into my joints slow and painfully. "Tristan can never be your mate. Not now, not ever."

I bit back tears. "He's going to come for me."

His presence was gone from my side, and I felt the tip of a steel boot against my rib cage. "Prince Calhoun will be thrilled to finally get what he wants."

I bit back my retort. As long as I drew breath, no one was going to touch my mate.

"You look hungry. Eat."

Experimentally, I stuck my hands out in front of me in search of the plate or bowl he had brought. Maybe he was treating me like an animal and I was supposed to eat off the floor.

"Where?"

"Figure it out, Kanji. And maybe next time, you'll reconsider your stance."

The room shuddered as he slammed the door behind him, and then there was silence.

"WHERE AM I?"

Christophe paused his ministrations of petting my hair. With the way he liked to touch me, it was a wonder he didn't ask to give me a deep conditioning treatment.

"The Sidhee world still. Have you reconsidered?"

I took a breath, my stomach growling in both protest and anger. After I'd located the hard piece of bread and meat, I'd only managed to choke down a few morsels. Christophe hadn't said anything, so I assumed he didn't care.

"Where specifically?"

My eyesight was getting better. Now I could make out the dark brown wood of the floor and the logs of the four walls around me. But because I didn't want Christophe to know I was getting better, I kept my eyes firmly shut.

"Does it matter?" He was irritated with me, making me wonder why he even bothered returning.

Christophe knew I would never give in; I could feel it in the way he touched me. And yet, without fail, he was like my shadow.

I waited. He'd either tell me or he wouldn't.

"Outside the main city. Even in their domain, they dwell underground. The air is difficult to swallow, even if you do belong to their world."

Underground? For the first time since arriving, I felt the true sting of fear. He not only wanted to take me away from Tristan, but away from the sun?

"How are the others doing?"

"I am done answering your questions."

He tore away from my hair so fast he took a few strands with him. "Will you submit?"

Childishly, I turned away.

"Time is running out, Kanji. I can't protect you forever."

The pieces clicked together. "The Sidhee prince doesn't know I'm here, does he?"

"No. And if you have an ounce of preservation, you will become mine."

I heard the familiar click of the door signaling I was once again alone, but I held my breath and waited. When I was absolutely sure he'd gone, I opened my eyes. Locating the stiff bread he'd brought, I allowed myself a small smile. Where there had just been colors and shapes, now there was an outline.

"WHAT DO you even do all day?" I wondered aloud, not expecting Christophe to really answer.

After picking at the bread, I'd crawled to the nearest wall so I could sleep upright. The blanket he'd given me was still clutched tight in my hands and even though I needed the warmth, I hated needing him.

Christophe scoffed and I heard the scraping of boots across the floorboards. I let out a gasp as he roughly took hold of my chin and held my face still. Stubbornly, I'd kept my eyes closed and as a result, I hadn't known how close he was.

Despite my attempt at staying strong, I was starting to break. It had been days since I'd been taken to the Sidhee world, maybe even longer. I had no way of knowing how time worked here and even if I did, the cold kept my body numb and Christophe kept me half starved. Meaning the moment I was done exercising my eyes, I passed out.

"What do you care?"

His breath was cold, his tone colder. I let out an involuntary shudder and tried to turn my face, but he was too strong.

"Just wondering what's it's like."

With a sigh, Christophe accepted my peace offering and released my face. My chin was still sore but I didn't dare move. "Nothing. They do not yet trust me. I simply overlook the miners."

"Miners?" I repeated.

"Yes." Christophe was impatient. "The ones who continue to cultivate the stones. The same way we had you overlook our trees, I suppose."

I swallowed, not trusting myself enough to speak. Even without him saying the words, I knew my kind were the ones being used as slaves. If Christophe had no problem exploiting them, why would the dark Sidhee?

"Will you become mine?"

"No."

Air whooshed beside my head and I heard the sound of flesh colliding with the wall inches from my ear. "Next time I come, I will not accept no."

I didn't answer.

"Kanji." He lowered his voice, but instead of feeling comfort, I felt fear. "Listen to my warning. If you do not obey me, I will still have you."

He found the hem of my shirt, fingering the frayed fabric supporting the last of my modesty. Christophe's meaning was clear.

Submit to him or next time, he wouldn't be arriving with bread and blankets. He'd destroy the last shreds of my dignity.

CHAPTER EIGHT

"TRISTAN, PLEASE, we have to—oh God."

"If you can still form sentences," Tristan murmured against my inner thigh, his lips hotter than the candles burning around us, "then I need to work harder."

I'd slumped back into the sheets, one hand over my mouth to muffle the sound. Micky and Shinji were watching movies with Ciaran until we prepared to leave for Pasky. Zain and Seth were glaring at each other because they knew they'd have to share the long car ride to Pasky. And Tomas was still grumbling about us not bringing him.

So with every tribe member otherwise occupied, Tristan and I found ourselves alone in our small cabin.

"Why are you covering your mouth?" Tristan asked seductively as he reached up to tug my fingers away.

My eyes rolled back as he gave my cock a few pumps with his large hand. He knew I wanted more, knew I was desperate, but he made me wait for the pleasure to come.

"Don't want to," I moaned as a lubed finger pushed past my tight ring of muscle. "Make too much noise."

"I just want to hear you." Tristan's voice was pleading.

"Then tell me to," I told him quickly, allowing my fingers to run across the golden skin of his shoulders and slender neck. "Whatever you want, just command me and I'll obey."

"So submissive. Can't say I hate this side of you. Just as long as I'm the only one who can see this."

I let out a strangled cry as he pressed a kiss to the tip of my cock, where precum was leaking down the shaft. He placed one hand on my hip to keep me still, but I writhed in anticipation. Again, he closed his mouth over my hardened flesh, but I barely felt the suction of his lips before he withdrew.

Another finger was added to the first.

"The way you look at me," Tristan breathed, his smoldering green eyes alight like precious stones. "Makes me want to tie you to the bed so I can see more."

My breathing hitched, but before I could speak, he interrupted. "Don't worry, my precious swan. I'd never take away your freedom."

"I'd let you," I admitted hoarsely as he yet again teased the slit with a finger and his tongue, the two expertly working together to drive me mad. "I already told you I'd give you anything you want."

"Your wings are something magnificent, Kanji. Don't ever let anyone take them from you."

"They don't mean anything without you."

Tristan paused, his lips pressed to my leg as he stared up at me through long lashes and golden hair. "Kanji," he started huskily, "how do you want me to take you?"

"Deep," I managed to whimper, the sound more fitting of a puppy than a swan.

Without warning, he leaned forward and swallowed my cock down his throat. The sudden movement combined with his fingers twirling inside of me nearly sent me over the edge. After all of his teasing, I was leaking in his mouth.

His mouth was amazing. The way his tongue pressed against the seam and darted into the slit, all the while keeping a steady suction, flooded my senses with pleasure. But the best part wasn't even anything sexual. My face flushed and my breathing hitched when he took my hand in his and held it tightly, as though I were precious.

Long ago, I'd given up on the idea of even having a mate.

And even when I had imagined a mate, my visions were nothing like the gorgeous fairy I saw before me.

Just watching his head bob up and down over my length was enough to make me squirm with desire.

"Enough," I whispered breathlessly. "Take me."

He released my hand, taking possession of my wrist instead. With strength unlike any other, he spun me around and lifted my hips so he was able to gain access to whatever part of my body he wanted. Positioned on my hands and knees, there was nowhere to hide.

Tristan noticed my shudder. "Are you scared?"

"No, I...." But the words wouldn't come out right. How could I tell him how much I desired him? How badly I wanted to revert to being the old Kanji, just so I would never feel worried about being thrown away.

No words were necessary for my mate to understand. After withdrawing his fingers, he grabbed the lubricant from the side of the bed, and I heard the clicking of the cap as he prepared to enter me.

Taking the sheets between my lips, I resigned myself to being silent. The last thing my tribe needed was to hear were my moans as I was ravished.

But the moment I felt his thick, hardened length sliding deep into my channel, all hope of silence shattered. As I bucked against him in an attempt to get closer, Tristan did not make me wait like he usually did. There was no slow entry followed by careful teasing. No. This time he thrust into me until my eyes rolled back and heat pooled in my stomach.

"Do you feel me? How deep I am inside of you?"

How could I not?

Fingers scraped sheets in an attempt to find grounding, toes curled, voices cried out, and the overwhelming sensation of pleasure swirled until I wasn't sure what belonged to Tristan and what remained of me.

The mattress creaked beneath our weight, but I couldn't have cared less.

"Come on, Kanji," Tristan teased, grasping my leaking cock so he could milk me the exact way my body craved. "Let me hear you."

"You win." I hung my head in defeat, giving in to the pleasure I knew he wanted. "I can't hold back anymore."

I could almost feel his smirk as he tightened his grip on my hips. "That's supposed to be my line, love."

Gasping in overwhelming pleasure, I was pushed over the edge when he bent to kiss my neck. His hair was like silk on my spine, his lips urgent.

"I can feel how close you are," Tristan said, his command gentle and persistent. "You're squeezing around my cock. Go ahead and show me how much you like being ravaged."

Holding out wasn't an option.

"Tristan," I screamed, convulsing as I came violently.

His thrusts increased, our bodies molding into a tangled web of passion and desire. "Kanji," he said once, the one word enough for me to know he had found his release and was thrusting through the aftershocks.

Not until my arms gave out and I collapsed did he withdraw from me. And then it was only to pull me close.

"How are you cold?" Tristan finally asked with amusement. "I'm on fire."

"Always cold," I muttered, grateful for the blanket he pulled over us.

He caressed my cheek with a single finger, my face clouding with heat. "Then I suppose I'll have to take you again. This time, much, much slower."

THE MEMORY of Tristan was enough to send ripples of warmth through my frozen body. Really, it was a miracle Christophe hadn't come back and found a chunk of ice waiting where he'd left me.

My stomach grumbled in protest, but the last time Christophe had come, he hadn't brought me food. At least he hadn't told me he did. Because I'd been so careful to keep my eyes closed, I was sure he thought I was defenseless.

All I had to do was open my eyes now he was gone, but fear held me back. What if my eyes still hadn't adjusted? The possibility of being permanently blinded was more frightening than never flying again. Even if I were grounded to the earth, Tristan would be there. But without my sight, I felt alone.

Shrugging the blanket from my shoulders, I took a deep breath and pried my eyes open. I wasn't even sure the last time I had tried, but I knew it had been at least a few days.

Seeing only shapes and bits of color was dejecting.

At first, I saw nothing. Then ever so slowly, my eyes began to adjust and I saw glimpses of what looked like a table. Sure enough, I saw a small wooden table situated low to the ground so chairs weren't necessary. When I could make out the frame of a bed and a sink, I lunged for the water.

I knew wishing for warm water was too much to ask, but I was grateful the sink worked at all. I splashed my face, scrubbing my hands and arms practically up to my shoulders in an attempt to wash away the grime. There were no mirrors and I was pretty sure I didn't want to see the horror that was my reflection anyway.

When I felt less like an animal, I hastily dried myself off with the towel I found and headed to the door. To my surprise, the wooden door instantly gave way, but because of how weak I was, I had some difficulty getting it all the way open.

I smiled at Christophe's cockiness. Because I had kept my eyes closed, he assumed I was blind. Until a few hours ago, he'd probably been right. But leaving the door unlocked meant I had a chance at freedom.

My face fell when I saw why he hadn't bothered.

The elder Kuro had talked about the Sidhee world as being dark and desolate. There were no pictures, not even drawings to go off, so I'd been free to imagine the worst. As I took a step outside, I covered my mouth with the back of my hand and coughed violently into my sleeve. Christophe hadn't been lying when he said the air was difficult to swallow. In fact, I was amazed my legs continued to support my weight.

In the distance, I saw mountains as gray and dismal as steel and iron. The sun wasn't just dim, but absent altogether. Clouds were in abundance, but they formed willowy wisps like stained lace. Where the light was coming from, I had no idea.

Standing in front of the little wooden cottage I'd been confined to, I saw a long path of gravel leading to a small village. In that moment, I couldn't have been happier I'd refused to let Tristan give up his life to the Sidhee prince.

There were no trees.

No flowers.

No semblances of kindness within the barren rocks forming what looked like a town. If I wanted to run, there were two choices: I could go toward the mountains and Christophe, or farther into the formation of ravines and twisting labyrinths.

The Sidhee had used my kind to fly, so there was that option too.

But I knew the moment I took flight, every Sidhee, Dryma, and Kuro would spot me.

I'd already abandoned my kind once and wouldn't do it again. So finding water seemed like the best option.

Prince Kanji, are... are you really here?

The desperate plea invaded my thoughts.

Chiaki? I dared to wish.

Oh my God. His relief was contagious. *Where are you, my prince?*

When I had first realized Tristan was my mate, I had consulted Chiaki on how to hide my affections. I'd thought that him seeing me in a vulnerable state would've lessened the respect he felt he had to show. But no matter how many times I felt unworthy, the Kuro swans remained loyal.

I glanced up at the sky, trying to make out a landmark I could describe to him. Apart from the rock that looked like a blob and the rock that looked like a cat, there wasn't much else.

Why don't you tell me where you are?

This was the first time since being brought to the Sidhee world I had heard anyone. Sometimes, there had been a swarm of noises like a set of headphones had been placed over my ears, but nothing as clear as Chiaki was now.

My hopes soared as his presence became more tangible the farther I got into the tiny village of cottages. There was a rank scent, and I located the fish heaped into the garbage cans at the entrance to the village. The large cans looked like tiny barriers at keeping others out, but the stench was overpowering.

I'm... hang on. Chiaki's mind went blank and I saw the interior of a cottage identical to the one I had fled. Instead of just a sink, there was a separate bathroom. "Prince Kanji?"

Spinning around, I almost tripped on the rocks beneath my boots. Standing before me like an angel was Chiaki. If there had been anything in my stomach, I would've lost it when I saw him.

Chiaki and his mate, Aiden, had always been different. Large blue eyes were characteristic of Kuro swans, but theirs were like ice. His pale blond hair wasn't the same golden hue as Tristan's, but rather like chiseled ice warmed by the sun. Even starved, cold, and sun deprived, Chiaki was easily the most beautiful Kuro swan I had ever seen.

But I felt sick at seeing the obvious torment he had endured.

My feet were cemented to the ground, refusing to propel me forward. Surrounded by the rancid odor of fish and the cold tundra of this world I felt immobilized.

If our kind had been able to provide adequate training, Chiaki would've made a great healer.

As perceptive as ever, he smiled and gently slid his hand into mine as though I was the one who was sixteen. "Prince Kanji, come inside, please."

I welcomed what little warmth was inside the cottage and bent to take off my boots.

"Doesn't matter." Chiaki shrugged, stopping me with a single headshake. "The floor is always wet."

It didn't escape my notice he'd lowered his voice. "Why are you—"

Then I saw what he was protecting. Rows of cots lined the floor, pushed against walls to make room in the center. In two of the cots were small figures curled into balls. I couldn't be sure because of the thick blankets laid over top, but one looked female and one male.

"What happened to them?"

I knelt beside the girl and realized she was Shinji's older sister, Carmine. Chiaki was at my side with a rag and gently dabbed the side of her cheek.

"We haven't accepted the Sidhee, so this world is like poison." He withdrew the rag and sat on his heels. "The Sidhee let the really sick ones rest, but every Kuro gets better eventually."

"Because of you, no doubt," I commented.

He blushed the color of fire.

"Where do they take them?"

"To the mines."

I glanced at his hands, soft and absent of calluses. "They don't take you?"

Chiaki bit his lower lip and shook his head. "They leave me so I can continue to heal."

At least there was one small blessing. I turned away from Carmine, unable to watch her quiet breathing and coma-like state without feeling disgusted at myself. "Has anyone... died?"

"No," Chiaki said softly. He lifted the blanket more securely around Carmine's shoulders and then went to the long table in the center of the room.

"They gave you candles?"

"Christophe did." Chiaki shuddered when he spoke the captain of the Dryma Guard's name. "Said he wanted me to make some for the fairies too."

I surveyed the little lumps of wax. When Chiaki lit a small blue one, I instantly felt calm.

"I took some of the soil and infused the candles with it," Chiaki explained bashfully as he blew out the match and added it to a small pile. I realized he had lit the candle especially for my benefit. "Helps make it easier to be here."

The flame danced before my eyes, like a delicate ballerina deciding on the final movement. The candles, the rocks the Sidhee wore around their necks, the water Ciaran had used and the Dryma trees… they were all connected. But my mind wasn't allowing me to make a plan the way Tristan would've.

"What are you thinking about?" Chiaki suddenly asked. "You look so happy."

I hadn't noticed. "Thinking about how to create a portable tree for the Dryma."

Chiaki coughed so loudly, I thought he was choking. Then I caught sight of his incredulous expression and realized my mistake.

I'd taken Tristan's acceptance by my tribe for granted and had assumed every Kuro knew. But the Kuro here had no idea I'd found my mate, much less that Tristan was a Dryma. Not even Joel, one of my oldest friends.

"Why do you care about the Dryma?" Chiaki asked, his blue eyes twinkling with interest. Before I could answer, he looked at his hands and quietly questioned, "Your mate is one, isn't he?"

"Yes."

Chiaki stretched his legs out in front of him. "I figured as much. Why else would you need to deny your bond?"

Laughter bubbled from my stomach and I was helpless to stop it. "You'd make a hell of a healer. No one else realized."

Candles were relocated so he could lift a wicker basket full of dried twigs onto the table. With intricate precision I could only ever hope to have, he twisted the thin strands together to form what looked like bracelets. They were brittle and kept cracking, but Chiaki managed to create a few.

"No one is going to love you any less for having a Dryma as a mate." Chiaki ducked his head, as if afraid he was giving unwarranted advice. "At least none of the Kuro will."

"I know."

He worked in silence, the howl of the wind the only sound apart from our labored breathing and the snapping of twigs. "What is his name?"

"Tristan."

Chiaki's smile doubled in size. Any bigger and his face was going to blow up. "Thought so. I liked him. He's kind."

"When we leave, Tristan can teach you more about healing."

His smile turned sad. "Sure."

"Listen." I gave his shoulder a slight shake. "We're going to get out of here."

"Only Christophe ever left," Chiaki pointed out. "And he came back without Mari."

Her loss was still painful, even though I'd had little love for our dead friendship. "Only because he used her as a sacrifice to return. If you haven't given in to the Sidhee, then we just have to figure out how to get back."

"The water pools beneath the caves. Aiden told me one of the Sidhee guards was talking about them. That's how they've been getting out."

"What if we flew instead?" I asked. Because Christophe had knocked me out before our journey, I didn't even have the smallest of details.

He reached into the basket, but the twigs were already used up. Only five small bracelets lay completed on the wooden table. "At the very top of the mountain, there is a separate pool. It's where Christophe took Mari."

My mind reeled. "That's what we'll do, then."

"The Sidhee have Dryma watching us around the clock. Even if we could fly, the Dryma who have turned would stop us."

"How many Dryma turned?"

"Maybe seven, including Christophe."

Such a small number, but I knew it was enough. The elder Kuro and Dryma and children weren't here, so the only ones who remained were the strong and fit. If the others were as weakened as Chiaki, it would only take one Dryma to stop ten Kuro.

"We need to get to the mountain," I decided.

Even in this desolate world, I knew if Tristan were with me, there would be light. Long ago, Kuro were able to leave the Sidhee world without portals, but with the added weight of the Dryma, we had no choice but to locate them.

If we could somehow find a portal leading to Pasky, I could only hope Tristan would be waiting. Hopefully with a bloodthirsty Seth, Zain, and Tomas; my friends would certainly be a sight to see.

Chiaki's faith in me was unshakable. He didn't even question me. "When you're ready, Prince Kanji."

A sound like a bomb warning sounded above, shaking the entire frame of the tiny cottage. Chiaki didn't move, but I flinched violently.

"What the hell?"

"Happens every day when the Sidhee are letting down the barrier from the mountain so the others can return," Chiaki explained.

"I never heard that before now."

"Christophe kept going to that cottage on the hill. Somehow he's used magic so only he is able to get up there. We knew something was going on, but we never imagined he was keeping you there."

"Clearly the magic hides noise too. There's no way I wouldn't have heard something that loud."

Then my jaw dropped when I realized Christophe was coming back. And this time, he wanted my answer.

"Shit."

Chiaki sensed my alarm, his eyes widening. "What?"

"I have to get back before Christophe realizes I'm not there."

"No." He lunged at me, wrapping his arms around my waist and holding on despite still being on his knees. "Please, please don't go back. We'll protect you."

"I have to." I disentangled myself quickly and headed for the door. "I'll come back, I promise."

"Prince Kanji, please."

"I have to," I insisted. "He won't hurt me."

Flashing the most convincing smile I could, I could see Chiaki was torn between running after me and obeying. Eventually, the need to respect my orders wiped away the indecision. But along with the conflict, his hope was also gone.

CHAPTER NINE

NEVER IN my life had I run so fast.

Chiaki had said the alarm signaled the return of the prisoners, which was why the mountain seemed to split into two as it dispelled the nondemons. I understood how the Kuro would fear Dryma, but it wasn't until I made the steep climb back up the hill that I caught sight of the Sidhee guards.

Every point of entry had a Sidhee standing guard. Even from this far, I could see their imposing figures and bloodstained eyes. The only way to get out of the village was along the path I'd taken, but going this way was a dead end because, as Chiaki had pointed out, they weren't allowed to cross the threshold.

Surrounding the cottage on all sides was a simple wooden fence. I wondered how on earth anything like that could keep even a human out. It was as if my prison literally hung suspended in time because apart from the path, every other direction blanked into absolute darkness.

Inspecting the post in search of magic, I saw small flowers tangled around sections of it. I uncoiled one and slid it into my pocket to show Chiaki before relinquishing my freedom.

Everything was silenced.

Not even the loud alarm reached my ears.

Like the submissive captive I was meant to be, I resumed my place on the floor. Now I could see the squalor of my lifestyle, I felt sick.

Closing my eyes, I waited for Christophe.

Time passed slowly and more than once I had to stop myself from flying back down to Chiaki and sparing him from further pain. But I knew if I left, Christophe would be furious.

An hour passed, maybe longer and still, he did not come. A couple more passed just as slowly as the first until I felt like I'd bite my own nails off.

Finally, I couldn't take any more.

With agility I didn't realize I had, I went to the door and opened it just enough for a small sliver of light to enter. Nothing greeted me, not even noise, so I ventured farther until my feet had carried me once again to the fence overlooking the small village.

I struggled with what to do.

Part of me knew this was what Christophe wanted. He was testing me, waiting to see if I would wait and accept him. If I abandoned the place where he kept me confined, it would be my way of denying his proposal forever.

The choice was easy to make; I only hoped my kind wouldn't suffer as a result.

Taking off at a run, I navigated my way back down the hill at a much faster pace until I was once again standing in front of Chiaki's cottage. Smoke billowed overhead and before I took the time to scan the area, I darted inside.

Several sets of eyes were upon me, each and every one full of unrelenting fear. Chiaki and Aiden were closest, occupied with the task of putting plates onto the table.

"My prince," Aiden said humbly as he lowered his eyes.

As surprised as he must've been, his discomfort at having me there didn't go unnoticed. In such a place, maintaining reverie was next to impossible.

There were several other Kuro, almost all of them Joel's wards. Thin, spindly teenagers stared at me with their mouths agape as though they were torn between crying and laughing.

Two or three bent into a slight bow, but I quickly waved my hand and gave them the warmest smile I could muster. Time stood still as the Kuro seemed incapable of movement. Then it dawned on me why the atmosphere was so suffocating.

Thoughts invaded my mind before I could stop them. Images of waiting and yearning and hoping I would come. Even when we'd been made into the servants of the Dryma, they hadn't been holding their breath for me to start a war.

But now they were ready.

The resolve was stronger than their frail bones as they stood firm and continued to wait for my orders.

I turned away, grateful the long strands of my hair could serve as a curtain to shield them from my tears. "I smelled fire," I said lamely.

"We were cooking," Chiaki said. A few eyes widened as he took a step toward me, but I was grateful for his close proximity. Being treated like a stranger was lonely, but being treated as superior was downright isolating. "I'm glad you're okay. Joel was getting ready to…."

He trailed off as he glanced behind me, but before I could look, strong arms wrapped around my torso. At first, I thought Christophe had caught up to me, and I prepared to fight. But the aura was wrong. Instead of feeling desolate, I felt love light fire to my bones.

"Kanji," Joel whispered, his voice hesitant as though he were unsure. "Are you really here?"

I turned around to face my old friend, hugging him as tightly as my arms would allow without breaking. "I'm here, Joel."

With a heavy sigh, he released me and slowly the crowd gawking at us began to disperse. The only ones who remained were Chiaki and Aiden, who continued to watch my movements as if expecting to be of service.

Joel brushed his soft light brown hair away from his forehead, revealing a crimson gash just above his eye. The gesture must've been unconscious because when he realized I had seen, he tried to hide it.

"Come outside with me," I whispered, indicating the many hushed voices behind us. "And tell me what happened."

There were Kuro older than me confined to these hovels, but Joel and his unwavering friendship was what made me trust him the most. Just seeing him in the flesh was enough to make my heart flip.

Huddled together like lovers, we made our way to the back of the cabin where a bonfire had been set up. A few Kuro about our age were standing there with fish in baskets as they prepared to cook. They had the same awestruck reaction when they saw me.

"I'll never get used to that," I told Joel as he gestured for the others to go into the house. Wrestling a basket of fish in his hands, I made to help, but of course he refused.

"Used to what?"

"Loyalty."

"It's a hard thing to shake," Joel said with a smile, reminding me how much I missed his optimism.

He quietly laid a single fish over a wrought-iron grate, and we watched as it sizzled slowly.

"Is this what you've been eating?"

"Sometimes bread too." Joel refused to meet my gaze, the glow of the fire shielding his angry wound. "The Sidhee don't want us to pass out."

"Who struck you?"

"Just let it go, Kanji."

"Tell me." I hated using my command, but I had to know.

"Christophe."

My hands tightened into fists. "Why?"

"Ever since we were little, I knew he wanted you, but I had no idea how much." Joel shook his head, a sad smile tugging at his weather-beaten lips. "Zain and Tomas used to joke about beating him up."

"I didn't know that."

"They didn't want you to be upset." Joel gingerly plucked the fish from the grate and placed it on a separate cooling mat. "Christophe is obsessed with you. I told him I knew he'd brought you here and asked to see you."

"So he hit you," I said plainly. "Bastard."

To my absolute surprise, Joel defended Christophe. "I think him loving you is the only part of him left. He didn't want anyone to find out you were here."

"Because he doesn't want me to leave?" I guessed bitterly.

"Because he doesn't want to lose the last part of himself," Joel corrected softly.

I stared in amazement. "When did you get to be so… insightful?"

Joel hung his head, the rush of the wind distorting the fire and with it, my friend's image. "When I fell in love with Seth. I always hoped he would love me, but I think being kind to me was his way of atoning for his behavior towards the Kuro."

He was too much.

"Joel," I said seriously, resting my head on his shoulder. "That fairy is desperate to get you back."

"Really?"

"Really. Seriously, he was even sending Kuro to look for you."

I couldn't see his face, but I could feel the thump of his heart and knew how he pleased he was. Thinking of his own happiness reminded me of Tristan.

"The prince of the Dryma is my mate," I divulged.

Joel sighed contentedly, leaning into my touch. "I know."

I jolted. "How?"

"Maybe I'm not a healer, but I've always been pretty good at realizing who is in love with who. I knew about Chiaki and Aiden for months before they announced their bond."

"Matchmaker Joel. You can bring all the Kuro together with their true mates."

"Or Dryma," he added softly.

"Yes. Or Dryma."

Silence followed our admission, but as the fire began to dwindle away, I found the courage to give voice to my concerns. "Are there any Dryma who managed to escape?"

The other Kuro might not have known, but Joel's acute attention to detail was probably what had aided him in surviving thus far. "Yes."

"How many?" I gulped.

"About five. Why?"

"I think the grave Seth found in Pasky was them," I murmured, feeling my stomach sink.

Joel frowned. "They had already joined the Sidhee. Why did they die?"

I closed my eyes. "So we were wrong."

"About?" Joel was struggling to keep his cool.

"Seth hoped they had been amongst those evacuated, but that made no sense. Even the elders whose trees are permanently damaged never had a disconnect with their trees and are more human than fairy, but still alive."

"So?"

"So I wondered if… perhaps they had joined the Sidhee as a way of tricking them so they could escape."

"I still don't follow." He withdrew the last fish, adding it to the pathetic pile. "Why did they die?"

"Because they didn't get their trees to heal quickly enough. But the way they looked…. It was the same way Mari looked when Christophe used her."

"The Sidhee purposely let them go to serve as a warning to the other Dryma."

"Even in this wasteland, they would feel the death of their kin," I whispered. "The same way I could feel your suffering."

"Kanji, what will happen to the Dryma when we return?"

"Tristan believes if he can finish the flowers they will go into a coma-like state, the same way he was when his tree was damaged. But he worries some of the trees that weren't just damaged, but completely destroyed, will mean death for that Dryma if he doesn't work quickly enough."

Joel sighed heavily, shifting his weight from foot to foot in deep concentration. "You are far too kind."

"Joel, I—"

"In this desolate landscape, we are all the same. Prisoners. Yet, the Dryma refuse to speak to us. Refuse to share their food. Refuse to even glance at us."

"Where are they?"

He gestured to the row of cabins behind us. "On the other side of the road."

At first glance, the cabins appeared the same. Rundown little logs stacked upon each other precariously. But when I really looked past the dark mist and swirling fog, I realized that even in hell the Dryma had their glamour. The harsh lines of the windows seemed softer somehow, the doors gleaming in the overcast light.

"Are you sharing your food?" I accused, looking at the small pile on his tray. "Don't tell me you are."

"They would starve otherwise. We give them all of the bread too."

"We?" I echoed in complete disbelief.

"Chiaki and I."

The softhearted healer didn't surprise me, but Joel certainly did. "I know you're kind, but why would you let them treat you like this?"

"Dryma and Kuro are very different," he mused, turning back toward the cottage as if following a silent shout. "But we are the same too. I don't want to watch anyone suffer if I can help."

"Hence why your house has always looked like an orphanage." I laughed.

"We need to escape," Joel said, suddenly reminding me of the most important task at hand.

"In order to do that, we need to know how the Dryma did."

Joel kicked a stone with the toe of his scuffed boot. His clothes had seen better days, especially the mud-caked boots. In the glow of the dying fire, I caught a glimpse of yellow sticking to his shoe.

"Take off your boot."

"What?" he choked, nearly dropping the platter as I dropped to my knees and took hold of his ankle. "Kanji, what the hell?"

"I recognize this," I told him, quickly removing the flower I'd pocketed. "It's the same kind Christophe put around the cottage."

"So?"

"I couldn't see or hear anything, which means the flower acts as some sort of magical barrier."

"Why does it matter they're on my boots then?"

"Look around you. Do you see any flowers?"

"No."

"Exactly." I was talking too fast, excited by the prospect of having discovered the Sidhee's method of keeping their portal secret. "Flowers would be pretty rare here, and I don't think the Sidhee are big on décor. Which means they probably exclusively use these flowers as a concealing method."

Joel stared. Finally, his face broke into a smile as he came to the same conclusion. "They're hiding the portal right in front of us."

"And only other Sidhee can see, which is why the few Dryma who turned could."

"Where are you going?"

"Inside." I took the platter before he could object. "If we stay out here any longer, we'll freeze before we can escape. Plus, I want to see every other Kuro's boots too."

Joel grinned, wisps of brown hair crossing over his devious eyes. "Your tribe is going to think you've gone mad."

"Think they'll protest?"

"Never. Wait, Kanji. There's something else."

My heart stopped at the fear in his voice. "Yes?"

"When Christophe takes us to the mines, they take us through a tunnel under the mountain."

I gave a quick nod. "And?"

Joel cleared his throat. "I know you haven't noticed, but we… we're at the bottom of a gorge."

"What?" My voice nearly failed me as I realized what he was saying. Standing at the top of the hill, I hadn't noticed anything strange about the village apart from the narrow mountain passes clinging to the sides of the houses. But now I was really looking, I could see past the mist to the thick rock surrounding us. "Damn."

Never mind climbing the mountain, we first had to climb out of the gorge entrapping us within the crumbling village. Flying would be faster, but we couldn't risk being seen in this flightless world.

Our best bet at succeeding in our escape was still focusing on finding the secret portal.

"We'll find a way," I told Joel, trying to sound as convincing as possible. "Now I need to look at some boots."

He gave me an incredulous look, but true to his character, he simply shrugged and followed. "Whatever you say."

Opening the door, I found myself staring into several sets of eyes. I realized Joel's house served as a sort of gathering place because there were Kuro pressed against walls, leaning on the table, and on the floor.

"Where are the wounded?" I asked Chiaki, who had approached me with a small plate in his hands.

He held me the tray as an offering, smiling so wide his eyes sparkled. "At night we move the sick and injured Kuro next door so they can rest undisturbed."

I eyed the food. "Is this for me?"

"Of course."

Some Kuro were holding plates, but most were empty-handed. My stomach grumbled at the scent of grilled fish, but I started to give a gentle shake of my head.

"Please," Chiaki insisted, boldly taking my hand and touching the plate to my frozen fingers. "Eat."

It wasn't much, but to him, the act was what mattered.

Giving in, I nibbled at the fish, swallowing away my shame. "I need to see every Kuro's boots."

A murmur swept around the room, and even Chiaki seemed confused.

"Our boots?" Aiden repeated.

"Yes. It's important."

Aiden wrapped his arm protectively around Chiaki as if the simple gesture were enough to keep his mate safe. "Whatever you want," Aiden agreed, his voice huskier than I remembered.

When I'd seen him last, he'd had a rounder face. After gaining muscle in his arms from obvious hard labor, he looked much older. I could feel his hesitance at letting anyone close to Chiaki, even his prince. Really, I couldn't blame Aiden for being so nervous when his mate was all he had left.

As the Kuro shuffled off their boots and brought them over for my inspection, I saw Aiden surreptitiously whisper to Chiaki. "Did you eat?"

"I will after you."

A shadow crossed over Aiden's delicate features, darkening his light blue eyes. "Baby, eat mine."

I was relieved when Joel called my attention back to the several pairs of worn shoes waiting for inspection because I didn't have to hear Aiden and Chiaki's defeated banter. Still, their love gave me hope.

"All right." I clapped. "Let's get started."

Surveying boots sounded easier said than done. I thought I'd find some sort of pattern on the shoes and then I could determine where the portal was based on where certain Kuro worked in the mines. But the reality was much more complex.

In fact, only Joel's boots had the undeniable stain of yellow flowers. Frustrated and confused, I racked my brain for an explanation, but came up empty. The idea I could be wrong depressed me to no end. And every moment meant more time away from Tristan, something that weakened me further.

"Don't go back, Kanji," Joel pleaded, stopping me with a single hand wrapped around my wrist. He wore a dark coat pulled over his lanky arms, but the large garment made him look like a child. "Christophe has changed."

"But he still won't hurt me." My voice lacked conviction, but with few options, I had to rely on Christophe's professed love in order to advance my plan. "You said so yourself. I'm the last part of himself."

Even though he didn't speak, I could see the accusations behind Joel's eyes.

But he wasn't the reason I came undone.

Like glittering stars in a moonless sky, Chiaki and Aiden stared out of the window, lips pressed shut and eyes unmoving as if fearing even the slightest movement would shatter what they had.

CHAPTER TEN

MY HIGH spirits were instantly crushed when I saw a small offering of bread and cheese upon a silver platter. The platter was placed in the very center of the bed invitingly, making my blood run cold.

"Where have you been?" Christophe had his hand wrapped around my throat before I had time to turn around. "I've been waiting."

My voice was silenced, his hand literally squeezing any complaints straight out of my lungs. "I—"

"You went to see your kind, didn't you?"

I bucked against him, writhing like a worm on a hook.

"Doesn't matter," he said softly, gently placing me back onto my feet. The ground swayed beneath me and even though I despised him, his hand around my waist was what kept me upright. "I'm glad you got to see what the Kuro have become."

"The Dryma are suffering too," I panted, my hands against the wall as I dragged in air. "Everyone down there is dying."

The former captain of the Dryma guard gave the slightest of pauses. I could almost hear his thoughts as he considered the meaning of my words.

"I'm tired of waiting, Kanji." Christophe's voice was deadly. "Your answer?"

Chiaki was counting on me, as were the other Kuro swans who had remained true to who they were. If I accepted his proposal, would I be able to gain enough sway without destroying my identity?

His hand was persistent in my hair, raking his fingers through the long locks over and over until I felt like ripping them out. "Kanji," he purred, "be mine. Please."

Christophe's "please" was startling.

I tried to take a step back but was only greeted with the hard lines of his abdomen. While I'd been occupied with my thoughts, he'd trapped me. My answer was decided for me when I saw the slight tinge on his boot.

In the dim light, I could've been looking at dust. But I recognized the yellow tint like watercolor across a darkened canvas. Had I not just spent most of the night trying to spot the flowers on the Kuro's boots?

Yellow flowers like the ones surrounding the cottage.

"But what will happen when Prince Calhoun finds me?"

His disgruntled sigh made me cringe. "No one will find you."

I needed more to work with. "The Kuro couldn't find me either."

"No, because I used the same charms the Sidhee use to protect you."

Like a prayer, he'd given me what I needed. The yellow residue on his boots could've been from walking along the hill, but it wasn't. He knew exactly where the portal was.

I'm so sorry, Tristan.

Swallowing what was left of my dignity, I bowed so my forehead was leaning against the cold wood of the wall and gave a slight nod. "Yes."

Instead of sounding happy, he seemed astonished. "What did you just say?"

"Yes. I'll be yours."

I was crushed against his chest, my breathing once again cut off by the sheer strength of his embrace. Nauseated, I did everything in my power not to empty the contents of my stomach, as he made a strangled noise, not quite human.

"The next time I come, I'll bring the necessary stones for you to become part of this world."

"Okay."

"You're so beautiful," he murmured, stroking my jaw.

I closed my eyes, thinking only of Tristan and my undying devotion to him.

"Come with me."

"Where?"

"To bed."

My legs buckled, but Christophe was so far gone he didn't realize he was dragging me across the dirty floorboards. "Wait."

"No." His voice was hard as he slammed me into the mattress. The cushion was so flat, I was practically lying on the hard bed frame. "No more waiting. You agreed to be mine. Now show me what that means."

Oh God, no. I mentally cursed myself for not realizing this was what he would expect. Of course Christophe wouldn't be satisfied with a simple declaration; he would want what he'd been seeking for years.

Betraying myself through words was one thing.

But I'd be damned if anyone other than Tristan was allowed inside of me.

"Christophe, please."

His touch felt like jagged shards of ice as he pinched and prodded my chest as though I were a piece of meat. His face was a blank mask of indifference as he yanked my hair and pulled me upward into a kiss that tasted like ash.

"One more day!" I knew my voice was desperate, but my options were few. "I want to talk to the other Kuro."

The feral noise that echoed from his chest was more suited to a bear. "Never. You'll never see them again."

"They will change sides," I pointed out desperately. He had me pinned down with one rough hand on my neck. "Let me speak to them and they'll change."

In the dark, his eyes glowed the color of molten steel. "Why should I wait to claim what's mine?"

"They'll think I was forced," I rambled as I twisted my arm from beneath his knee so I could touch his face. As far as I knew, this was the first time I'd willing touched any part of the Dryma. Closing his eyes, he sagged into my touch, his heart craving far more than I could ever give. "Tomorrow night, you can have me."

We were still in a compromising position, his hand inches from my belt. If he refused, I would be helpless.

"Tomorrow night," Christophe repeated. His red hair was plastered to his face, the color a faded reminder of the great beauty he had once been. "Speak to your Kuro, but should you try to escape, I will utterly destroy every one of them."

Shuddering at his threat, I didn't doubt he would.

When Christophe rolled onto his side and placed a hand across my hip, I knew it was going to be a long night. Too afraid to sleep with him smothering me, I focused on Tristan and the many things I had to say to him when we were reunited.

FOR EVERY bit alive Christophe was, I was dead. A slight glow had returned to his face, giving him a youthful appearance that would draw human males and females alike. Barely able to sit, I wondered if becoming a Sidhee had given him the ability to drain others' energy.

"I will give the Kuro a shorter day," Christophe began as he buttoned his shirt and hastily ate a slice of bread from the silver tray. "So you can speak with them before I return."

"And then?" I was almost afraid to ask.

"You will stay here until such a time when you can be introduced to Calhoun."

My jaw clenched. "Which means?"

"When he has Tristan, his adversity to you will disappear."

I was glad he had his back to me so he couldn't see my rage. No matter what he thought, Tristan was never going to be confined to this world. His light was too radiant to be locked within darkness.

My limbs were lifeless, one leg hanging off the bed as though it were detached from the rest of my body. Christophe dressed painstaking slowly and even though I refused to meet his gaze, I knew he was staring. Finally, with a single touch upon my head, I was once again alone.

As much as I wanted to sleep, I knew there wasn't time. After hastily pulling my coat over my shivering shoulders, I ran to the fence line.

If I had wasted even one more minute, I might've missed my target.

Marching like marionettes manipulated by invisible strings were rows and rows of Dryma and Kuro. Clustered together, distinguishing between them was impossible. Most of the figures were male, which meant some small part of Christophe must've remained. With any luck, he'd allowed the females and children to stay behind in the mess he called a village.

I tried to locate Joel or Aiden, but the only figure I recognized was Christophe's. He was at the front wearing a suit the color of blazing fire.

True to his haughty nature, he had his head held high and shoulders pulled back. I recognized a few former Dryma guards following closely behind, but the defeated way they held their bodies expressed the shame and anger they felt at having been betrayed.

But even in the face of defeat, they had maintained their worth, which made me respect them all the more.

Moving quickly, I grabbed fistfuls of the yellow flowers, ignoring the way they stained my pale fingers. I wiped the residue along my cheeks and at the base of my neck before shoving the rest into various parts of my clothing. I was sure I looked like a comical version of GI Joe but if my plan worked, then appearances didn't matter.

"Kanji? Where are you going?"

The delicate voice startled me. Standing with a small bowl of what looked like fresh water was Chiaki.

"You can see this cottage?" I asked.

He gave a small nod. "The others couldn't, but I always could."

Thus proving his innate ability as a healer. "I was going to follow them."

Chiaki gave me a once-over, his pale eyes grazing over my flesh curiously. "You'll be seen."

"You think?"

Time was running short. Christophe had already made a turn deviating from the village path and was headed toward the mountain pass.

Chiaki bit his lip. "I could see you."

"But you said the others couldn't see this cottage, so I'll have to bank on the Sidhee not seeing me either."

It wasn't as though my plan was to walk out in the open. I just needed enough of a disguise to sneak past the guards and into the pass so I could follow Christophe.

"Please don't. It's too dangerous," Chiaki murmured. "If the captain sees—"

"Do you love Aiden?"

He flinched as if I'd slapped him. "More than anything."

"I feel the same way about Tristan. And about my kind, which is why I have to follow Christophe. Wherever the portal leading to the human world is, only Joel and Christophe go there."

Chiaki gingerly plucked a flower from the fence. "Buttercups."

"Hmm?" I asked distractedly, my keen eyes trained on Christophe.

"They represent the memories of childhood. I wonder how the Sidhee make them work as a shield."

Without warning, Chiaki plopped one of the flowers into his bowl of water and stirred with the tip of his finger. Taking a sip, he smiled shyly before offering me the bowl. "Using flowers topically is good for wounds, but when it comes to internal changes, it's better to ingest."

His words flashed vibrantly in my mind. "Flower tea?"

But I was no longer thinking about the buttercups. The reason Tristan hadn't managed to make his flowers work for the other Dryma.... Was it possible he needed to take Chiaki's advice and use them internally? Ciaran had essentially done the same thing with success, after all.

"Why is ingesting better?"

"Some humans believe the soul is in the blood. In our case, because we are so connected to the earth, it's true."

After slamming the tea, I expected to feel different, but nothing changed. I even held my hand experimentally in front of me to see if I'd disappeared, but there was my dirt-laden hand.

"What are you doing?"

Chiaki had loaded up on flowers and started down the hill. "I'm going with you."

Of all the things he could've said, this was the most unexpected. Maybe that explained my dumbfounded expression as I stared. "No."

Chiaki was one of the most loyal Kuro I'd known, but he shook his head and defied my order. "I have to, Prince Kanji. They took everyone today. I'm the only one left."

I blinked. "I didn't see any females or children."

"They left earlier," Chiaki said sadly. "With a different guard."

Christophe had promised I could talk to the Kuro, but he had taken all of them. Which meant he wasn't taking any chances of me escaping.

"Aiden had a really bad bruise over his ribs," Chiaki admitted. "My place is with him."

In his eyes flickered a resolve I couldn't ignore. "Stay with me."

Instantly, he brightened. "I will."

The moment I had his hand, we were racing down the hill. The jagged rocks slowed us down, but our determination was stronger. There was never the relief of hitting flat ground because even the valley was uneven. I wanted to be cautious, but there wasn't time.

Either the flowers would work or they wouldn't.

When we hit the end of the rows of houses, there were tall rocks narrowing until the wall of the mountain was too high for us to climb.

Ducking behind a cluster of the rocklike trees, I watched as the last of the Kuro and Dryma disappeared into a narrow opening in the side of the mountain.

Standing guard like rows of toy soldiers were five Sidhee wearing the same red and black garb Christophe had been draped with. They held no weapons, but the sheer size of them made them more than capable of taking us on. Taking a breath, I noticed the two guards closest to the opening had dark chains hanging around their necks. A few of the beads were glowing like luminescent versions of the buttercups.

I waited, the sound of Chiaki's heartbeat thundering in my ears, but the guards never left.

Do they stay here? I channeled.

Yes.

Even though you're the only one?

I think they're afraid others might be hiding. There isn't exactly a roll call.

My stomach clenched as I turned back. *And you're sure there is no one else left?*

If we had an opening to escape, then we had to take it. But I was loath to leave any Kuro or Dryma behind.

Chiaki's thoughts were jumbled as he struggled to form an answer. Sensing his distress, I took hold of his wrist as an act of comfort and stepped into the open.

I'm sure there's no one left. Try not to breathe, Chiaki suggested.

I took a final breath as we approached the guards. Our footsteps sounded like thunder, and my heart hammered so fiercely I was sure the Sidhee could hear.

Chiaki was shaking violently beside me, but it was too late to turn back. There was the smallest of openings left and for a moment, I thought we'd miss our opportunity. When one of the guards shifted slightly, my body tensed in preparation for a fight. But the attack never came. Within seconds, we had bypassed the demons as stiff as statues and were swallowed up by consuming darkness.

The only reason I even knew where to go was because of the faint light glimmering just ahead.

Have you ever been here? I asked Chiaki, still impressed the flowers had worked.

No. His face was masked by the darkness so I couldn't see his expression.

Then we have to keep up.

Quickening our pace, I moved as fast as I could. But with the small allotment of light, moving was easier said than done. If we weren't careful, the rocks beneath our boots would take us down. Even with the illusion, I was sure we'd be noticed if we fell.

I now realized the cold I'd felt before was nothing compared to what I felt now. With such frigid temperatures, it was no wonder the Kuro looked sickly pale and weak. Sidhee were tall beings, but there were parts of the tunnel where I had to lower my head in order to pass through. Over and over, I collided with the walls of the narrow cave. After a while, the pain dulled to a slight throb and I just ignored the constant sideswiping.

We followed the group for what felt like an hour, until we finally came to an opening with other tunnels jutting off in every direction. Christophe held up a hand, signaling for the Dryma and Kuro to come to a stop.

His voice was loud, and with the echo, it boomed. "Joel, come with me."

Chiaki's whimper made my heart clench. *Why just him?*

I don't know. But now the reason Joel's boots were tinged with yellow, as were Christophe's, made sense. Joel took a step forward, his head held high in defiance and pride.

Where does he take you?

I hadn't meant to channel my thoughts, but my fear for my friend overrode logic. Joel flinched, but somehow managed to continue looking forward.

Kanji, what are you doing here?

Following you.

How did you get past—

Not now. I cut him off gently as I watched him follow Christophe down a tunnel farthest to the left. If there was a more treacherous path, I didn't see it.

The Kuro and Dryma had broken apart and were following Sidhee clad in red down the other tunnels.

They all lead to the same place, an underground cavern, Joel explained quickly as Christophe stood behind him as if to make sure he didn't run. Hatred for the Dryma captain formed in the pit of my stomach. *But Christophe takes me to a small crystal cavern.*

Crystals?

Yes. Don't ask why. I don't know.

Then they were gone. As far as I knew, my ability to speak to the other Kuro through my mind wasn't limited by distance. But without being able to see Joel, I didn't want to continue our conversation in case Christophe became suspicious.

I'd blocked Chiaki from the conversation so Joel wouldn't worry. The small healer was staring at me with eyes darker than the clusters of rock surrounding us. "Where is he going?"

"Crystals," I whispered back, trying to formulate a plan.

Had Christophe been with the others, escape may have been possible. But with the portal so far away, flight felt hopeless.

"Follow Aiden," I told Chiaki, knowing his thoughts had been with his mate since the moment the group had been separated. "Look at everything and anything that could help me make a mental map of this place."

With a single nod, he ran after the largest cluster of Dryma and Kuro. Chiaki was so consumed with making sure Aiden was okay, he didn't pause to ask for details. I hated dividing my mind, but I had to make sure to keep tabs on what Chiaki experienced.

Prepared, I raced after Joel.

The only source of light was coming from tiny rocks scattered across slabs of rock and dirt. They were so small, it wasn't until I looked closer that I realized they were crystals. Apart from their unearthly glow, there was nothing separating them from the kind of cheap plastic crystals sold at drugstores.

I felt like a shadow, isolated and trapped within my own body as I moved forward into the unknown. What made matters worse was my difficulty in adjusting to the dim light. I felt blinded.

Voices were up ahead and as I got closer, I realized they belonged to Joel and Christophe. I rounded the corner and nearly fell off the side of a jutting cliff to the pit below. I pressed my back to the wall with my arms and legs pulled close to my body so I was as small as possible. The flowers had helped Chiaki and I get into the Sidhee mines, but I could feel my lack of confidence as the tea started to burn through my bloodstream.

Joel and Christophe were about thirty feet down. The only way into this cavern was from the way I came. Looking up, I saw turret after turret piled on top of each other leading to a rocky roof. I searched frantically for any sight of water or flowers, but there was nothing apart from the crystals.

They were so mesmerizing my mouth dropped as I stared upward into what I imagined the night sky would look like without a trace of pollution. Even the view at Pasky couldn't compare to the sight laid out in front of me. With a disheartened sigh, I felt a tug in my chest as I longed for Tristan. There were no words to describe how desperately I wished he were here.

And not just to share this sight.

But to provide me with the strength I needed.

"What are we doing?" Joel finally asked.

If Joel had been mining the crystals, I wouldn't have second-guessed Christophe's motives. But the former Dryma was the one inspecting each and every crystal before carefully handing it to Joel. After a moment, he would take the crystal and place it in one of two large buckets.

Because Christophe used only his bare hands to pry the crystal away from the mother wall, the process was painstakingly slow.

"All this time, you've never said a word," Christophe commented, his voice harder than the crystals within his hands. "Why now?"

Joel kept his fear from his voice, but I saw his hand shake slightly. "Curious."

Christophe grunted but didn't reply.

"Why only me?"

"If there was a second-in-command for the Kuro, I assume it would be you."

Joel weighed the crystal in his hands, but his expression was confused. "What importance does that have?"

Christophe contemplated his answer and when he craned his neck upward, I thought he had sensed my own apprehension. My fear felt contagious.

"The Sidhee want their flight back."

Joel didn't move.

"But they don't want to have to use the Kuro as they once did. Somehow these crystals are able to catch the essence of another. They can trap, as well as release."

I stared at the luminescent crystals just above my head. When I started to comprehend his words, I felt what little contents were in my stomach starting to make an appearance.

Kanji. Joel's voice was shaking. *Leave now. Run.*

Not without you. Even if I could, there was nowhere to run.

Kanji, please. I was wrong about Christophe. He's a monster now. And he really was.

"What are you doing?" Christophe suddenly screeched as he stood up, toppling over his chair in the process. Before I could blink, his hand was tangled in Joel's light brown hair and he was forcing my friend to look at him.

Joel didn't answer, but his face gave him away.

Releasing my friend, Christophe kicked the chair out from under him and slowly turned toward the entrance to the cave.

"Kanji." His eyes searched until he found his target. "I should've known you'd follow."

I'd lost the element of surprise, but trying to deny my existence would only put Joel in danger.

"I'm here, Christophe." I edged away from the wall and placed a foot on one of the stones of the cliff. Using them as stepping stones, I started to descend, but Christophe's commanding voice stopped me.

"Fly, Kanji. I know you can."

Joel's eyes widened. Just as the Kuro had been kept in the dark about Tristan, they hadn't learned what I'd done in order to release our flight. Was it possible they had denied their natural compulsion to fly for fear they were wrong?

Stripping my jacket and shirt from my chest, I felt my skin stretch as muscle and bone contorted to make room for the silky wings jutting from either side of my shoulder blades. The soft feathers grazed my ankles, but as large as they were, I still could not use them to hide.

I could've anticipated Joel's surprise at seeing my wings, but not Christophe's. His green eyes reflected the glow of the crystals, but also his awe.

"I've wanted to see... for so long."

"Were you serious about using these crystals against my kind?" I demanded, folding my wings back into my body. With how tightly we were confined, I didn't really have a choice. I'd made sure to purposely land in front of Joel so Christophe would have to go through me first. "You mean to sacrifice my kind for the Sidhee?"

Christophe's bloodless eyes reverted back to the demon he was becoming as he stared at me and simply said, "The Kuro will not die. Their magical powers will simply be returned."

"To the Sidhee?" I echoed.

"No, to where you and I once came from."

"What are you talking about?"

"This was once our home, but the Kuro and the Dryma decided on wanting pleasures only the human realm could offer." Christophe recited an ancient text I wasn't sure existed. But the definitive way with which he spoke made me wonder why he would lie. "Kuro and Dryma will give up their powers and return to the human realm. But as humans."

"And if they refuse?"

The answer was in his grimace. "They will become Sidhee."

"I won't accept this," I whispered, my voice hollow. "And neither will they."

Christophe waved his hand around the barren landscape. Apart from the two chairs and buckets, there was no semblance of human objects. Nothing to help maintain the humanity we'd chosen.

"I've decided, Kanji."

I blinked. "On?"

"I won't convert you to a Sidhee. And I won't take away your wings. I just want... you."

This was the only proof I had of his so-called love for me. I prayed it was enough.

"Why did you change your mind?"

"Because I can have you anyway. Right now."

There was a shuffle behind me and then Joel was acting as my shield. At some point he must've fallen because he cradled his side with his arm as though wounded.

"Stay away from him."

Christophe mockingly put his hands up. Even though they were the same size, Joel could never have the same look of anger and hate Christophe did. "Or what?"

Joel's growl turned my stomach. "I will fight you."

Rather than laughing like I thought he might, Christophe smiled knowingly. "You are far too weak to be a decent fight."

"I—"

"Kanji." Christophe silenced Joel with a simple word. "Tell your boy to move aside or I will rip him apart until I can reach you."

"Get behind me, Joel." My command was urgent, but I literally had to force Joel behind me with a strong hand and stronger order.

Prince Kanji, the entire roof is covered in those flowers.

Chiaki's voice confirmed my beliefs. The reason Joel and Christophe had remnants of buttercups on their boots was because we were in a more concentrated area.

What else do you see?

Images flooded my mind. Chiaki had managed to find an alcove similar to the one where I'd been concealed until I'd been found out. Even though there were different tunnels, they all led to the same place: a large basin fifty times the size of the one I found myself trapped in. Sidhee stood at the entrance of every tunnel, barring any escape.

Look up.

When he did, I felt an abrupt change in his demeanor. *Kanji*, he said excitedly. *I can see you.*

What?

The ceiling is the portal. There is an illusion keeping you from seeing it, but there is a lake atop the mountain.

So I was right. The buttercups were what hid the water from view.

With Joel obediently, but angrily, standing behind me and Christophe silently staring at me like a well-cooked steak, I realized my answers came too late.

"Tristan," I whispered. "Love...."

Christophe's hands were even worse than before, quickly undoing the jacket I had hastily put back on after my flight. My body and mind went completely numb, and the only reason I knew he was progressing was because of Joel's possessive hiss. He hated what he was witnessing, but his loyalty was too strong to disobey a direct order.

Helpless to his roaming hands, I knew he was touching my stomach, my ribs, and my lower back. Then he suddenly pulled me to the ground and pinned me between his legs. I tried to turn my head to the side, but his sadistic streak was making an appearance, and he yanked me back into place.

Kanji, why are you letting him touch what's mine?

Why did I have to hear Tristan now of all times? Was my subconscious trying to destroy me too?

No, my beautiful swan. I'm coming for you. Tristan's voice was too vivid. *Get ready.*

There wasn't time to question his declaration. My mind kicked into overdrive. *Chiaki, show me everything. We're going to have to fly fast.*

Silence was my only response. Because I was the prince, I was able to break into the confines of Kuro's minds. When I was suddenly assaulted by a wave of anger from Chiaki, I dove into his mind and saw what had struck a chord.

The usually peaceful Kuro healer had launched himself to the floor of the basin in an all-out assault. Wings he wasn't used to having stretched and beat madly as he attacked. I knew at once what he was fighting for.

Only the safety of his mate would be enough to alter his demeanor.

I was pulled from his thoughts just as several wings burst through the rocks above Chiaki and the others. It was chaos, the screams deafening enough for me to hear even without being connected.

Christophe seemed in a trance, unwilling or unable to hear the disruption echoing from the other tunnels. When he reached for my belt, I let out a choked cry. Before I could fight, Christophe slowly slumped on top of me. Struggling with his weight, I pushed him to the rocky floor.

"I couldn't let him," Joel said shakily. "I'm sorry, but I just couldn't."

The crystal that had once seemed like a delicate flower had been transformed to a blade of death. With a sickening crack, it shattered as Joel let the object slide from his hand.

"I know." I rolled away from Christophe's limp form and grabbed what was left of my clothes. In his frenzy, Christophe had destroyed most of my coat. At least my pants were intact. "Come on."

"What's going on?" Joel demanded, his limp exposing his wound. "Kanji?"

"Tristan is coming for me." I corrected myself, "For us."

He blinked. "How would he—"

"Look up. What do you see?"

"Nothing." The crescendo of noises from the other tunnels grew louder, and Joel cringed at the sound. "We have to get to the others."

Even wounded, he was brave. I was halfway up the drop-off when I looked down and saw he hadn't moved.

"Joel, let's go."

He stared at me in confusion.

"Didn't you fly down there?" I asked, exasperated as my boots hit earth.

"No, Christophe forbids me to. He flew me down."

I wanted to command him to fly, but his expression reminded me of the very first time I'd felt my wings. The surprise, the shock, the denial… none of those emotions were anything in comparison to the surge of life.

"Joel," I called softly. "Please, just allow your body to feel."

Images were being forced into my mind at such a rapid pace I was sure they did belong solely to Chiaki. He had managed to free his mate from a Sidhee, and the two lovers were flying toward the roof where several other Kuro and Dryma had already fled.

Joel took a breath as he stripped from his clothes. His wings were lighter than mine, a hue closer to his shade of hair. Nervously, they beat together as if they had a will of their own and then he was beside me. Joel seized my hand and dragged me down a cavern with his newly found confidence.

Kanji, where are you?

Tristan's voice nearly sent me sprawling to the ground. Something in my expression told Joel what had happened.

Our speed was nothing to scoff at. Before I knew it, we'd burst into an opening of the main basin. To say there was chaos would've been an understatement. Kuro and Dryma were trying to flee through the glittering portal overhead, but because the Sidhee couldn't follow without being prepared to take sacrifices, they did everything they could to keep their prisoners in place.

The anguish I heard from the throats of Kuro and Dryma told me some had fallen.

"Chiaki," Joel screamed, his voice warning. "Take Aiden and leave."

The two healers stood out with their bright blond hair. Chiaki had managed to free Aiden, but they were in the midst of fighting an oversized Sidhee blocking their path.

My presence didn't go unnoticed. While the Dryma continued to surge upward with what little strength they had, the Kuro came to a screeching halt. Confusion and panic swept throughout their minds as questions flitted across chapped lips.

Leave, I commanded. *Help everyone you can, but do not wait.*

"Chiaki." The name had barely passed Joel's lips before he was gone from beside me and swooping to the ground.

I prepared to follow but was stopped by the sound of a familiar tread behind me.

"Did you think he killed me, Kanji?"

I closed my eyes. "No."

"And yet you ran from me."

I needed to run. I needed to get away… back to Tristan. Scanning the sky, I couldn't see him, but I could feel him. His presence was as thick as smoke, filling me with absolute elation. Yet it was as elusive as air, running through my fingers just as I started to close them.

"Let me go, Christophe. Tristan is coming and he's angry."

I didn't trust myself to turn around for fear that seeing the rage in his face would make me lose concentration. Tristan was a Dryma first and a Kuro second. But the faint part of swan within him belonged to me and sooner or later, I'd pinpoint his exact whereabouts.

"Do you really think I'm frightened of him?"

"He was your prince," I whispered defiantly. "Doesn't that mean anything?"

"Not where you're concerned."

Christophe was getting closer… too close. I saw Joel had Aiden and Chiaki tucked into his sides, their wings interconnecting like a giant butterfly. They were so close to the portal I knew they could smell the fresh air, but they lingered.

Three pairs of eyes were upon me, and I knew they were waiting. My order meant nothing if I wasn't coming too.

"I'm sorry you became this, Christophe."

"I'm not letting you go."

"Following us would be a mistake."

Then I spiraled off the ledge. Instead of flying up, like I knew he'd expect, I just fell. The whoosh of air in my ears combined with the clattering of steel against iron created an out-of-body experience where nothing was real.

But his arms were.

And his hand pressing my face close to his heart was too.

"Tristan," I murmured.

"What the hell were you doing?" His eyes flashed brighter than the fire pits used to light the basin. "Why didn't you use your wings?"

"I knew you would catch me, Tristan."

"Get to the portal, Kanji."

I flung all of my weight into his arms so he wouldn't have the option of running. "Not without you."

"Christophe will follow," Tristan warned.

From his perch, the former Dryma captain looked like a mask of pure rage. If he hadn't been breathing, I would've mistaken him for a statue used to guard fortresses.

"Tristan," I pleaded, my voice small. Now my mate was finally holding me, my kidnapping sunk in. "I can't anymore. Please...."

My cries meant more to him than his anger at Christophe. So knowing full well Christophe would lead an undefeatable army to the human world, we retreated. Joel, Aiden, and Chiaki disappeared into the portal.

"Look at me," Tristan commanded. He held fast to my jaw and turned me so he could take possession of my lips. The kiss was searing, sending heat straight to my neglected cock.

Moaning into his mouth, I watched his body tense.

"Part of me wants to claim what's mine, be damned who sees," Tristan admitted, once again leaning down to kiss me. His lips were full of need and desire. "But I will never willingly allow another to see your bare skin."

"No," I whispered. "Only for you."

As rocks and clay morphed to sky, I felt the echo of thoughts around me and knew Zain and Seth were there as well.

Almost there, please, keep flying to your freedom.

In this moment, all I could offer my tribe were words of comfort. I prayed the encouragement was enough for every Kuro to escape through the slim portal that had appeared like a beacon of light upon a shadowy shore.

CHAPTER ELEVEN

THE DAYS in which I'd painstakingly waited for Tristan to awaken had been the worst of my life. I had been so desolate, so full of helplessness, that even a twitch of my mate's fingers was enough to elicit cries of despair.

Never had I thought I would ever feel that way again. Not until Christophe tore me away and proved losing my mate was worse than his sleepless slumber.

How did you find me, Zain?

Lying beside me like something from a dream was Tristan. He had given up most of the room in our bed, so his legs were pressed together. Breaths no louder than butterfly wings rose and fell from his chest. An arm beneath his head told me he'd kept watch over me until sheer exhaustion overtook him.

Not wanting to let go of this moment, I closed my eyes.

Then Zain answered my question and proved this was my reality.

I heard you call for me. Portals don't immediately close, so there was enough time for us to pinpoint exactly where the portal was. It took a few days of that Asrai boy trying to reopen it, but he managed.

Years ago, Christophe and Tristan had foolishly hoped the same thing. If I had not saved them, neither my hunter nor lover would be alive. *You could've died.*

Your prince jumped in without hesitation. Zain tried to sound unimpressed but failed. *Then Seth and I followed. I'm not sure, but I saw the Asrai kid go all blue-eyed so I'm assuming he did something to keep us from drowning.*

Which made sense. His magic ran deep.

Rest while you can, Kanji. When I see you, I'm going to punch you for letting that bastard take you.

You're not really mad at me, I countered.

No, he sighed. *I'm mad at myself.*

Don't be. Then a shift in the figure beside me made me sever my connection with Zain.

"Baby, are you awake?" I felt a soft touch as Tristan stroked my cheek.

"Yes." I opened my eyes.

Seeing his pain almost made me wish I hadn't. My mate was a wreck, simply put. He had dark shadows beneath his round eyes, and there were indentations in his lower lip where I knew he'd bitten too hard.

I couldn't contain my sob as I rested my cheek on Tristan's arm, the simple act more intimate than if he'd kissed me.

"Don't worry about being brave, Kanji. Did you doubt I would come for you?" Tristan asked softly.

"No." I shot up, my button-down shirt falling open. Not only had I been changed, but bathed. "I knew you would come. But I was afraid he would hurt you."

Tristan blinked back his surprise. "Who?"

I took his hand and held his fingers to my lips. The raw taste of his earthen skin instantly calmed me.

"Love, who?" His eyes softened at my touch.

"Calhoun."

Tristan's green eyes flashed black at the mention of the Sidhee prince's name, as if remembering Calhoun was like remembering another life. "Calhoun still desires me?"

I could only nod. "Why do you sound so uncertain?"

"Because I thought by now he would find a different conquest."

"No one could ever get over you," I assured him. "We make quite a pair, don't we? Christophe wanting me and Calhoun wanting you. Makes me think they should just get together and leave us alone."

Tristan pressed his nose to my cheek and laughed. "If only, Kanji."

I swallowed my fear. "The others? Did they make it back?"

His face was a mask of sadness. I had been away for days and the only thing I seemed capable of was making the love of my life upset.

"The Kuro are exhausted, but otherwise fine. Zain and Tomas are taking care of them."

"And the Dryma?"

He hesitated. "Sleeping, but alive. Their souls belong to the trees still harbored in this world, but with the roots tying them to the human world, they might not... survive."

"Your flowers will work this time," I assured him. "Chiaki is back and you can use the water like Ciaran did."

"Fewer Dryma have returned than were taken," Tristan said sadly. He opened his mouth to continue, but I just leaned into his chest so he would know I understood. "Perhaps those with utterly destroyed trees knew they wouldn't make it back and chose to join the Sidhee rather than risk death in the human realm."

Christophe had said there were Dryma who turned, and accounting for the five fairies who had come back to this world to be made an example of, who knew how many of their kind had turned their backs on humanity forever?

"Ciaran?"

His eyes brightened. "He's doing great. He even speaks to me now."

My jealousy surprised me. Even without thinking about Ciaran, I'd subconsciously missed him.

"He wanted to find you," Tristan told me, easing my fears. "That's why he opened the portal."

"Did any Sidhee follow us back?"

"Not yet, but they will soon."

"There's more you're not telling me, isn't there?"

Tristan's eyes raked my body as if determining whether or not I was strong enough to hear his words. "Two of my brothers have not returned, which means we are down to four princes. Our hierarchy is not as loyal or determined as yours is. Landon and Aron are asleep, but Seth and I agree on the best path."

"What choice is there other than to fight?"

"I think you will find the Kuro are afraid of what would happen to them should they revive the Dryma."

Then his caution made sense.

"If we don't fight, the Sidhee will destroy all of us. It's only a matter of time."

"You see that, love." He kissed my lips as he pushed me onto my back and straddled my waist. "And so do I. But our relationship is unheard of to say the least. Kuro and Dryma alike may not be supportive of our ideals."

With Tristan fondling my chest, I was starting to lose focus. "You sound like someone went against you."

He was silent.

"Did they?"

"No, but I heard some of the Kuro talking."

"About you?"

"About Seth."

My hand on his cheek startled him, but he leaned into the touch. "Tristan—"

"Seth isn't the most approachable, so I understand where your kind are coming from. But whatever is decided, know this." He undid the single button keeping my shirt together. "You will never be taken from me again."

His promise made me tremble.

"Did Christophe do anything to you?"

I considered lying but couldn't bring myself to. "Christophe almost strangled me, but that's it."

"That's it?" Tristan repeated almost angrily. The bed dipped as he pinned me down with his legs on either side of my hips and one hand holding fast to my wrists. "You're making light of the fact he could've killed you?"

"I can't explain why, but I knew he wouldn't."

Tristan slid his fingers upward until he rolled my nipple between his forefinger and thumb. He still had his other hand wrapped around my wrists so I couldn't move, but instead of fear, I felt desire.

"Ciaran was the one who showed me how to get into the Sidhee world," Tristan confessed, moving to the other nipple and pinching until the bud was hard. "I knew the moment we'd entered the Sidhee world because I could hear your thoughts. Christophe had you pinned to the ground in a barren cave and you had ordered your friend not to help. That cowardly son of a bitch. A few more minutes and he could've had his way with you."

"Never," I vowed. "I wouldn't have let him."

"He's stronger than you."

"I still would've fought him."

Tristan just stared at me with amusement before bending his head to take my nipple into his mouth. I cried out in pleasure as he abused the sensitive flesh with his talented tongue, swirling and licking the way I wished he would around my cock.

"My body," I moaned, "is only for your pleasure. I promise."

Tristan cut me off with a possessive expression I wasn't used to seeing on his chiseled golden features. "Even with his hands on you, I could feel what was in your heart. The way you look at me with such loyalty, there's no way I could ever doubt your love. And I hope you never doubt mine."

My mouth fell open as I stared up at the most beautiful creature I had ever laid eyes on. His golden hair had fallen over his face so he had a mischievous look about him that made me squirm. Tristan wore a loose sweater opened at the hollow of his throat so I could see his pulse. My eyes went lower as I stared at the bulge in his pants where his beautiful cock was waiting to be pleasured.

I groaned.

"What do you want?"

"You. In my mouth," I clarified.

Tristan gave me a questioning look and I knew why. Our sex life had mostly consisted of quick encounters in strange places. Like our relationship, there had never been a time where we could casually make love.

"I have a lot of desires," I warned him. "Things we haven't even gotten started on yet."

Tristan released my wrists so he could take a fistful of my hair. He was so gentle, I only felt a faint tug as he brought his lips to mine. His tongue entwined with my own, made my thoughts swirl. As he pulled away, I saw reluctance.

"Are you sure you want me to be rough with you?"

"Do your worst," I challenged, making him roll his eyes.

With a determined sigh, he took both of my wrists, pinning them to the bed as he edged his way up. His cock was so hard I could practically see the outline of his head straining against the jeans fabric.

I used my teeth to pull down his zipper, but he released me for a second to undo the button and free his cock. The length was so hard, so thick I leaned forward and took him down my throat without giving myself time to adjust.

Tristan cried out in surprise, his pleasure evident. "Damn, that feels good."

He took the lead, which was exactly what I wanted by initiating this position. With his hands holding down my wrists and his cock buried in my throat, he could do whatever he wanted. Closing my eyes, I relaxed my mouth and sucked as hard as I could. Without the use of my hands, I felt clumsy and incapable of taking much of his length, but my mate didn't seem to mind.

His moans of appreciation combined with his intense chanting of my name sent unadulterated pleasure straight to my hardened flesh. As he adjusted me, used me to suit his whims, I completely gave in. My dripping cock was a constant reminder of how desperately I wanted my own release, but with Tristan's encouraging cries, my needs took a back seat.

"Kanji, I want to fuck you."

His words made me jerk. Never before had he sounded so possessive, so dominant. Before I could blink, he'd flipped me so I was on my hands and knees. Pulling at my pants and my briefs, he tugged at the fabric until I was naked beneath him.

Never had I felt so vulnerable.

And at the same time, so wanted.

There was a pause, long enough for him to retrieve oil, and then his fingers were slick at my entrance. I was already leaking and hard, but when he pressed against the tiny bundle of muscles deep within me, I arched back and whimpered.

"Tristan, please." I buried my face in the pillow in an attempt to gather my bearings, but everything held his scent. "I want you inside of me."

"Don't these desires of yours want me to tease you too?" He ceased his movements inside me, leaving me empty. "My sweet Kanji?"

As badly as I wanted to come, I wanted Tristan's pleasure first. "Whatever you want to do, go ahead. I want to please you."

His fingers started moving again, harder than before. "Oh, you do, love," he assured me. "You have no idea how badly I want to give in and take you."

I lifted my hips suggestively, but before words could form, he'd taken hold of my cock and stroked. I was so close to coming; it was a wonder I hadn't already.

When he removed his fingers, I trembled in anticipation. Slowly, he eased himself into me, giving me little time to adjust before delivering a merciless pounding. Every time he took possession of my body, he grew more intense.

Murmuring and crying out in a mixture of pleasure and pain, he continued to alternate between slamming into my prostate and stroking my leaking cock.

"Can you take it?"

I nodded into the sheets.

My entire being became a vessel for his pleasure, something to be used. But when I started to meet his thrusts in earnest and tiny cries escaped my throat, he took mercy on me.

"Come for me, Kanji," he ordered, his voice calm among the chaos I felt raging in my body. "Now."

My muscles clenched and my balls drew up as I emptied my release onto the sheets. The pleasure was so intense, when he raised me onto my knees so both his arms could imprison me against his chest, my head fell back onto his shoulder. Thrusting upward, he bit into the soft flesh of my neck.

"Again, Kanji, come for me again."

I instantly reacted to his touch, my legs shaking and convulsing as he supported my weight. Tristan's scent combined with his alluring voice was enough to drive anyone crazy, but I wasn't just anyone. I was his true mate. And what he wanted, I gave.

Rolling my hips, a strangled sound escaped my lips as he stroked my revived member until I released completely. There was no strength left in my body, not even enough for me to lie back down.

Craning my neck so I could look into his eyes, I saw glittering emerald orbs staring at me.

"You're my life," Tristan whispered. "I'll never let you go."

SOMEONE WAS shouting. Because the sound died off so quickly, I assumed the noise had been part of my dream. But as the crescendo of voices steadily increased, I could no longer ignore them.

"Tristan?" I forced my eyes open, but instead of Tristan, someone else was waiting. "Ciaran?"

With his pale hair cut short and very human clothes, I wasn't sure I was looking at the same Asrai.

"Kanji." His voice was like a soft summer breeze. "Missed you."

"Huh?" My response was less than dignified. "What did you say?"

Judging by the hastily stitched T-shirt and loose-fitting jeans, one of the younger Kuro had altered the outfit for him. Although his skin looked less like diamonds and more like flesh, his startling eyes hadn't lost any of their sheen. The absorbing blue was enough to take my breath away.

Ciaran frowned. "I said I missed you."

At first, I'd expected some sort of accent in his words, but the only sound I heard was that of my mate.

Now I could explain the sense of calm I found at being so close to the Asrai boy. Looking at him was like looking at a younger version of Tristan.

Without warning, Ciaran slipped from the bed, his small feet leaving the tiniest sound as he made his way to the empty bowl where Tristan's flower had been. My heart clenched, my mate's safety always of the utmost importance. But I felt shame when he just retrieved a water bottle and handed it to me.

"Thanks." I eyed him suspiciously but his large button eyes were void of emotion. "Any idea what's going on out there?"

"Fighting."

"Yeah, I gathered that." I cleared my throat. "Do you know why?"

Ciaran held out his hand for the bottle when I was finished. "Not everyone is happy about you being with Tristan."

I sighed, piling my long hair into a ponytail. "That's... complicated."

"Not really." He already had my coat in his hands. "What you are shouldn't matter."

"Unfortunately, it does."

"That's why I don't have any parents."

"You've got me and Tristan."

I didn't have to read his mind to know he didn't believe me.

Still, his sudden closeness was comfortable. He followed me from the room to the main living area like a shadow. When I saw his boots neatly stacked beside mine, I almost gagged from cuteness. Before he would have to ask, I took his hand and pulled him into the frigid weather, my boots hastily laced.

The anger I felt emanating from the crowd outside my door was suffocating. If I hadn't seen looks of relief from my tribe, I would've gone right back into the cabin.

"Stay behind me."

Obediently, Ciaran dug his small fingers into the fabric of my coat. In my mind, I knew no Kuro would ever harm me, but the hostility was unnerving.

Tomas and Zain were at the forefront of the crowd, their eyes the color of cold steel. Tristan and Seth had their feet firmly planted on the dividing line between the Kuro's cabins and the Dryma's.

"What's going on?" I struggled to find my voice, fear for my mate overwhelming as I saw the pure hatred in my friends' eyes.

"Kanji." Zain sighed in relief.

A path was cleared so he could make his way to me, Tomas not far behind. His dark roots were like a beacon among what used to be his bleached hair.

"We're deciding," Zain told me.

My eyes flickered from him to Tristan. "On?"

"What we're going to do." Tomas rolled his eyes.

"Fight. You have to fight." Seth was angry, which explained why the only one brave enough to stand on his side was his brother. "You don't have a choice anymore. You have to stop hiding."

"For what?" Tomas screeched, his voice bitter. "For you? The moment we fight, we'll be reverted into slaves."

A shout rang out among the Kuro. The fear was contagious, as were their doubts. Even though we had been reunited with our brethren, there were still far too few of us. We'd barely escaped from the Sidhee world and it was due to Christophe's carelessness.

"Please." Tristan's plea was enough to silence even the most stubborn of my kind. He was my mate after all, their prince. "We swear never to imprison you again."

"You cannot make such a promise." Zain was trying so hard to keep control, but long gone were the niceties. "Without our protection, you will die."

"We already are dying," Seth roared, causing a few of the Kuro closest to him to take a step away. "Don't you get that?"

Shouting resumed.

Through a sea of faces, I saw Micky and Shinji standing beside a tree in the far back as if they wished they could disappear. Micky closed his eyes, a silent plea for help.

"We have to fight," I said quietly, knowing my words would be heard. Silence echoed across the desolate campground as disbelief crept into tired faces. "I know how much you have lost. How much you have suffered. We are weakened and we have enemies, but the Dryma do not need to be one of them.

"If we don't lure the Sidhee here and fight on our terms, who is to say they will not return? If we want to live our lives in peace, we have to draw upon our strengths and face them. After all—" I looked around at the deep-set eyes of my kind. "—we have something the Sidhee have always craved: flight."

Zain was shaking, his eyes burning into my soul. "If this is what you want, you know I'll follow. But Kanji, reconsider."

I put my hand on his shoulder, his body sinking into the touch. "We have a choice to make, my friends. Walk away and live in fear or fight the Sidhee on our terms."

My words hit their mark.

The looks of adoration upon the Kuro's faces I expected, but not the one I saw on Tristan's. He wore dirt-stained jeans, a loose shirt, and a jacket with one too many holes and yet, he was more regal than I would ever be. No amount of glam, illusion, or magic was ever going to diminish his grace and beauty.

I finally realized he was the one who fueled my strength. With the way he was looking at me, the Sidhee could attack in that moment and I wouldn't hesitate to defend those I loved.

There was a life I could deserve, if only I maintained the courage to protect it.

"A choice? What choice could there be to make?" Seth was still angry.

"I know you are scared the others won't wake," Tristan said kindly. "I am too, but if we want to ask for help, we cannot act like this."

"You are blinded by your lust for Kanji," Seth argued.

"I love him," Tristan countered, his voice dangerous. "That won't ever change. If there is ever a choice to make, I choose him."

I released a breath I didn't realize I'd been holding. Tristan's public declaration meant more than he could've realized. Tomas bowed his head in defeat, his shoulders giving in. Zain gave a curt nod in Tristan's direction, his silent sign of approval.

"I won't make you fight." I turned my attention away from the conflicted brothers. "You can join the others in the south if you wish."

Tomas grumbled, muttering something that sounded like "asshole" under his breath before saying, "You already know my answer."

"Mine too." Zain sank against my side. "Of course I'll follow you."

Christophe taking me meant more than the loss of my freedom, but a loss of who I thought I was. The tiny hands on my jacket, the glimpse of hope in my tribe's eyes, and my mate's beautiful smile all reminded me of how much more I stood to lose.

Opening my mouth to speak, I was silenced by three familiar figures crossing the threshold between what belonged to the Dryma and what land belonged to us.

"Joel." I let out a sigh of relief.

When I hadn't immediately spotted him among the waiting Kuro, I had feared he'd been hurt. But my worry was misplaced because other than a small butterfly bandage across his forehead, he appeared unharmed. In his hands were a bowl and some washcloths stained the color of rose petals.

I felt slightly sick when I realized the color could only be from blood.

Chiaki and Aiden flanked him on either side. Their fair hair was so pale the strands stood out against the snow. Aiden's eyes flickered to his mate before he made the decision to cross past Joel and join Chiaki.

"Where were you?" I asked.

Joel's eyes crinkled as he smiled. He wasn't what someone would call unforgettable, but his overwhelming kindness paired with his soft features made him irresistible.

"Checking on the Dryma." He deferred to Chiaki almost instantly, showing not only his wisdom, but his willingness to concede. "Chiaki checked their vitals."

The closest of my Kuro surrounded me, leaving only the smallest of openings, which my mate claimed.

Tristan's jaw clenched as he hung on Joel's every word. "The flowers are helping?"

"They seem to be," Joel said uncertainly.

"Don't sell yourself short," I chided, reaching up to touch Tristan's jaw with the tips of my fingers. "We knew the flowers alone wouldn't work."

"No," Joel agreed. "But they are helping. Before Chiaki and I set them up, their breathing was labored. At least we know we have time."

Chiaki desperately wanted to speak. I could see the urge in the way he bit his lip and shuffled his weight from foot to foot.

"Chiaki knows how." I beamed, making sure the young Kuro met my eyes. "Tea."

"Tea?" Up to this point, Seth had been trying his hardest to remain calm, but this was the last straw. "How on earth is tea supposed to help? Should I make some finger sandwiches?"

Tomas's earlier hostility returned. "Would you let him explain before you lose your fucking mind?"

I nodded to Chiaki to continue, but my approval wasn't enough.

Only when Aiden took his hand and held tight was he able to find his voice. "I made tea from the buttercups the Sidhee use to conceal. Kanji and I were able to conceal ourselves."

Tristan's eyes flashed fire. "Ciaran was able to wake me up because of his connection to water. So if we use his abilities, Chiaki's tea, and my flowers, we stand a good chance of reviving the Dryma. And if we have any hope of defeating the Sidhee, we need more than just the Kuro. We need the Dryma to fight with us."

"Our kind are little more than bodies," Seth argued, his voice empty. "Yet you think you contain enough power to bring them back with enough time to fight, little brother."

"I have no idea what you're talking about with tea," Zain commented, withdrawing a bag of sunflower seeds. I knew better than to think he was hungry as he shoved a handful into his mouth. "But having the Dryma as reinforcements sounds like a plan."

A slight tug on my hand brought me back to the small figure waiting for my attention. I had never been very nurturing to the younger generation, hence why the orphans lived with Joel, but something made me crouch down so I was at Ciaran's level.

"What's up, Ciaran?"

"If I help you," he started nervously, "can I stay?"

His words broke my heart. That precise moment was the one I realized how attached I was becoming. I was too choked up with emotion to speak, but my mate understood. He was already on his knees at my side.

"Of course, Ciaran. You don't have to worry about us sending you back."

I realized how lucky I had been. Even with the loss of my parents and my flock in shambles, I'd grown up loved and knowing where my place was in the world. What must it feel like to never know what the next day held?

I had a newfound respect for the strength Shinji, Micky, Chiaki, Aiden, and the others went through every day. But even more so for Joel, who stood beside them.

"So what now?" Joel sighed. When he shivered, I finally saw a break in Seth's composure. I saw how badly the Dryma prince wanted to comfort Joel, but he held back. "I know we have to make them this tea, but how do we plan to lure the Sidhee here?"

"Easy," Tomas scoffed, toeing the dirt with his boot. "We make them an offer they can't refuse."

Zain lost a mouthful of sunflower seeds as he cackled with laughter. Tristan stared at me, obviously waiting for me to explain Tomas's humor.

"He means we should lure them out by using ourselves as bait," I explained softly, feeling both Ciaran and Tristan clench either of my hands in worry. "They've always wanted the Kuro swans for their flight. And now the Dryma are... resting, we're the only reason they'd bother coming back."

"No." Tristan's voice was hard and unrelenting. "Too dangerous."

"Are you volunteering to be bait?" Tomas asked Tristan, the hard look in his eyes worse than what I felt in the pit of my stomach.

"Not an option," I said firmly. "Don't mention it again."

"Our prince will remain safe." Zain eyed Tomas as he continued to laugh. "And so will his mate. The Sidhee aren't stupid enough to come without a plan so they'll probably send a few scouts first."

"How can you be so sure they'll bother?" Micky asked nervously, constantly eyeing me to see if I would reprimand him. After I gave him the go ahead, he continued. "I mean, if you already escaped once, why would they think you wouldn't again?"

"Oh, they'll come," Tristan said darkly, his arm snaking around my waist like a twine. "Christophe can't help himself."

"And Calhoun either," Seth added.

I now understood what had driven the Dryma to wanting to align with the Sidhee: desperation to maintain their lives. I only wondered if after having been there, they would feel guilt at almost sacrificing their prince.

"We will have to divide up tasks," I decided. "Micky and Shinji, you'll prepare the Kuro for flight. Chiaki and Joel will watch over the Dryma and give Tristan anything he needs. Aiden, you can help. Zain, Tomas, and I will go back to Pasky—"

"No." Tristan's voice was flat.

"Tristan. I can retrieve the leaves from the trees for you."

"Yes, and I will come with you."

"But Ciaran used water from where he came, which means he has to stay here—"

The small Asrai boy shook his head, his hands covered in the oversized sweater as he tried to push back the sleeves. "I think it would work to get the water from where the trees are. That water is closer to your soul."

"I already lost you once." Tristan leaned in and kissed the corner of my mouth. "You aren't going without me."

"Maybe we all need to go back," Chiaki suggested softly, his voice the melodic break we desperately needed. "If the Sidhee come and we aren't ready, who knows what could happen?"

"What about the rest of our kind?" Seth asked. "You can't seriously want to leave me here alone."

"They can't be moved," Joel said quietly, the only one brave enough to outwardly defy Seth, and he still look pained doing so. "But Chiaki is an expert healer. I am certain he can find a way to hide the Dryma's presence here."

"Is this true?" Seth demanded.

Chiaki gave a small nod. "I will try."

"We have been here for weeks," Tristan added, "and they haven't found us yet. Should they attack, I think they will be more set on the Kuro than the Dryma anyway."

"I could remain here as well," Joel offered quietly.

Seth was staring at his Joel like he'd never seen the Kuro before.

Seth's voice, when he finally found it, was frazzled. "You mean, I would stay here with you and we would watch over the Dryma until they awoke?"

"Chiaki and Aiden will stay too," Joel added softly.

"Tristan needs the healer too," Seth pointed out. "He can't hide the Dryma and heal them from two different locations."

"I'll take Chiaki and Aiden with me, then send them back with what they need. This way I can stay in Pasky and monitor the behavior of the trees. And we'll still communicate, Seth. If things get worse here, I'll return."

"With Kanji?" Seth narrowed his eyes.

"Yes." Tristan sighed. "With Kanji and Ciaran."

Whether Seth was concerned for the safety of the Dryma or excited at the prospect of being alone with Joel for a few days, I couldn't guess. But the look in his eye told me he was going to stay.

"I have to check the flowers, love." Tristan brushed aside my hair so he could kiss the nape of my neck. His touch made me wish we were alone with only his naked, beautiful body to keep me company. "Then we can start getting ready to go."

I nodded, my throat sore. "Joel, can I talk to you for a second?"

"Sure." He carefully stepped around Seth, making sure not even a thread of his coat touched him. "Chiaki, Aiden, go with Tristan."

"Sure thing." Aiden took Chiaki's hand and steered him after Tristan, who stood patiently waiting.

I looked to see if Ciaran would go with him, but he had stopped and was talking to Micky and Shinji. Talking wasn't really what he was doing. Rather, he was staring at the two Kuro with keen interest.

"When did Ciaran get so comfortable around them?" I asked Joel as we headed to an empty bench built beneath a large tree. The tree was barren, but the familiarity of the trunk against my spine felt nice. What was left of the earthen scent of dirt felt even better.

Joel collapsed next to me. "While you were gone, they took care of him."

"Wait." I eyed him. "How would you know? You weren't here."

Joel chuckled, the corners of his eyes crinkling happily. "Micky told me. The kids tell me everything."

Which must've been nice.

Joel fidgeted with a thick ring around his finger, a gift from his father. Over and over, the metal caught the sunlight and created illusions across Joel's face. "So," he started quietly, "what did you want to talk about?"

"Seth."

He turned away. "What about him?"

"Don't do that," I warned, searching for my mate even though I knew he'd be gone. Tristan was already past the hill leading to the other side of the campground, but I could feel his presence. "You love him and trust me, I know what that's like. Even when you think you don't care, or don't want to, he's all you think about."

Joel took a breath. "Tristan is your mate. Different circumstances."

"Seth cares about you." I paused, ascertaining what my assumptions about Seth might lead to. "The entire time you were gone, he was a wreck. He wanted to go back and search, every day, remember? I already told you how he feels…. Why run?"

"He hasn't said anything to me."

I knew right then my words didn't matter. In all things, my voice was the reason and backbone of our kind. But when love and mates were concerned, I didn't doubt Joel would ignore me forever.

"Then say something to him. If you don't before this is over, you might regret it."

"Speaking from experience?" Joel teased.

I shook his shoulder until he'd meet my gaze. "Yes," I admitted. "If we hadn't made the decision to go to the Dryma Ball, I might never have mated to Tristan. Our lives could be very, very different. Trust me, Joel. You don't want to end up wondering what could be."

He squinted against the backdrop of the sun behind me. "I didn't know matchmaking was part of our prince's duties."

"Is now. Got a problem?"

"Nope."

"Good, then let's get going."

The last thing I wanted to do was uproot my kind yet again and trek my tribe back to the place where we'd barely lived. But the decision had been made; the only thing left was to finalize plans.

Zain and Tomas had their heads bent together with a few other Kuro. When they saw me, Zain started to follow, but I shook my head. "I'll be back in a minute."

Shrugging, he happily munched on his seeds. I was pretty sure he was ecstatic to be doing something other than cooking.

"Where are you going?" Seth's voice lacked conviction.

"Tristan" was my simple reply.

I could tell he wanted to stop me, that he was already upset with the amount of Kuro on *his* side, but he couldn't find a reason not to trust me. Not now we'd decided to side with the Dryma.

He shifted on the picnic table, where he was keeping watch. "Where's Joel?"

"By the river," I told him, biting my lip. "He's a great guy, probably the nicest Kuro I've ever met."

"I know that."

"Then get over yourself and tell him how you feel."

Seth was instantly on his feet. The change of stance didn't go unnoticed by my friends. "What do you know about how I feel?"

"If you feel anything like your brother does for me," I said with certainty, "you hardly breathe when you're away from Joel."

He smiled cruelly. "And if I can breathe just fine?"

"Then fucking let him go."

We had arrived at an impasse. Joel had only shared his thoughts with me after I'd found him crying at the river's edge months ago. Seth had broken off their relationship, but the look he got in his eye when he saw Joel suggested they were anything but over.

"It's not my business," I added softly, trying to ease the tension I saw rising in Seth's shoulders. "But he's one of the best friends I've ever had. I can only imagine what kind of lover he'd be."

As if on cue, Joel started trudging back to the campground. The moment Shinji and Micky caught sight of him, they ran up to him like lost puppies. I looked around for Ciaran and wasn't surprised to see him bounding across the campground. When he reached me, his cheeks were flushed, but he had a smile so vibrant I grinned right back.

"Can I come with you?"

I thought about opposing but realized there was no point in trying to shield him from the state the Dryma were sure to be in.

His hand in mine was comforting, and I wasn't sure I hadn't brought him along for my sake.

Even though the Dryma were technically alive, the scent of death was everywhere. The still, quiet air reminded me of the many nights I'd lain beside Tristan, holding on to the hope he'd awaken.

"KANJI, BABY, what are you doing?" Tristan looked at me in alarm, making me realize he hadn't wanted to test my emotional state. "Are you okay being here?"

"I'm not going to collapse." After being imprisoned by Christophe, I wanted to. "I just want to help you."

"Me too," Ciaran chimed in, shifting so he was within Tristan's sight.

We'd entered the first cabin and were standing in the small common area. From what I could tell, the Dryma were in the single bedroom, but there were probably more upstairs. The cabins Seth had reserved had enough space for eight individuals to sleep comfortably. If we had been given even one of these, every one of Joel's wards could've slept under the same roof.

I pushed away my irritation and turned to the matter at hand. "I know I can't help check their vitals or adjust their flowers, but I can do something useful."

Tristan's eyes flared so bright, the emerald hue the true essence of spring. He touched the back of my neck and drew me close so his words were only for my ears. "When we are alone, I am sure I can find many ways you can be useful to me."

With regret in his eyes, he pulled away and glanced at the winding staircase. "Chiaki and Aiden are upstairs. I have to teach Chiaki how the flowers work."

"How?" Ciaran asked.

"I'll show you."

We weren't quiet; there wasn't a reason to be. Two male Dryma, barely older than us, were lying on the double bunk beds, with two females resting on the queen bed. There weren't enough space heaters to go around, and the air was like death.

Tristan was already sliding from his thin coat, exposing a V-necked sweater unlikely to keep him warm. "Here."

"I don't need—"

"Kanji." His voice was patient and kind as always, but there was a warning in his tone. "I have to focus and I can't if I'm worried about you getting sick."

The promise of warmth was hard to resist.

"I'm not cold," Ciaran said, looking at me curiously. He released my hand so he could inspect the flowers on the nightstand.

"Kuro swans tend to be colder," Tristan explained patiently as he led me to the nightstand. "Beautiful, aren't they?"

At first, I thought he spoke of the sleeping females, but his eyes were only on the flowers.

"You speak with such passion," I said, slightly ashamed. "I don't see them the way you do."

"Let me have your hand."

Ever so slowly, he moved our entwined hands until my fingers were inches from the petals. Like gravity, I was pulled to them. The colors were as soft as rabbit fur, but the fierce heartbeat was more suited to a lion.

The Dryma were still… breathless. The only proof of life came from the flowers.

"Dryma fairies and Sidhee used to be one race," Tristan explained to Ciaran. "We craved the sky, the air, and the trees so we left that world. We were granted our desire for nature, but at a price. We became tied to the earth, our souls entangled with the very roots of the trees we cherish. I'm sure you know this from the stories concerning the Asrai.

"Our kind were too proud to serve as our own protectors, so we trapped the Kuro. In hindsight, using slavery because of our own fears wasn't beneficial for either of us." He paused, suddenly realizing he was speaking to a child. In Ciaran's defense, he looked anything but bored. "I fell in love with Kanji and wanted to free his kind, so I studied and tried to connect our lives to flowers instead so we could carry our souls with us. It wasn't enough, but at least they are keeping my kind alive."

Ciaran looked confused. "Then why can't I heal the flowers for them the way I did for you?"

Tristan coughed. "I'm a little bit different."

"How?"

I held my breath. Even though technically Tristan was half Kuro, I had never been able to see him as anything less than the regal fairy I'd first met.

"Because he's like me too," I answered softly.

Ciaran looked from me to Tristan, the blue of his eyes vibrant. "Beautiful?"

Tristan practically collapsed from laughter. He took Ciaran's hand and mine, leading us both out of the room before my shocked expression multiplied.

"Yes, beautiful." Tristan finally caught his breath. "Like Kanji. My soul belongs to him. The other Dryma need their flowers even after they awaken."

"What's going on?" Aiden's voice was almost as cautious as his stance. He had Chiaki shielded behind his back, but the moment he caught sight of our faces, he looked confused. "Are you okay, Prince Kanji?"

"Ciaran called him beautiful," Tristan explained. "And you really are, Kanji."

Aiden pushed blond strands from his forehead, his eyes twinkling mischievously. "Not like my Chiaki, though."

"Oh yeah?" Tristan played along, bubbles of laughter still dripping from his voice. "Did you hear that, Kanji?"

For a moment, there was panic on Aiden's face, like he thought I would be insulted.

I was anything but.

"Ciaran has us all beat." It felt so good to laugh and not feel like I had to.

The small Asrai stared up at me, his head cocked to the side, giving him the appearance of a puppy. "I am?"

"I second that." Chiaki dragged Aiden down the stairs, the two pale-haired Kuro looking every bit connected. "Sorry, baby. I still love you."

Aiden's pale cheeks flushed scarlet as he mumbled, "Love you too."

"So we've decided, then." Tristan commanded our attention, both with his vibrancy and his attractiveness. "Asrai beat out Kuro and Dryma where looks are concerned. Glad we settled this age-old feud."

If I'd giggled any harder, I would've been on the floor.

Our reprieve was cut short when a gust of air slapped against the exposed skin of my ankles and a disgruntled-looking Seth appeared. Tristan, as good-natured as ever, opened his mouth as if to explain, but then closed it. Even if laughter was good for healing, I was sure Seth wouldn't appreciate the break in his serious mask, however brief.

"How are they?"

Tristan touched my shoulder, his hand lingering on my upper arm for a few seconds as he stepped in front of Ciaran and me. "As good as can be expected. I read their vitals, but because they aren't humans, the lack of pulse is normal. But the recovery seems to be stronger in some. I can only assume this is due to the nature of their individual trees."

Which explained why the flowers breathed even though the Dryma were still.

"I want to go check on the others just in case, but I'm sure the results will be the same. The best thing for me to do is get back to Pasky with Ciaran and Chiaki so we can start on the tea."

Seth coughed. "I couldn't agree more."

Watching the two brothers broke my heart. I realized I'd hoped Tristan's revival would bring him to a closer relationship with Seth. Deep down, I always knew it wasn't meant to be. Seth wanted to choose Joel, I knew he did, but duty and obedience kept him from giving in. Seeing Tristan love me so freely had to hurt.

And even though there was no way I'd ever give up my mate, I could sympathize.

"Kanji, love." Tristan trained his eyes on my shaking frame. "Maybe you should go back to the cabin. We don't need to bring a lot, but I'm sure there are things you wanted to pack."

Apart from Zain's Jeep, there were only a handful of cars. Because most of the Kuro would not be coming back, I assumed we would load up everything we had to in the cars and then fly.

"Ciaran and I are going to drive with you, Tristan," I decided.

His eyes softened. "If you want to be with your kind, I understand."

"My prince." Aiden dutifully stepped in. "Chiaki and I can drive Ciaran if you want to fly with the rest of our kind."

But I knew from the reserve in Tristan's eyes he wasn't ready to fly in front of the others. "I'm okay with driving. You two deserve to use your wings. And we can always make pit stops and change out."

They seemed content with the idea, more so in fact. Aiden was looking Chiaki up and down with an excitement more fitting of a child about to receive a present. Such wonderment could only be there because he was finally going to see his mate's wings.

The moment was shattered when Seth cleared his throat loudly and jutted his thumb toward the other cabins. "Tristan?"

"Coming, coming."

A cry of pain slipped out as more of my mate disappeared out the door. Before I could take a single step, Tristan had swept me off my feet.

"Crushing me," I whimpered, trying uselessly to put some space between us. "Lemme go."

"Don't care." He nuzzled the side of my cheek, my neck, anywhere he could reach. "Just want to hold you."

"I'm not going anywhere."

He stared, eyes full of apprehension.

Placing my hands on either side of his face, I looked deep into the emerald orbs. "Promise."

Satisfied, he gathered Chiaki and Aiden and followed after his brother. I could still hear Seth's curses long after they'd left our sight.

CHAPTER TWELVE

PACKING MOVED quickly. Part of the speed was due to every Kuro helping load our few cars, but part was because of our lack of things. I'd always thought the reason we did so well in our confined community was because our flock was what really mattered. Material things were nice, especially coats and blankets, but really, I couldn't think of one thing I owned I couldn't lose.

Zain and Tomas were annoying as usual, forbidding me to help pack anything that wasn't mine. What was more, they'd decided to split up so one could lead the Kuro back to Pasky, while the other stayed behind to drive one of the cars.

"Can't let your Jeep out of your sight, can you?" I teased.

"Shut up," Zain scoffed as he slammed the door. "You know I'm not about to let you drive there without me."

"We're not even driving together." I pointed to the sleek silver car behind his. Tristan was loading Ciaran into the back and the sight should've made me happy, but I was still pretty pissed at the car.

"Seth's a bastard, isn't he?" Zain groaned. "He had money all this time and never even thought to buy some damn food."

Dryma were wealthy beyond belief. "We thought he had a good reason not to use his money."

Zain rolled his eyes. "The Sidhee are after us. Not the FBI."

I couldn't come up with a defense so I just shook my head. "We agreed to stay at Crystal Cove so there should be plenty of food there."

"A bunch of us living in mansions…," Zain mused, signaling for Shinji to hurry and get into the Jeep. "This is like a bad sitcom waiting to happen."

"I'll record the shenanigans."

"Yeah, sure. They would all just be pictures of your boyfriend."

And he was right. Even with Kuro exposing their creamy skin in preparation for flight, my fully clothed mate was the only one I had eyes for. The sun had finally graced us, but the beams seemed to only find Tristan's golden curls. He appeared slender, but I knew beneath his clothes were hard lean muscles.

I ached with the need to kiss and worship every inch of his body.

The moment we were alone, I was going to do just that.

Tristan searched the campground, his gaze piercing. Once we locked eyes, he easily crossed the space between us until his arm was around my waist.

"Ready?" Tristan asked, feeling my fingers. "The car is warm."

"Good, see you there, Kanji." Zain jumped into his Jeep, silently shooing me away.

"Are you sad to leave?"

I eyed him. "You're kidding, right? I hate this place."

Tristan stopped me from opening the door by sweeping me into his arms and carrying me to the passenger's side. He deposited me on the comfortable seats before draping a blanket over me.

"You don't have to take care of me," I muttered, my voice thick with emotion. I wasn't used to being taken care of, but because Tristan did it so easily, I always forgot he wasn't either.

He just gave a light chuckle and started the car. The hand not on the steering wheel held fast to mine, our fingers drumming silently on the armrests between us.

We'd barely driven a mile before Ciaran slumped over in the back.

"He's passed out, isn't he?" Tristan smiled.

I reached behind to make sure his head was resting on a blanket and not a box. "Sure is."

Silence caved in around us as thick as smoke.

"What is it, love?"

I bit my lip. "Why did you lie?"

"About?"

"Earlier. When you said you started learning about the flowers for me."

Tristan's jaw locked. "I didn't lie."

I touched his cheek with the tip of my finger, his body instantly slumping into my touch. "But—"

The seriousness in his voice startled me. "Christophe is not the only one who fell in love with you that day."

Subconsciously, I touched the back of my head where I had fallen. "Do you think I'll ever regain my memories from that day?"

"I'm not a doctor." Tristan brought my hand to his lips. "But I hope not."

I frowned. "Why?"

"Because then you might remember the way Christophe looked when you pulled him out."

"No matter how much he might love me—" I cringed. "—I'll never want anyone but you."

Tristan sighed in frustration. "I know you won't. I know and yet... I can't help but be worried. You are so kind and I know you feel bad for him. Every time I think about him taking you, I want to hide you away."

I jolted in my seat. "What?"

"Don't you feel bad?" Tristan stole a sideways glance in my direction, as if waiting for me to deny it.

Instead of responding, I leaned forward until the seat belt was digging into my ribs and laid my head on his thigh. His answering shudder showed how much he liked where I was.

His hand in my hair was rough, his fingers scraping against my scalp. "I hope you don't have any plans of moving."

I adjusted myself so the seat belt was a little more comfortable. "Nope."

We'd left the campground late so I wasn't surprised the sun had already abandoned us. We were making great time because of the lack of traffic, but every time a car zoomed by, I choked up. Seeing the bright lights zoom across Tristan's face was like being in the Sidhee world all over again.

The second Tristan's face was distorted by the lights reminded me of the way Christophe had looked when he was angry.

"You're shivering," Tristan pointed out, reaching over me to turn up the heat. "Are you all right?"

I didn't want to worry him. "Yes."

"Are you sure?"

I gave another nod, burying my face into his thigh so I could inhale his earthy scent. Despite everything, I found I missed Pasky.

"If you're tired," Tristan murmured, his fingers threaded in my hair turning gentle, "go ahead and sleep."

"I should help drive," I mumbled.

Absently, I stroked his thigh, relishing the hard muscle. He stiffened and made a pained noise in the back of his throat. At least I knew I wasn't the only one who didn't want to hold back.

"When we get back, every Kuro is going to look at you for guidance," Tristan started, his hand slipping from my hair so he could adjust the radio. Instead of the upbeat music, the tune had gone soft. "You should rest while you can."

I used caution with my words just in case Ciaran wasn't as asleep as we thought. "I want to be alone with you when we get there."

"Of course. Any Kuro is welcome in my house, but my suite is much larger than those cabins and is private."

I resisted a chuckle. "Twice as big?"

He played along. "More like four times."

"So that means Ciaran… he's going to stay with us."

Out of all our concerns, this was the most human and the most important. He might have been an Asrai, which meant there were things about him we would never understand. Some of those things were the way he'd been raised before he'd been expelled. If what Tristan said was true, one day the Asrai females might try to call him back.

I noticed Tristan was holding back. "What do you want to do, Kanji?"

"Mari used to plead with me to mate to her. Over and over and over until I thought I'd lose my mind."

"Yes." His voice was emotionless. "You're very popular."

I poked the firm flat lines of his abdominals. "The only time I ever wanted to give in was when I realized I wouldn't have children if I didn't."

"So you've thought about children?"

"Of course. Have you?"

"Yes."

There was a tense moment of silence where I waited for Tristan to speak. When he didn't, I realized I could feel his longing. The same desire to belong, to have a family, was as ingrained within him as it was within me.

"I don't care if he's not related to either of us," I said, finally breaking the silence. "When a Kuro had been abandoned, Joel didn't think twice about bringing them into his home. I never understood that before."

"And now?" Tristan was holding his breath.

"I don't want to let Ciaran go."

"We'd have to one day," Tristan reminded me softly. "If he wanted us to."

I chewed the inside of my cheek. "Yes, but at least we'd have this time."

Tristan's laughter startled me. "Sometimes you surprise me."

"Why?"

"Because you always say exactly what I feel."

There was an immense relief at finally being able to talk about what had bothered me for so long.

"Sleep, Kanji."

"On one condition," I pressed. "Put your hand back on my head."

I craved his touch more than he would ever know. "Whatever you want."

WHEN THE brick mansions of Crystal Cove finally came into view, I sighed in relief. Despite having been there with Tristan to help him gather materials from his greenhouse, I was excited to be there with some degree of permanence.

Tristan's house was the largest, meant to house the Dryma king, queen, and several of his brothers. The estates looked old but had been built less than a hundred years ago. Instead of taking advantage of every house, I wasn't surprised Zain, Tomas, Micky, and Shinji had decided to stay in the guesthouse.

Crystal Cove was already private, having been designed as a gated community. But Tristan's home was on an entirely different level. Not only were there tall fences surrounding the property, but the guesthouse was also composed of a sturdy brick. The winding vines added to the appeal, making the smaller house look like something out of a housekeeping catalog.

Although I doubted Sidhee would try to take over Crystal Cove, Zain and Tomas insisted they stay at the guesthouse. Their argument was simple: if the Sidhee invaded, they'd meet my friends before getting to me. I didn't really mind, not if it meant they would be close enough for me to reach in an emergency.

The other Kuro took refuge in the neighboring mansions, unwilling to be farther.

I knew this would happen, knew my kind would be timid of the sudden wealth we'd been offered, however temporary. But knowing money didn't change my tribe's heart was very reassuring.

A mansion meant for two Dryma housed five or six of my Kuro.

And I was glad of the closeness.

"What are you grinning about?" Zain's eyebrows disappeared into his dark hair. His yellow Jeep was parked next to Tristan's rental car as we helped direct traffic. There weren't many of us, so apart from the guesthouse and Tristan's, there were only three other mansions in use.

"I was wondering how every Kuro would handle this change," I mused. Shinji and Micky carried their things into the guesthouse, eyes wide. Tomas was farther down the road, his bleached blond tips making him easy to spot. He barked orders, the others eager to please. "We always wanted to live here, remember?"

"I remember." Zain fingered the buttons of his dismal coat as if in deep thought. "Kanji?"

"Yeah."

"What do you think we'll do?"

"What do you mean?"

"After."

Zain had only offered one word, but I knew what he meant. As tied to nature as the Dryma were, so too were the Kuro.

"We'll have two communities, one for the summer and another we'll go to in the winter."

Zain sighed. "Sounds nice. What does your mate think?"

As if on cue, Tristan appeared from one of the many doors to his house, a towering stack of blankets in his arms. I was about to go to him when Micky beat me to it, hands outstretched for the blankets. They handed them out together.

"Tristan wants what I do," I told him, contentment bubbling in my veins. "There's no way he'd ever want to leave nature, so I'm thinking we'll move closer to another nature reserve down south and keep Pasky here too."

"With me, right?" Zain's voice was so quiet I almost missed it.

I blinked. "Of course with you and with the others. We'll travel in flocks when we go from the south to the north and vice versa. Just because I have Tristan doesn't mean I'll give up leading our kind."

"Sounds like we'll be real swans."

"We are," I reminded him. "Just the new and improved version."

He laughed at that. In truth, I knew how difficult moving our entire tribe from the north to the south every year would be, but I knew we could. Kuro grew restless being tied down to one place and lonely if we were alone. Knowing we had two homes where we were all together was the only real solution.

Ciaran tottered out after Tristan, his arms full with the only blanket he could cradle in his tiny arms.

"You're freaking me out, Kanji."

"What? Why?"

"You're grinning again."

"Can't help it."

"I know." Zain's sadness was crushing. "Maybe someday I'll have what you do."

My reply was automatic. "You will. I waited twenty-six years."

"Good thing we live longer than humans."

Fears were left unspoken as we wondered how long we'd actually live. With the Sidhee on the horizon, our every day was uncertain.

"Tomorrow, I want you to and Tomas to round up all the weapons from the Dryma estates. Then form patrol groups. Chiaki and Aiden have to prepare to go back, but every other Kuro needs to be sectioned off."

"Got it. Anything else?"

I thought for a moment. "Yeah. You and Tomas go buy some hair dye. He's starting to look like a beauty experiment gone wrong."

Unlike Tomas, who had refused to cut his hair, Zain had cut every strand of dyed hair from his head. Luckily his hair grew fast, but there were still patches shorter than the rest.

He started to protest, but I cut him off. "Tristan and I talked. We're going to be borrowing some of the Dryma money. He figured it's the least they could offer us."

"Man, I'm glad Seth isn't here."

"Me too. Get some sleep."

He raised his hand in farewell, catching Micky and Shinji on the way back to the gatehouse. "See ya tomorrow."

I lingered at the thick wall separating the royal house from the others. Cars had been unpacked, and doing a mental check, I realized every Kuro was here. Recognizing the burning feeling in my chest as loneliness, I went in search of my mate and Ciaran.

Tristan's backyard was more of a garden. There were wrought-iron gazebos, tables, chairs, and benches, all handcrafted and unique. I was grateful for the heavy iron because it gave me a place to rest.

"Need anything else done?" Micky asked, bouncing in front of me.

"Nope, just get some rest."

His gaze slid sideways. "Are you sure?"

"Micky, I'm not mad at you."

"I went with Seth," he said quietly. "I'm still sorry."

"Consider yourself forgiven," I said softly, running a hand through the tangles he was trying to pass off as hair. "Go rest. You're staying in the guesthouse, right?"

"Yes."

I gave a stiff nod, the ache in my shoulders finally catching up to me as I watched him bound away.

"Still tired, love?" Tristan asked, massaging my aching muscles. He focused his energy where my skin was pulled taut over my hidden wings. "We can rest soon."

Ciaran plopped onto a nearby bench, his hands shoved deep into the pockets of his oversized sweater. "I'm hungry."

"We'll get you something." I attempted to smooth down the pale strands of Ciaran's hair, but it was a lost cause. "What about you two?"

Chiaki and Aiden looked cautious, like they'd intruded on a private moment. But even when Micky and I had exchanged words, I knew they'd heard. Everyone in my tribe had a need to be near me, something I could hear in their thoughts and in their hearts. Since returning from the Sidhee world, the desire had only grown stronger.

"Yes, please, Prince Kanji." Chiaki closed the gap between us, tugging Aiden along like a living doll. "I'm starved."

Tristan let his fingers graze my neck just enough to leave me wanting and helpless for more. "Then let's go see what we can salvage of the kitchen."

I took a breath, willing myself to remain calm.

But then Tristan gave me a look and my resolve faltered. His expression was definitely hungry, but not for anything we were likely to find until we were alone.

"FINALLY."

I hadn't heard Tristan come back after putting Ciaran in a bedroom across the hall. The only other time I'd been in Tristan's room was right after I'd learned he was also a Kuro. The memories were bittersweet.

"What are you doing standing there, Kanji?" Tristan put his hands on my shoulders, slowly inching down my back until he found my skin beneath my shirt. "I think you're overdressed for the occasion."

"This is your room." I softly trailed my finger across the thick wooden pillars arching up to the ceiling. There was the wisp of a canopy and no shortage of greenery. "I feel like we're outside."

Tristan leaned forward so he could run his teeth along the side of my neck, stopping at the hollow of my throat so he could inhale deeply. "Yes, I always loved my room. Good thing too."

There was sadness in his voice. "Why?"

"The others never liked me much."

"Others?" I was surprised my voice had stuck around this long.

Already, Tristan had shed my sweater and shirt from my body and was working on my buckle. I felt his arousal pressing against the small of my back, and my mouth went dry at the thought of taking him into my mouth.

"Other Dryma always thought I was strange. So I spent a lot of time alone."

"Idiots," I murmured.

His chuckle was dark in my ear. "I only need you and Ciaran to love me."

"And we do," I whispered, turning so my back was pressed against one of the tall columns. I muttered his name as I slid to my knees, my hands entwined with his on his hips.

"You look so good down there." He sighed.

"Let me taste you," I pleaded, staring at his long legs and the small patch of skin where his shirt didn't quite meet his pants. "Please."

He groaned, sliding a hand through my long hair and catching the strands. Until he wanted me to, I wasn't going anywhere. "If this is what you want."

My response was to pull at his zipper until his beautiful, hardened length was exposed. I flinched as he slammed his hand against the column to steady himself, preparing to take what I was willing to give.

Experimentally, I swirled my tongue around the head, catching tiny drops of precum. His legs tightened in expectation, so I took him farther into my mouth until I was seeing stars from how tightly he was holding my hair.

"Don't torture me," Tristan pleaded.

I pulled away, feeling the length of his cock in my hands. "Never."

Then I took him deep into my throat, making sure to pay attention to his heavy balls. How long had it been since I'd had him in my mouth like this? Since I'd felt the raw need to please him until he wasn't able to ever doubt what I felt?

Our relationship had been a whirlwind, even at the beginning. There was never a moment where things had been easy, but hearing his wanton moans swirl with the frantic beat of his heart told me everything I needed to know.

I needed him.

His pants grew louder as he thrust his hips. His cock was so slick, I hardly noticed the impressive length sliding into my throat. The earthen scent of his body sent jolts of pleasure straight to my cock.

"Enough." Without warning, he lifted me to my feet, turning me so my face was pressed to the wooden column.

Gone were my briefs until I was at his mercy. A strong hand stroked my length as he dipped the tip of his finger into my slit. I cried out in pleasure as I felt his cock sliding between my crease, our joining so close I couldn't bear to wait.

"Don't move while I get the oil."

There was the sound of a zipper and rummaging cloth as I imagined he rifled through our bags until he found the oil. I heard the snap of a cap and then his slick fingers were at my entrance. With his other hand, he once again pleasured my cock until I thought I would give in.

"Tristan, please. I'm already so close."

"Come for me, then."

"But you're not inside," I whined, my voice a mix of desperation and pleasure.

Two fingers caressed me from the inside, pressing up and against my spot until my legs were as wobbly as jelly. "Are you ready?"

"Yes," I cried, arching my back as he removed his fingers and impaled me in one quick thrust.

"So tight," he hissed, stilling his movements. "God, can I move?"

Rather than respond, I rocked back into him, eliciting a loud moan from my mate. My actions were more than wanted I realized as he began pounding into me. His arms around my waist kept me from falling, but I was just as eager to please as he was. I met every thrust, a startled cry ripping out of my throat when he grazed my sensitive bundle of nerves.

Pushing me onto the bed, where there was still nothing for me to hold on to, Tristan seemed pleased he had more traction. His grip turned fierce as he literally fucked me into the sheets.

That earthen scent was everywhere.

Inhaling the scent clinging to the comforter, I tried to possess every bit I could. Tristan turned my head to the side, holding me in place with a firm hand around my neck. The pressure was intense, but not something I couldn't handle.

If anything, my restricted movement made my cock leak as I rubbed against the bed.

"Am I only the one who can have you this way?" Tristan asked breathlessly.

"Yes, only you."

His shudder raced through his body to mine. "Will you come for me?"

The abrupt change in his voice caught me off guard. Even though I'd been returned to him, I could feel how anxious he'd been. What he needed was my absolute submission. "If you want me to, Tristan."

"Yes, yes, right now."

My body was sliding against the bed, my nipples and cock rubbing the sheets so I was lost in mind-numbing pleasure. Tristan put his fingers in my mouth so I could taste him as my orgasm threatened to shatter my very existence.

There was nothing delicate about the way he was taking me, but I wouldn't have wanted it any other way. The sheer, raw power he possessed over me was enough to make both my mind and trembling body submit.

It was only a few moments before I was screaming in pleasure, his cock so deeply immersed within me I thought I could feel his pulse. I tried to turn my head but he held his hand still with my fingers scissoring in and out.

"Please," I whimpered, coating his fingers in my hot spit. "You too. You too."

"Don't worry, love," Tristan's usual tone returned. "I'm coming."

When I heard the noises he made as he sought his release, I was sure no one had ever managed to sound so regal and animalistic at the same time. As he slowed his thrusts, he replaced his fingers with his lips.

Shaking, sweltering, and utterly spent, I stared up into the emerald hue of my mate's eyes. "Sleep?" I asked.

Tristan's eyes laughed. "As long as you stay right where you are."

Being anywhere but his arms sounded like torture.

CHAPTER THIRTEEN

THE NIGHT before, I'd been far too eager to be in Tristan's arms to care if we were in a mansion or a tin box. But now I had been claimed, I couldn't ignore the beauty around me. So impressive was the architecture, I found the meticulously kept mansion felt like a prison. Pressing down on all sides was a life I'd always wanted but knew I'd never have. Even with Tristan as my mate, this wealth was his. Something I could borrow but never possess.

Not wanting to disturb the fish, I gently pressed my finger to the glass and watched as the colorful creatures darted away. Tristan's room was tranquil and silent like the forest, but the guest room where Chiaki and Aiden were had an aquarium taking up half a wall. The entire castle was unearthly, which made sense considering the Dryma had poured much of their magic into the structure in an effort to preserve their culture.

I found it remarkable the trees could be wounded and even destroyed, but the fish in the magical aquarium looked more alive than I felt.

"They went to see Zain and Tomas already." Tristan startled me as he leaned against the doorframe. He looked perfectly at ease watching me. "I saw them leave when I got Ciaran some cereal."

"I should be out there," I said softly, turning my hand from side to side as the fish crept closer. "The woods are dangerous."

"Maybe I'm wrong," Tristan suggested, "but I think this house made them uncomfortable. They'd rather be in the guest house."

"How could anyone not want to live here?"

Tristan crossed the room, his touch on my spine. "Living here is lonelier than you think. Even with so many brothers, there were days I wouldn't see anyone."

"Why didn't you come find me then?" I pressed my face against the cool glass. "Even as your servant, I would've been happy."

There was remorse in his sigh. "Every day I thought of you. And there were times I almost broke and came looking. But I stopped because I was sure you'd hate me."

"Because you are a Dryma?"

"And because I was the reason for your imprisonment."

I turned to face him, wrapping my arms around his neck. "Not your fault."

"No." He grimaced. "But I still feel guilty. If you hadn't saved me…."

I silenced him with my mouth on his. Twisting in his embrace, I tasted the jam and bread we'd eaten for breakfast, a sweetness I wanted to hold forever. "Just for a moment, let me pretend the Dryma and the Kuro got along. That we were allowed to be friends."

"Kanji." His eyes flashed the color of sea foam. "I'll pretend as much as you like."

"Good. You might not know this about me, but I love to run."

Tristan raised his eyebrow. "You? Run?"

"Yeah," I teased. "So last one to the guesthouse loses."

"Loses what?" Now Tristan was intrigued. "Just what are the stakes here?"

"Race me and find out."

Then we were taking off through the hallways, laughing like small children. For all my talk, Tristan was faster, his long legs obviously the source. He darted past me in a flash of blond hair and golden skin. Seriously, the Dryma could have been a model if he hadn't been so inclined to use his intelligence.

Just as the guesthouse came into sight and I knew I'd have to concede, I stopped and bent over in laughter at the sight greeting me. As thin as I was, Tristan's clothes hung off me and made me feel like a child. But my appearance was nothing in comparison to Zain and Tomas's.

"What on earth are two you wearing?"

"They're called parkas," Tomas gritted out, obviously annoyed with the oversized yellow coat. "We don't have our uniforms, and these were lying around."

"So at least we'll look somewhat authoritative while stripping trees," Zain said proudly, revealing the parkas had been his idea. "If anyone stops to ask what we're doing, we'll say we're nature volunteers."

I raised my eyebrow. "Nature volunteers, huh?"

"Or something…."

"I think that's hilarious," Tristan added, slightly breathless. "Where do I sign up for one of these things?"

Tomas's jaw locked, but I saw he was just trying to hold back his laughter. "Ask Zain. This was his brilliant plan."

"Shut up, Tomas."

"Okay, okay." I broke up the party, as amused as I was. "Where are the others?"

"At the front gate," Tomas informed me as he pointed to the greenhouse. "Chiaki and Aiden are in there waiting for your boyfriend."

"Guess that's my cue." With a kiss that would never be enough, Tristan left my side. His presence remained for a good couple minutes, none of us able to speak.

"You guys know you don't have to do this, right?"

"Give it up, Kanji." Zain spat a handful of seeds to the ground, kicking them away with the toe of his boot. "We've already been over this."

My heart clenched. "We have no idea of when they'll come."

"How are you sure they will?" Tomas asked, seeming to realize the absurdity of his question the moment he was done.

"Christophe is pissed," I told them quietly. "Even if the Sidhee didn't care, they can't ignore his wishes now he's one of them."

"Never liked that bastard," Tomas growled. "How dare he take our prince?"

"Point is," I said, attempting to soothe his anger, "maybe the Sidhee only took prisoners because they were available. If no one is here apart from Tristan and me, then maybe…."

"If you are even suggesting we give you back to Christophe," Zain muttered, "I'm going to kill you myself."

"Tristan would never let that happen." I shivered at the thought. "But if they could sense how many of us were here, maybe they'd only send a few."

"That's bullshit and you know it." Tomas surprised me by touching my shoulder. I was glad to see his hair had once again been restored to a beacon of white light. "Neither you or your boyfriend are going to act as bait."

"Agreed." Zain threw his arm around my other shoulder. "The Sidhee can send ten or a hundred... doesn't make a difference. I'm not leaving until you do."

Any argument I had died when I caught sight of Ciaran. "Okay, which one of you guys gave him a parka?"

Zain rolled his eyes. "Not it."

Laughter bubbled from my stomach. Not only was the parka absurd against Ciaran's pale skin, but the bottom had been cut so he could walk. Despite the alteration, he still looked like he was drowning in the cheery yellow fabric.

"Don't like it?"

"No, I think you're very cute."

Zain nearly dropped his bag of seeds while Tomas stared at me dumbfounded.

"What?" I was unnerved by their responses.

"He's really grown on you, huh?"

Ciaran was more than just an asset to my kind. "He's like a little brother."

As uncomfortable as the Kuro were around Tristan and Seth, they were even more intimidated by Ciaran. In the few days since I'd returned, I couldn't sense his presence until he wanted me to. From afar, he looked like an ethereal being with a power all his own.

But even knowing how much strength he possessed, when he was standing beside me with one small hand in mine, it was hard to see him as anything other than a child.

"Are you almost ready?" I asked Ciaran.

"Yes. Tristan is talking to Chiaki."

"Aren't the plants pretty?"

Ciaran stared at the ground, seemingly debating how truthful he wanted to be. "Not as pretty as water."

We all laughed then, especially Zain. The crinkling of his eyes and his booming laughter told me he'd been waiting for an excuse to crack up.

I sensed my mate before I saw him. His hand on my hip, gently turning me so he could press his nose to my collarbone, was enough to silence my thoughts. "Ready?"

Mutely, I nodded.

Tristan gazed at the sky as though he were able to predict the weather. I wouldn't have been surprised if he'd managed to add meteorology to the long list of subjects he studied in college.

"Do you want us to put these in your car?" Aiden's voice was cautious as he cradled a small plant to his chest.

The flowers had all been taken to the campground on our first trip, but without knowing exactly how to strip the trees, Tristan had plants he planned to practice on.

Unlike his mate, Aiden had short hair, but he'd pulled back his bangs with a single clip so I could actually see his face. His blue eyes I expected, but the flush of color in his cheeks was startling. He seemed more alive somehow.

"Go ahead and put them in the Jeep, kid." Zain nodded to his beloved car. "That princely car isn't worth shit when it comes to storage."

Tristan agreed, releasing me so he could relieve Chiaki of the object in his hands. He must've seen my eyes go wide because he brushed away a stray stand of my hair and whispered excitedly, "I'll show you what these do when we get to Pasky. I worked on developing them for a while."

"They look like giant hollow honeycombs," I joked.

"Similar idea I suppose." Tristan loaded the car with four of those bulky objects, even having to take up the passenger's seat to do it. "I'll meet you there."

I started to protest but Tristan silenced me. Only my mate's authority was strong enough to sway me. "It's okay, Kanji. You should be training your kind."

"Besides." Chiaki stepped up, wiping the dirt from his palms onto his pants. "I can fit in the car with him, so I'll go."

"Me too," Ciaran chirped, his voice as lovely and small as a bird's.

My pulse quickened at the thought of not being with Tristan, no matter how short the time. But necessity called for my presence.

"Be safe."

Tristan's eyes glistening were the only reply. Fear had silenced all other voices.

To say we had a plan was like saying trees planned when each leaf would disconnect. There were too many factors to consider and even though we had one goal, I wasn't confident in our abilities.

Like Aiden, the other Kuro had been rejuvenated after being reunited with the rest of our kind. But the hollow feelings of desperation they'd been taught remained.

Tomas and Zain stepped into their roles perfectly. As friends, they were loyal and honest. As leaders, they were fair and understanding of limitations. Unfortunately, there were too many limits to work with. Most of the Kuro were hesitant to select one of the few weapons we found within Crystal Cove. As a result, we resorted to finding large sticks we could use for fencing practice.

I tried my hardest to stay out of their thoughts, but the lure was so strong, I found myself drowning among the self-loathing and doubt.

"Again," I told Zain. "Let's run through the drills again."

We were in a part of the reserve where the land was mostly flat and devoid of trees. With a view of the lake and trails, the area was mostly used for camping.

"I know you're tired," Zain started as he took a step away from the hill I was perched on. "But our prince says we should practice again."

There was no malice in his voice, but I could hear his exhaustion. Every Kuro had a partner whom they were sparring with, the sticks buckling and bending. I would speak to Tristan about finding more weapons within the Dryma castle with the hopes the dazzling armory would be enough.

Zain and Tomas were excellent fighters, which was the reason I'd selected them as leaders. Before, when Christophe had been in charge, he hadn't considered our unique build. We weren't bulky and muscular like the Dryma, but we were strong enough to hold our own. Zain and Tomas recognized our attributes and trained accordingly.

I heard soft pants as the clash of stick against stick struck over and over like the detonation of a bomb. Screeches tore through my kind's throats, a combination of swan and human. Aiden was nearest to me, training mercilessly with Micky.

Zain had a blank expression. Tugging on a newly dyed strand of red hair, he clearly wanted me to enter his mind.

What's up, Zain?

Have you noticed a change in Micky?

I took note of the sweat pouring down Micky's face, the look of determination in his eyes as he pivoted away from Aiden and swayed to the side. *What about him?*

Zain shrugged inconspicuously. *Micky's always wanted to impress you. But he seems more gung-ho than usual.*

He apologized again for coming back here without permission.

There's something more going on.

I dipped into Micky's thoughts, surprised by the beautiful face I saw. *I think he's drawn to Ciaran.*

Zain frowned, tilting his head to the side as he took note of Aiden's powerful jab with his makeshift sword. Aiden and Chiaki were the youngest mates I'd ever heard of. Ciaran wasn't even a Kuro and he was way too young, but he was very powerful.

Micky might be his protector someday.

His protector? Zain echoed. *Like Ciaran's knight in shining armor? Bet the kid will love that.*

Considering all our kind has been through, it might be nice to be put on willing protection detail.

Could be fun. I call dibs on the next hot female Asrai, then.

Sure thing.

Why Ciaran had chosen now to appear was a mystery to me, but without confronting the female Asrai who had expelled him, I might never know. What was more was that he'd lived years with the Asrai before being thrown away. Was age something the water fairies considered, or had he simply bided his time while looking for a place he belonged?

Thoughts swirled, but answers evaded me.

Prince Kanji, do you have a moment?

I wasn't expecting to hear Chiaki's voice. Instantly, panic spread through my body like a virus. *Chiaki, is something wrong?*

There was a moment, then: *No, sorry if it seemed that way. Prince Tristan was just wondering if you wanted to see how the basins work?*

Yes, be there soon.

Zain wasn't privy to the conversations I had with other Kuro unless I allowed him to be, but my expression must've given me away.

"We're all tired, Kanji." Zain rolled his shoulder a few times. "And stiff as hell. Tomas and I will take every Kuro to the armory and then go back to Crystal Cove."

I eyed him warily. "The armory is at the castle."

He gave me a knowing look. "Yeah, and?"

"Why do you—"

"Because I'm not letting you outta my sight again, okay?" Zain huffed. "So when you're done with Tristan, go to the castle and we'll leave Pasky together."

"Your logic doesn't make much sense," I chuckled.

Rolling his eyes, he shooed me away as though I were little more than an insect. "Meet us at the castle within the hour. Just in case we can't get in without Tristan."

"Will do."

Unzipping my jacket, I prepared for flight. It wasn't until I consciously felt every eye on me that I froze. Seeing me without my shirt wasn't in itself extraordinary, especially because I'd always been very slender. But the glazed look of the Kuro told me their inquiring eyes meant something more.

For the first time, they were going to see their prince's wings.

This moment was more important than I'd ever thought possible.

I almost slipped my jacket back over my bony shoulders, but swallowing the lump in my throat, I focused on the toe of my black boot and breathed deeply.

There was always pain when shifting my wings out.

Usually, I acted quickly and the discomfort was equivalent to a dull ache. But as the center of attention, I was hyperalert to my surroundings. I felt everything.

The spacing of my shoulders came first, followed by the rip of my skin to make inserts for my wings. The skin healed as soon as my wings were tucked back inside, as though they had never existed. My shoulder pain was what remained. I'd hoped after managing to shift a few times, my body would revert to the agile ones my uncle had spoken of.

But the truth was difficult to accept. After being restrained for most of my life, I'd adapted to the life of a human and there were things I would never have.

I tried to ignore the gasps of my kind as my wings gained full volume, spreading out on either side of me like inky quills patchworked together like a work of art. I had to admit, my wings were what I clung to, and it was because they were the result of Tristan's selflessness.

Gaining flight, I gave up my footing and with my sense of ground, my humanity. No longer was I bound to the mortal rules of life. If the

Kuro watching me gained anything from the mad beating of my wings, I hoped they could see the elatedness I felt.

I felt the air against my face as I dove through trees and past shimmering lakes. In this form, mere moments separated me from Tristan.

His heartbeat was so loud, it muffled the sounds of the woods. Zain's words were in the back of my mind because of course I knew what we were doing was risky. With so many factors unknown, there was nothing to do but trust the woods.

I was well aware of how many humans believed the trees were inanimate objects for their own use. But I could feel the way the trunks breathed, even when the breaths were shallow. The Sidhee were foreign visitors here, and their presence was even unwanted by the trees.

Trusting in the rolling landscape of green, black, white, and brown was all we could do.

I landed in a small clearing where I could see the wire baskets and other equipment poking out from the checkered pattern of trees.

"Did I take you away from something?" His voice was as melodic as the trickling of the lake flooding into the smaller ponds. "I didn't mean to."

Tristan was behind me and I could feel the ghost of his hands on my skin, sliding down my bare arms. My hair had come loose from my hair tie, so he gathered the strands and let them fall over my shoulder so my back was bare for him.

"So beautiful, my Kanji. So delicate and perfect."

I stifled a laugh. "You're the one who is perfect, my prince."

"I have to admit—" He pressed a kiss to the crook of my neck. "—I like you calling me that."

I swallowed. "Why?"

"Makes me feel like I own you."

"You do."

Finally having had enough, Tristan turned me. He instantly cupped my face, his eyes searching. There was a moment of utter silence where I tried to comprehend how I had gotten so lucky to find my mate, let alone the epitome of a god. Then he smiled his reassuring beam and nodded toward his tools.

"Are you ready for me to show you?"

I let him tug me along like a doll on a string. "Don't be disappointed if I don't understand."

"Of course you'll understand." Tristan's faith in me was unshakable.

Kneeling on the ground with his hands pressed to the trunk of a tree was Chiaki. He had his pale hair swept beneath his hood to keep the wind off of his face and his sleeves pushed well past his elbows. Ciaran was sitting on his heels less than a foot away, his hands outstretched.

I didn't want to interfere with their concentration, but Tristan pulled me until I was close enough to kiss the tree.

Gracefully, Tristan sank to his knees beside Ciaran. Chiaki was tracing circles on the tree with the tips of his fingers, and at first I didn't understand what they were doing. Ciaran put his palms flat against the roots after flinging a few droplets of water to the ground. Their movements, although pretty, didn't appear to have any meaning.

Then as Chiaki and Ciaran caught a few of the leaves that detached, I realized how methodical they were being.

"The idea is to make tea," Tristan explained, his soft breathing like thunder against the silence. "Rather than separate every tree and reunite with an individual Dryma, we're taking a collective approach."

After the leaves had been safely deposited into one of the wire baskets, Ciaran and Chiaki moved on to the next. They barely needed to move because of the close proximity.

"Chiaki sends the healing water through the tree so the leaves that fall are oozing with Dryma essence." He guided my fingers to the top of the basket. I expected cold, but the wire was as warm as a heartbeat. "Then Ciaran gathers the leaves he feels have the most life."

"But we're in the middle of winter," I said quietly. "How can there be leaves?"

"Weren't there always?" Tristan raised his eyebrow.

"I—were there?"

Tristan kissed the palm of my hand. "There were less, but Dryma trees always retained a sense of their beauty. Without leaves, our kind would've reflected the ugliness of the trees."

"They aren't ugly," I defended, incapable of ever thinking of Tristan as anything less than stunning. "Just... different. I never noticed because I didn't look up."

He tilted my head back. "And now?"

I closed my eyes, melting into his touch. "I see everything."

And I truly did. Where there had only been black and white among the landscape of winter, there were hundreds of hues I could never replicate. Everything I saw and felt was because of him.

"How many more trees, Prince Tristan?" Chiaki's voice was quiet as he was probably trying to not intrude.

I had had to keep a notebook detailing every fairy's tree, but Tristan only had to look into his mind. "In area nine, there are a few more."

"Tristan," I started, looking over the three full baskets. "Will the Dryma have to take this more than once?"

"I felt whole after only one of Ciaran's healing treatments. Hopefully they will feel the same. Plus, I have something up my sleeve."

"What?"

He rose to his feet and offered his hand. "You'll see."

Short of begging, I was pretty sure nothing I said would make him divulge his secret.

"Where are the others?" Chiaki stretched his arms above his head, his fingers stained green and brown from the leaves.

I knew he really wanted to know about Aiden. "At the Dryma castle gathering supplies."

Ciaran jumped up so quickly I thought he'd been possessed. "There's a castle?"

Tristan gave him one of the softest looks I'd ever seen. "Sure is. My kind hid it away from humans, from…." He tossed me a cautious glance. "From everything."

It was no secret the Dryma liked their kind to be isolated. If anything expressed that fact, it was the way they kept their castle private.

"Kanji, you said the Kuro are already on their way there?"

I nodded, angling my face up so I could take note of the sky. With as many Kuro as there were, when they took flight, the very air would be stirred.

"They won't get far without codes," Tristan noted as he surveyed the wicker baskets. They were so full, leaves spilled from the top. As unimportant as they looked, each miniscule leaf held a greater purpose. "We can swing by and gather the leaves from section nine and then go to the castle from there."

"Great. Let me help you."

The baskets were heavier than they looked and now I knew exactly why the hours the Kuro had spent training weren't enough. Pasky was an endless stream of trails, trees, and lakes. Even if you thought you were a part of Pasky, you could easily end up on someone's property because of the way everything was interconnected.

Most of the sections had a parking lot, so the Jeep wasn't far, but because the trees were sometimes difficult to get to, it ended up being very time-consuming.

Periodically, I checked Tomas and Zain's minds, just to make sure they were doing fine. Either the Kuro were more tired than I thought or my kind were still reluctant to fly because they hadn't even reached the castle by the time we reached section nine.

I was pretty sure the short trek to Pasky from the campground hadn't been enough for many of the Kuro to regain their confidence in flight. The rest of the leaves were gathered smoothly, mostly because Ciaran and Chiaki had perfected the art in a way that made me jealous. Tristan was there to help, but before he could catch the leaves, he pulled away.

As we trekked through the overgrowth to the hidden water castle, I kept in line with Tristan. Chiaki and Ciaran were behind, talking quietly about different plants and trees whose names I had already forgotten.

"Can I ask you a question?"

Tristan's fingers twitched at his side. "Of course."

"Earlier, why did you pull away?"

He blinked. "What do you mean?"

When he wouldn't meet my gaze, I knew I was onto something. "The leaves were falling and you had your hand outstretched, but then you just pulled away. Why?"

Glancing behind, he was checking to see how much of our conversation Chiaki and Ciaran could hear, I figured. Determining they weren't of concern, Tristan continued. "Not worthy. The magic within them was dead."

My boot caught a rock and just before I fell, Tristan scooped his arm under my stomach and held me upright.

"Love, are you all right?"

I gave a shaky nod. "Yes. Just a rock."

"Better hold on to me as a precaution."

"You just wanted an excuse."

His long lashes caressed his cheeks. "Do I need one?"

"No. Touch me whenever you want. But I was caught off guard by what you said."

"About the leaves being dead?" he guessed.

"Yes. What did you mean?"

Tristan gave a heavy sigh. "I'm trying to wake the Dryma up as quickly as I can. Without their strength, we don't stand a good chance at destroying the Sidhee. So I have to be selective with what part of the tree I use. If I take parts that are already dead, recovery could be slower. I'm trying to be careful, but all the while, I'm panicking."

I let his words sink in. "Even if they don't wake up in time, they will eventually. Until then, we will manage and Chiaki will keep them safe."

He pressed his lips together, but before he could continue, our attention was pulled to the castle.

The castle wasn't called the underwater palace for nothing. Hidden behind towering trees was a powerful illusion that concealed the castle in its entirety. However, much of the castle was concealed underwater where even nonroyal fairies didn't have full access.

This was exactly how Christophe had managed to conceal me before. At the memory, I shuddered and huddled closer as though the temperature was what had dropped and not my nerves.

"Beautiful, isn't she?" Tristan stopped and stared at the space in front of us. In his arms was a basket he gently placed on the ground at his feet.

Apart from a sporadic spread of blossoms, the landscape was bare.

"Um." Chiaki forced a smile. "What's beautiful exactly?"

"Our castle," Tristan replied.

Chiaki looked at my mate like he'd gone mad.

Tristan's grin burst from his cheeks. "You can't see the castle, but I can."

I frowned. "But I could before."

"Because we knew the Sidhee were coming. And when he held extravagant galas, we made sure extra protection duty was instilled to keep humans away."

"Hey, what gives?" Tomas thundered through the trees, the Kuro trailing behind. Toward the front of the line were Zain and Shinji, both with bewildered expressions. "We've been looking everywhere for this damn castle."

His frustration was justified, but I honestly couldn't do anything but stare in awe as Tristan raised his hands like a magician and lowered them. The illusion concealing the castle slowly peeled away like a banana's skin until the astonishing, breathtaking castle was all that remained.

The castle towered into the sky, complete with brick turrets and a steep set of stairs leading to a set of glass double doors outlined in crystals.

Where there was once gray and death, there was now a flourishing garden. Lotus flowers floated in perfectly placed ponds, and I was sure I heard the sound of birds overhead as they swooped into the miniparadise. There were stone steps guiding guests through the park and ornate golden benches.

Without warning, Tristan sank down next to one of the ponds. Carefully, he swirled a finger in the deep water and gave a small smile.

"The fish are gone," he whispered so only Tomas and I were close enough to hear. "Proof of our fading magic."

Touching his shoulder, I tried to be stronger for him. "We survived so long in this world, it was only a matter of time until we started to fade."

Tristan was a formidable presence and I knew he'd never break down, not in front of others. His shoulders trembled slightly as he ran a golden hand through his hair and down the back of his neck. Standing, he rubbed my hands, chiding softly. "I'm a terrible mate letting you get cold like this."

The concern I felt wasn't for me, but for the Kuro patiently waiting. They had more respect than to listen to our conversation, but I could hear the chattering of teeth.

By now, the castle had been fully revealed. Stone archways welcomed us as we padded over the path to the entrance.

"Are we in a Grimm's fairy tale?" Zain whispered in my ear as he caught up. "This place is creepy as hell."

Tristan's smile tightened, but if the comment bothered him, he didn't say so.

"You can say that again," Tomas agreed, shoving his hands into his pockets as though being smaller made him less of a target.

My friends weren't the only ones less than enthusiastic about entering the castle. When my boot slid over the entryway, a hush rattled my eardrums. There wasn't enough heat in the world to prevent the shivers racing down my arms and legs. Even the air was stiff and stale, as if waiting to claim us as forever occupants.

Zain cleared his throat as he pulled his hat low on his forehead. "So where is the armory?"

"Straight through this room and down a set of stairs," Tristan said. He wasn't bothered at all, just went to the wall and pushed a large button so all at once, the torches bathed the room in artificial light.

I recognized the large room as the one used at the gala. It was just as beautiful and breathtaking, even if the only form of music was the cry of the wind through the cracks in the mortar and brick.

"You don't need to take us there." Tomas struggled to keep his voice even. I wasn't sure if he was uncomfortable deferring to a Dryma or trying to save Tristan the trouble. "We can handle swords."

Tristan peered at a torch, running his finger along a crack I hadn't seen. "It's no trouble to accompany you, especially because the armory is more than likely locked."

Tomas grumbled an acceptance as he shifted his coat more securely around his body and tiptoed the length of the ballroom. Despite knowing I shouldn't, I couldn't resist looking up. Most of the ceiling was covered in unlit candles that appeared to float with ornate objects sparkling even in the dimmest corners. But the part of the ceiling I liked best was where there wasn't material at all. Just a gaping, endless hole.

And because of the way the looking glass was created, even the trees didn't reach the top.

I felt the wisp of a touch on my shoulder, the huff of breath at my ear, and the calm rush of love weaving into my heart before I felt nothing at all. No matter how hard I tried, all I could see was my mate, even when there was nothing.

Breaking through the foggy entrapment of my mind, I was startled to see only one other figure in the room.

He was small and seemingly insignificant, but his presence was only second to my mate's.

"Ciaran," I breathed. "Where did the others go?"

"To get the swords. Tristan told you so."

"He did?" Figured my mind was too trapped within the sky to have heard.

"Uh-huh. Said to take your time."

I softened my voice. "Why did you stay?"

"Because you're scared."

There wasn't a question in his voice, only an undeniable statement. At first, I felt anger creep into my face at the accusation, but he was right.

I ran a hand through my hair. "The Sidhee are pretty terrifying."

Ciaran's eyes were as blue and expansive as the sky I couldn't look away from. "Yes, they are demons after all."

This kid was as blunt as they came.

I felt the whisper of a shadow behind me just as my body was assaulted by the overwhelming urge to surrender. There was a primal feeling reverberating through my body, a need to submit to my mate.

Even without looking behind me, I knew the imposing figure was Tristan.

"There are more than just swords," Tristan said distractedly. I could practically hear the need in his words. "Ciaran, if you want, I'm sure you could find a weapon you'd fancy."

Asrai were smart and Ciaran was no exception. He was gone even before I had the time to gather my bearings.

"Stay as you are," Tristan commanded.

Like a small bird of prey, I stayed rooted to my spot on the marble floor. Eyes downcast, the only sight I saw was what Tristan allowed. His shoes, completely white despite his trek through the reserve, circled me once, twice, before coming to a halting stop.

"I love how obedient you are to me," Tristan murmured, his voice thick. A gentle but insistent hand cupped my chin so he could tilt my face. "But at the same time, your submission distresses me."

My brow furrowed. "I never meant to make you sad."

"You misunderstand. Kanji. I could never be anything but whole when I am with you. You saved me."

"From drowning," I retorted warily. "I know."

"And from myself."

"Huh?"

"When you met me, I was willing to give up on my own life in order to please my family and my kind. My submission was caused by weakness." He guided my arms to his neck and then touched my hips. "But yours is caused by strength."

I was embarrassed at his attention. "Whatever you say."

"Dance with me."

"There isn't any music."

Tristan tightened his grip on my waist, spinning me into an imaginary world where every step I took was perfect. "Then you aren't listening."

My mate was far too breathtaking with his long, muscled limbs and inquisitive eyes. His soft blond curls fell into his face, a chiseled jaw I couldn't resist kissing.

"I can hear your heartbeat," Tristan murmured, bending me backward so I had no choice but to rely on his embrace. "And the sound of our footsteps over the floor." He separated my legs with his hand, cupping me over my jeans. "Your heavy breathing when I touch you here."

"God." I hissed with pleasure as he ran a finger over my hardening length. I whimpered when his teeth scraped the hollow of my throat. "Tristan…."

"Think you can be quiet?" he challenged, the friction of his hand over my jeans electrifying. When he undid the top button, I nearly stopped breathing, "Do you want me to continue, love?"

My arms flopped uselessly to my sides, my legs barely carrying my weight as he continued to stroke and tease, driving me mad with lust.

Tristan's mouth found my nipple through my T-shirt, his teeth scraping across the nub. "Do you?"

I found enough strength in my arm so I could touch the hot skin of his forearm. "Yes." I sighed. "Please, Tristan."

Our dancing had led us to the center of the room where I had the perfect view of the sky window overhead. Soft wisps of cloud brushed across the window but I could hardly keep my eyes from rolling back as Tristan reached into my jeans and retrieved my cock.

"You're already leaking." He stroked the tip before letting his hand slide down my length. "Such a pretty cock, Kanji."

I jolted at his words, incapable of concealing my blush. Using what strength remained, I pulled myself up so I could look at his face. But he was staring at his hand wrapped around my shaft and there was something undeniably sensual about the way his eyes and hands didn't waver from their task.

I was so lost in the clouded lust in his expression, someone could've interrupted us and I wouldn't have noticed.

"Close," I panted, fingers tightening on his sleeve.

Gracefully, he fell to his knees in front of me, hands tight on my asscheeks so he could keep me close. Opening his mouth, he took me down the back of his throat before I had time to blink.

Over and over he swallowed me until I wasn't sure who enjoyed his ministrations more.

Where there had been only silence, was endless music. My fingers were in his hair, his hands caressing my lower back and thighs as my release threatened to take me down.

Screaming into the crook of my arm, I tried to muffle the sound as my orgasm shattered what was left of my sanity.

Tristan held on as I rode out my aftershocks, pulling away only when I was dry so nothing but his spit clung to my flesh. With his composure still intact, I felt my cock start to harden again. There was something unbelievably attractive about the way he could remain in control, even when I felt his desires burning holes through his emerald eyes.

"Later, Kanji." He fluidly rose to his feet, rebuttoning my pants and taking my arm. "The Kuro are waiting."

The Kuro were the only reason I didn't jump his bones right then and there.

CHAPTER FOURTEEN

SEEING MY mate with a broom in his hand while Ciaran held the dustpan did things to me I wasn't proud of. Half of me wanted to take over because cleaning was the least I could do. But half of me just wanted to stare at the seemingly innocent moment that really solidified us as family.

I cleared my throat. I hadn't wanted to intrude, which was why I had yet to enter the greenhouse. "Can I help?"

Tristan's eyes were more vibrant than the flourishing plants. Wordlessly, he handed me a spray bottle full of liquid that looked like earth.

I wrinkled my nose at the appearance. "What is this?"

Tristan laughed. "Some of the plants in here need more nourishment than others."

"Ah."

In the colossal greenhouse, I wasn't sure what was okay for me to touch. Seeing my distress, Tristan leaned the broom against one of the wooden tables and pointed to a bunch of plants in a horseshoe-shaped box. "Start here?"

Silently, I moved to start spraying the leaves, coating them in the brown substance. Most of the Kuro were still asleep, having been exhausted from days of training. Even though all of the leaves had been gathered the first day, Tristan had wanted Chiaki and Aiden to remain for a few more days to make sure the magic had been gathered.

"How will you know?" I'd asked.

Because the leaves were living proof of souls, they were kept in the private living area sectioned into Tristan's suite. I could hear the rustle as soft as breathing.

But the color hadn't changed, and Tristan said that could only mean one thing.

And he was right. An entire week had passed where I'd gotten frantic calls from Joel trying to remain calm about Seth's nervousness. Clearly, the Dryma prince wasn't willing to pick up a phone himself.

More than once, I'd wanted to ask Joel why he did what Seth wanted, but I already had my answer. Joel was in love with Seth and nothing short of betrayal was going to change that.

So after finding a handwritten note from Tristan this morning, saying he'd gone to the greenhouse, I'd gone to meet him. The sun had barely risen, the clouds thick and heavy in the gray sky.

"Did you see the leaves this morning?" I asked softly, watching Tristan out of the corner of my eye.

He had opted for a sleeveless shirt and a pair of loose pants. Every time he reached up, bits of his toned stomach were revealed. His arms were strong and lovely, easily able to redecorate the plants in whatever way he wished.

"Yes, they maintained their hue."

"I'll let Chiaki and Aiden know."

"Will they be happy to return, you think?"

I thought for a moment, watching as Tristan touched the inside of my wrist, so dainty and frail in comparison to his. "I think they will. Zain and Tomas are an entirely different story."

My two friends trained with the Kuro every day since we'd returned to Pasky. The addition of weapons had made the Kuro gain more confidence, but I could see the anxiety in Tomas and Zain's faces. The Kuro weren't ready, and they knew it.

To make matters worse, we all kept closely huddled in Crystal Cove at night, too alert to sleep in case the Sidhee made their attack. It was foolish to hope the demons had given up, but still, as the week had passed without a sighting, I started to hate the standstill we'd been forced into.

"Aiden is a talented fighter," Tristan agreed. "Taught Ciaran a few things, right?"

"Yep." Ciaran wiped his hands on his jeans, leaving a small trail of dirt. "The swords are too heavy, though."

"We'll have to find you a dagger, then."

The words came easily, but the thought of ever seeing Ciaran forced to fight was extremely painful. Tristan gave me a slight nod before I lowered myself to Ciaran's level. Down here, I felt he would see me more of a friend and less of a leader.

"Ciaran," I said softly. "We haven't thanked you for helping with the flowers."

He smiled, fidgeting uncomfortably at my close proximity. "That's okay. I wanted to."

"Honey, we want you to do one more thing."

"Anything."

His lack of hesitation made me smile. "Go with Chiaki and Aiden."

Whatever he expected me to say, it wasn't that. Spinning so he could glare at me, I saw a gleam of fire in his eyes that told me a fight was approaching. "What? Why?"

"Because they might need you," Tristan added, coming to Ciaran's other side. Our knees bumped together, and his hand on my back steadied me. "These flowers are too important for anything to go wrong."

There was truth in his words, but just as we'd predicted the night before when making our decision, Ciaran wasn't having it.

"You don't want me to fight," he accused.

"You're right." I chanced touching his hair. Since I had found him, holding his hand was the only contact we'd had. When he didn't move, I continued. "Tristan and I aren't getting rid of you. But you shouldn't be here. We don't know what's going to happen."

"Or when," Tristan said for added effect.

Seeing he had been defeated, he glanced down and shook his head. "I won't go."

I couldn't say I was surprised. "Why do you want to stay?"

If there had ever been any doubt about the way Ciaran felt, it disappeared with his next statement. "I have to protect you."

"I can protect Kanji," Tristan stated, his voice kind. "You believe I will, right?"

"Yes." Ciaran's words weren't jumbled like a small child's should be. They were thoughtful and steadfast. "But what if he has to protect you?"

In another life, one where Ciaran had been our child in every sense of the word, we would've made him leave. But the fierce loyalty with which he lived was characteristic of what he'd been through. Making a decision that could protect him wasn't right where Asrai were concerned. He had the foresight to make his own.

"A dagger it is, then." Tristan stood, raking his hands through his blond hair. "Our armories are not legendary for nothing."

There was still doubt across Ciaran's face.

So when I went in search of Chiaki and Aiden to tell them it was time to leave, Ciaran had become intensely interested in a heap of dirt beneath a table. When I returned, he leaped out from his hiding spot as though he'd never been gone.

Ciaran's and Tristan's hands in either of mine were all the comforts I needed. If my throat hadn't swelled with emotion, I would've told them so.

OUR DAY in and day out training had made my Kuro strong and able. They now held their heads high as they matched their strength equally with the swords of their choosing. A clash of steel rang through the forest. I was sure the trees could feel our desire to protect because where there had been shades of gray there were now amber and golden hues.

But nothing, nothing at all, was going to make up for our lost time.

Sidhee were bred at birth to battle, to combat, to kill.

My kind were not even close to those standards.

Tristan could fight well; I'd seen him. But his skills as a healer were second to none, so he canvassed the forest in search of herbs while we trained.

I was no exception and trained just as hard as the others, focusing more on the younger Kuro who needed encouragement.

"Ciaran," I corrected gently, shifting the dagger in his hands. "Try using this hand to jab and then this arm as a bluff."

He mimicked my movements, a glint of pride in his eyes. His sparring partner was downplaying his strength, giving Ciaran the illusion he was better.

Zain's expression was pointed. *Told you Micky wants to protect Ciaran.*

Secretly, I was pleased Ciaran had his own mini-entourage of Kuro dedicated to his protection. At first, I'd believed Shinji and Micky tailed him closely for my sake, but I'd seen the slight developments of friendship budding.

Asrai were strange creatures that could appear as young or as old as they wanted, but after all this time, I was sure he wasn't creating an illusion.

Are you actually going to let him fight?

Zain was across the clearing, sword at his side as he casually directed a line of Kuro back into a formation. I was less than surprised to find half his attention still firmly placed on me.

Chiaki and Aiden left yesterday so unless we hide him, he'll be here when the Sidhee attack.

Did we really have to let Aiden go?

I raised my eyebrow. *You think he would've let Chiaki leave without him?*

Zain's mind raced with curses. *They could've at least left my Jeep.*

Your Jeep is fine, I assured him. Apart from stopping to fill up the tank and use the bathroom, the two Kuro hadn't stalled in their drive to the campground. Joel was more than thrilled to see him, but in what I could see of Chiaki's mind, Seth was completely absent.

A high-pitched whistle overhead and a dark presence slamming into my chest snatched my feet out from under me.

Within an instant, Zain and Tomas were on either of my sides. I searched frantically for Ciaran, who was sandwiched between Shinji and Micky.

"The hell?" Tomas growled, using his hand as a shield.

The sun was absent, and there was darkness as thick as smoke.

"What is that?" Zain stared at me as he lowered his voice. "Sidhee finally making their move?"

I gave a slight nod. "Think so."

Zain didn't miss a beat. Didn't even hesitate before turning to the Kuro and issuing commands. "As we planned. Get your weapons and circle up."

Because attacks could be aerial, we needed easy access to our wings. Coats were shed, shirts discarded, and a burst of dark wings as vibrant as a flock of crows emerged. Zain and Tomas had managed to get everyone into a circle, so attacks that came from behind would be few.

Micky had Ciaran on his back as his boots thudded over the dismal landscape. The trek was short, but to me, the few steps he had to take to get to me were pure torment.

Another rush of dark magic vibrated through the trees just across from the pond. Searching the thicket, I could make out shifty outlines too fast to be anything but immortal creatures.

"Sidhee are cunning," I whispered to Zain and Tomas, not wanting to frighten the others. "They won't have sent an entire army. Not until they know the layout. But they need a sacrifice to return. Don't let them take anyone."

Tomas's blue eyes had taken on the light of the red flashes the Sidhee possessed. "No way are they taking anyone again."

Some of the Kuro had not even seen the wasteland the Sidhee called their home, but the fear was palpable.

My heart thudded against my rib cage like a tiny bird trying to escape. Pressure built in my lungs until I gasped for breath, my legs trembling like a fledgling.

"Tristan," I whispered. A single word that meant everything.

"Kanji, wait." Zain reached for me, just as Tomas did. But they were too slow to act and after I'd escaped their outstretched arms, there was no way they'd be able to catch me.

Tristan said he'd be close, said there would be no chance of him being taken. But if the Sidhee were already here, what if he'd been harmed?

Zain and Tomas knew better than to follow. I believed in their strength and courage, knew they could maintain the orders I'd issued. Even though they seemed to not mind Tristan's presence, protecting me would forever be their first priority.

But I had to get to Tristan. Make sure he was safe. And then we'd return in time.

A figure joined me and thinking they were a Sidhee, I prepared to lash out. My attack stopped just short of a wide-eyed stare as Micky trembled beside me.

"What are you doing?" I asked breathlessly, darting through trees and underbrush. The world around me was a blur, but Ciaran clinging to Micky's back… that image was crystal clear.

"Ciaran insisted we come with you," Micky cried.

There was fear in his voice. Fear of the Sidhee and fear of my disappointment.

"So you listened?"

Micky lowered his head just enough to be humble but without hindering his gaze. "I had to."

The pain etched in his voice stopped me short. Catching my breath, I reached over and scooped Ciaran into my arms, his as body as lithe and frail as a doll's.

"Why?" I demanded an explanation. "I know you care about him. He's special to our tribe after all."

"My prince." Micky gracefully swept into a bow, his arms at his sides as rigid as boards. "I assure you, my feelings are just out of loyalty. He's your son."

The word stopped me short. I opened my mouth to reply, but there was no sound.

Ciaran shifted in my arms, his light blue eyes fading to ice. "Aren't I?"

Of course, the notion hadn't escaped me. But to hear the word was so final, so binding.

My grip around Ciaran tightened protectively, his fair hair brushing against my bare shoulders a reminder of what I needed to protect. "Yes, you are, which is why you need to stay safe."

To others, understanding how easily I could accept Ciaran as my own was hard. Micky had lived his entire life without knowing his parents, without having a biological family. As far as he was concerned, I was to Ciaran what Joel had been to him.

My revelation was cut short when another cold aura reminded me of the imminent danger my mate was in.

I started to hand Ciaran back to Micky, but his arms wound tight around my neck. His heart beat madly, echoing in my eardrums. "Take him back to the others."

"I have to stay," Ciaran pleaded. "Have to."

I decided there was no time for him to go back safely. "Fine, stay close."

Micky started to turn away but my hand firmly on his forearm stilled him. "You too, Micky."

His face went blank, a hand going to his belt where his sword was still sheathed. "I'll kill anyone that tries to harm you, Prince Kanji."

Shifting Ciaran so he was on my back, I pressed a finger to my lips. We had slowed to a crawl, the trees too thickly clustered for us to run.

Flying seemed like the ideal option for finding Tristan, but if the Sidhee didn't know my location, they would then.

Tristan's satchel lay open, tiny tools and instruments scattered like internal organs across the snow. My heart clenched so painfully, I stopped breathing. I scanned the open ground for even the slightest hint Tristan had been harmed. Blood, hair, even the faintest tear of fabric would've been enough for me to realize he'd been attacked.

What was left of my rationality told me Tristan was safe, that he was stronger than I was and would've gotten away. But the image of the dark Sidhee prince clouded any reason I had. Even living in the darkened world, never knowing what Christophe truly intended for me was better than imagining the things the prince would do to my mate.

"Tristan—"

Something as hard as a boulder collided with my side, knocking me off balance. I clung tight to Ciaran's legs wrapped around my waist, but I felt the loss of his hands on my neck as he was thrown. Another rough collision sent me spiraling into Micky.

Grabbing for my sword, I used the cold handle as a way to ground myself. Micky rolled to his knees, unsheathing his sword and protectively crouching over Ciaran. We'd been thrown a good twenty feet, our bodies only stopping of the tree's will.

"You okay?" I asked huskily, remaining low to the earth so I would have a better visual.

There were bruises climbing up our arms and hiding beneath our clothing, proving we'd been attacked even though the perpetrator was gone. Looking closer, I saw the tiny ruby-red threads clinging to the vacant branches. As beautiful as the stones were, they were as dangerous as the Sidhee's violent tempers.

Humans couldn't see the small flashes of red, but they were full of hatred and if left untouched, could consume the purest of creatures. They were devices created by the Sidhee themselves to eat away at the trees.

Luckily, the trees they clung to did not belong to any Dryma.

Micky acted as a shield between Ciaran and the approaching threat. "Where are they?"

I pressed a finger to my mouth, my other hand wrapped around the sword. The bulky object was cumbersome and heavier now that I had to rely on its strength. With my eyes glued to the sky, I tried to locate even the faintest of movements. The forest seemed to move in slow motion, the thumping of my heart as loud as the birds.

From my right, I saw a dark figure leaping from the woods. Acting on instinct, I held up my sword in defense, the clash of steel loud as his blade met mine. Ciaran let out a yelp, but I couldn't let my eyes stray from my opponent.

With eyes glittering red and armor as sharp as thorns, there was no mistaking the creature attempting to pin me down was a Sidhee. If the threatening appearance and scaly skin weren't enough of an indicator, the abrasiveness of his cold breath was.

A flicker of recognition crossed his eyes as he surveyed my face. After all, he was probably sent here to retrieve Tristan and me.

When he started to lift his sword, I kicked his legs out from underneath him and rolled to the side. Grabbing Ciaran's hand, I pulled him across the clearing, Micky panting to keep up.

We should stay and fight. Micky's inner protests were too loud to ignore.

Too many, I offered by way of explanation.

I couldn't see his face, but I imagined his confusion. *There was only one?*

No. There are several. He acted first to assess who we were. Now he knows…. I let the sentence die. Now he knew, and there was no telling what he'd do to Ciaran and Micky if they stood in the way of my capture.

"Down!" I cried, cradling Ciaran's head to reduce the impact as we toppled to the ground.

Micky landed beside me with a thud, his lip bleeding from where he'd accidentally bit down. Covering his body with my other arm, I felt the scrape of nail and tooth across my back. The Sidhee were no longer hiding, at least four of them circling and vanishing within the trees as though they were playing a game.

To them, we probably were.

"Watch Ciaran," I told Micky, leaping to my feet and retrieving the sword I'd dropped when we fell.

The sound of metal told me Micky still had his weapon at the ready.

All at once, three Sidhee landed feet where from where we stood, their bodies massive and their height looming. They looked like dead trees that had been brought back to life, but absent of anything good about living.

"Come with us, swan," the middle Sidhee boomed, his voice as loud as thunder. "We are here for you."

Micky was in front of me before I had time to push him back. I started to pull his arm, but the strength and muscle surprised me. Our attacks had aged him, had made him a more capable version of the swan I had known. He wasn't a child, but he wasn't ready to take the same role Zain or Tomas would have.

Still, his courage touched me.

A melodic flutter of wings pushed Micky to the side as my mate took his place. The wings were as loud as a thousand birds chanting in unison toward one goal.

"Tristan," I gasped. "Thank God you're okay."

My mate looked over his shoulder, his eyes alive with a passion I only saw when I knew I was going to be worshipping him on my knees. "Of course." His voice was fierce. "I told you I would always come for you."

Momentarily, we had forgotten the Sidhee, but they had seemed just as shocked and intrigued by the addition, and they had yet to move. Our advantage gone, the Sidhee moved forward venomously, either not recognizing Tristan or not caring he was the one their prince desired.

Tristan was an amazing healer, better with herbs than swords, but even knowing he might not win, my place was at his side. My sweaty hands made the handle slippery, and the blade felt too heavy for me to lift. The Sidhee let out a crescendo of sound like a demon chorus echoing in the night. One flew past us and swiped at Micky, but he was prepared for the attack and deflected. Ciaran was pressed tight into my back, a solid wall of fright.

With Tristan joining us, the Sidhee only had the advantage of a single additional fighter. As briefly as I could, I intercepted Zain's thoughts.

I was right in thinking the Sidhee would only send a few to scout the area. The other Kuro had maintained their formation, but there was no need. The only Sidhee within our world were the ones violently clashing against our swords.

While defending myself against the Sidhee from before, another jabbed his sword in my face. If Tristan hadn't taken hold of his arm, I wasn't sure I'd have ever been able to look at his handsome face again.

"How dare you attack my mate," Tristan roared, sending the astonished Sidhee ten feet back. His backside landing on the ground created a sickening crunch as the very trees shook within their foundation. "If any of you tries to touch him again, I will destroy you."

Surprise was soon replaced by laughter as they mocked my mate. Micky's whimper behind me was loud, he and Ciaran obviously perturbed by the dead sound of the Sidhee's joy.

The demons had yet to break up our makeshift circle, and I realized why.

"They're playing with us," I whispered urgently, tugging on Tristan's jacket. "Or else they would've made a grab at us."

"I know. But without turning our backs and running, we don't have much choice."

He was right. Without the addition of flight, we had no advantages. The time it would take for us to gain flight would be all the Sidhee needed to win.

"Kanji," Ciaran whispered. "Look."

I spared the slightest of glances, but groaned when all I saw was the sparkle of water spilling from between a gathering of trees.

"Go, Ciaran, go to the lake." I pried his fingers from the loops of my jeans; his head shook frantically in refusal. "You can get away. You are still an Asrai."

Micky had jumped to the aid of my mate, both of them locked in a dance against three Sidhee where every move was deflected or downright ignored.

The fourth Sidhee jumped into my line of vision and narrowly, I pulled Ciaran to the side before he could taste the steel of the demon's sword. I realized the Sidhee was being cautious around me, his chapped lips turning downward in a snarl.

"I can help," Ciaran pleaded. "Trust me."

Tristan's lithe figure danced between the Sidhee's strong hold, his arms and legs as long and graceful as a dancer's.

Without hesitation, Tristan rebounded and wound his hand around my wrist like a snake. "Go, Ciaran."

"Wait, what are we doing?" I asked in confusion. "Micky?"

"Right here, my prince." Like a creature of smoke, the teenage Kuro was at our side, his spindly legs crossing over the rocky landscape.

The tip of my boot caught on a root, but Tristan maintained his hold on me. His breath in my ear sent shivers into the very marrow of my bones. "I'll never let you go, love."

I felt his arm around my waist, his hold tightening until he took the very breath in my lungs away. So close... only a few more steps and we would be at the water's edge.

As still as death, but as vivid as a dream, the water greeted us like an old friend.

Discarding his shoes, Ciaran waded into the lake like a parched creature near death. Water crawled up his arms like tiny earthworms, joining to his skin like the very veins pumping life through his body.

"Take a deep breath, Kanji," Tristan instructed me, dropping to his knees so he could undo the laces of my boots. "Then dive."

There wasn't time for him to explain because the Sidhee were just as fast as we were. Ciaran turned around, his large eyes glowing the same pale hue as when I'd first found him. The water was cold between my toes, chunks of ice farther out that had yet to melt in the absent heat of spring.

Trusting my mate, I inhaled sharply and dove to Ciaran. At first, the cold was so unbearable, I could do nothing but hover in a place where I wasn't sure I was alive.

Then my wings broke through my shoulder blades, even without my command. Skin melted into soft downy feathers, my neck stretching and twisting. A break in the water beside me made me realize Micky had jumped in too. Fascinated, I watched as his wings took over his body until the creature beside me resembled more of a bird than a human.

Breaking the surface, I was surprised to find I didn't gasp for air. Feeling the droplets of water roll off my now feathery skin, I caught the faintest glimpse of my reflection. The blue eyes I recognized and the pitch-black color of my feathers, but the rest of me was astonishing.

A swan. Our ancestors had been able to fully transform into graceful birds, but over time, the skill had been lost. Ciaran let his arms fall to his side, clearly exhausted. Thrashing in the waves, Micky appeared at my side, his wings fluttering desperately as he tried to regain control.

Breathe, Micky. I whipped my long neck from side to side in pursuit of Tristan. *I know you must be scared, but—*

Scared? His excitement startled me. *This is cool as hell. We're swans, like actual swans. My parents used to tell me stories about this.*

I admired his bravery, but only for the split second before I caught sight of Tristan. He was pinned down by two Sidhee, and another had his sword pointed at the fragile spot just over his heart. Whether their intention was to kill or to intimidate, I didn't care. Bursting from the water with speed I didn't know I had, I threw myself onto the Sidhee threatening the existence of my mate. I heard shouts, but every voice was indistinguishable.

All except for Tristan's.

There was blood, I was sure of it, but the finishing blow didn't come from me. My purpose had been to distract and weaken the Sidhee, but Tristan had delivered their endings. I had no conception of time, of space, or even my name. The primal nature locked deep within my heart pulled me back to the sky, to the blossoming hope there was warmth and sun.

Shaking my head, I released the tangle of red thread I had in my beak.

Facing me, a bleeding sword in hand, was the only source of comfort I needed: Tristan.

"Kanji." Tristan's voice was low as he slowly dropped his weapon. "Please. Come here, baby, please."

His hands were outstretched, vibrant green eyes glued in my direction. I could see the frantic darting of his eyes but wasn't sure why. Did he truly believe I would ever, ever run from him? From the only man I would ever belong to?

A terrifying thought rocked my core. What if he wasn't afraid I was going to run, but that I would attack? After all, I may have been beautiful, but my appearance wasn't the one he'd come to love.

Lowering myself to the ground, I tried to appear submissive so he wouldn't feel threatened. The tips of my wings grazed the earth; my face pressed close to his feet.

A slight whimper escaped, revealing how afraid I was that I'd scare my mate.

"Oh baby, no." Tristan was instantly on his knees, the fabric of his jeans soaked through in patches. "Don't be sad, Kanji. I'm here."

In this form, my words were silenced. I had yet to break the barrier separating his mind from my own and was unsure if I'd ever be able to. Even with Kuro blood running through his veins, he was more Dryma than swan.

The moment Tristan touched the curve of my neck, I shuddered fiercely. Feathers transformed into flesh as my wings retreated and my long hair fell over my shoulders. I stared at my fingers, almost expecting to see traces of webbing.

"You were remarkable, Kanji." Tristan's voice was full of admiration, his eyes twinkling. "So beautiful and graceful. You were like something out of a fairy tale."

His fingers caressed my neck, working their way up to my jaw where he held tight. Blushing, I turned so I could kiss his palm. "I didn't do much."

Tristan's laugh was boisterous. "You saved my life. Baby, you are so much stronger than you give yourself credit for. If you can't believe in yourself, believe me."

He tucked my hair behind my ear affectionately, his mouth on mine. I was lost in our scorching kiss, a flame only he could ignite burning in my heart. His hand on my cock sent me into a fit of embarrassment.

"I'm not wearing any clothes."

"No." Tristan chuckled, pulling my face into the crook of his neck where I breathed deeply. "I fear they ripped. Hold on a moment."

He shrugged from his jacket and helped put my arms through the holes. Because he was so much larger than I was, the coat went nearly to my knees, hiding my obvious arousal.

"I can't keep my hands off you," Tristan panted as he covered the expanse of my chest with his hands. "Are you hurt at all? Do you need me to carry you?"

By some stroke of luck, my boots had remained intact. Shreds of fabric from my jeans clung to my legs so I brushed them away and held out my arms.

"Kanji." Micky panted, bursting into the clearing just as Tristan had picked me up.

His hair was a mess, but his clothing had only stretched during his transformation. Perhaps because he was so slight and the clothes he wore were five sizes too large. Ciaran trailed behind him, his eyes alight with a gleam only the lake could provide.

"There was another Sidhee," I remembered, adjusting so I was standing on my own, but Tristan could still hold me. "What happened?"

The guilt in Micky's eyes gave me my answer. Still, I felt compelled to enter his thoughts. There had been an immense struggle, but unlike his human form, the agility that came with being a swan aided him. Before, he might not have had as fair of a chance, but with the added strength, he'd drowned the Sidhee in the lake. Ciaran had taken care of the body, a swirl of delicate water turning deadly as it pulled and ripped until only scraps remained.

"Ciaran," I breathed, taking his face between my hands. His flesh was searing and the hue in his eyes looked washed out. "How were you able—"

"Not here." My mate halted my curiosity. "Castle de Mar isn't far…. Have him explain there."

I gave a slight nod, taking hold of Ciaran's hand and holding fast.

Zain, what's happening?

We're all fine. Tell you more when I see you. His gruff response was expected. *Where the hell have you been? Did you find Tristan? Micky?*

Yes, we're all fine.

Good, tell Micky he's in for it when I catch up to him. There was silence as Zain tried to censor his concern. *Where are you going?*

The water castle.

Okay?

I think all of the Sidhee came after us, so you should be fine. Meet me at the castle.

Ten minutes.

Knowing Zain, he'd be there much sooner. Anxiety ate me alive. Not only was I concerned for the safety of my kind, but there was a giddy excitement deep within my bones I couldn't shake.

I had transformed, actually changed my matter into something I had long given up on. And the fact Micky had been able to as well was uplifting. Did I dare hope our full magic could still return?

Seeing Tristan told me I wasn't the only one nervous. Protectively, he hovered beside me, one hand on the small of my back, the other tight around his sword. Emerald eyes scanned the landscape, his jaw clenched and his body tensing at even the slightest noise.

The castle really wasn't far, but Tristan surprised me by stopping at the trickling pond at the golden gate.

"Don't go anywhere," he pleaded.

"I won't."

Reassured, he bent so he could scoop a handful of the water into his palm. When he brought the liquid to his lips, I could only imagine how it must've tasted. The lotus flowers would've given the water a slight flavor as soft as a bed of down feathers.

"Everything's connected," Tristan murmured.

"Come again?" Micky asked.

My mate consulting with himself was something I'd gotten used to long ago and from Ciaran's expression, so had he. When Tristan had gathered his thoughts enough to put them into words, he would speak.

"The Sidhee use the water as a portal. And Ciaran uses the water to heal." Tristan stood up excitedly, brushing his dripping fingers on his pants. "They're all connected."

I caught a strand of his glimmering hair. "Which means?"

"We can use the water too."

"How?"

Before he could explain, Zain's booming voice interrupted. "Kanji, man, what the hell?" He knocked me off my feet, his arms wrapped around my body threatening to crush my ribs. "You okay?"

I couldn't stop my lips from turning up. "Yes, I already told you I was."

Holding me at arm's length, he looked me over as if needing to ascertain for himself. Just when I thought I was in the clear, he blanched. "Why aren't you wearing any clothes? Don't tell me—"

"Of course not." I blushed, looking to my mate for help.

Tristan desperately tried not to laugh, obviously finding Zain's sexual insinuation hilarious. "I didn't steal his clothes. Promise."

"We turned into swans!" Micky exclaimed.

Truthfully, I was surprised he'd managed to wait as long as he did before divulging. Zain went as limp as his eyes.

"Did you say you turned into a swan?" Tomas repeated, nudging Zain out of the way so he could have a look at me. He reeked of cigarettes, one dangling from his lips unlit. At his exclamation, the cigarette fell to the ground but he didn't move to retrieve it. "Like real ones?"

Keeping his voice down wasn't part of the plan. As tired as the Kuro were, I could hear their hearts pounding in excitement. They hung back, resting on the ornate benches and wrought-iron tables laid out in the castle's garden. But even the farthest Kuro was hanging on my every word.

Tristan must've sensed my uneasiness because he turned so he was partially shielding me from view.

"I'm okay," I assured him.

"I'm not sure if my plan will work," he murmured so our conversation was concealed from anyone outside of our small circle. "I don't want to give false hope."

"We could go inside."

"But your swans should see you. That gives them hope too."

Micky nodded in agreement; Zain and Tomas were still shell-shocked as they tried to process the possibilities.

"Tristan, your plan… does it include Ciaran?"

"Yes." My mate gave Ciaran a sideways glance. "If you are willing."

For a child, his replies were always so serious. "I am."

"Did you know Ciaran could do that?" I finally asked, my fingers tingling with the urge to shift again. After having done it once, I felt addicted to the feeling. "Is that the only reason we could change?"

Zain blinked. "Ciaran did?"

My mate's heavy hand on my shoulder calmed my nerves. "Of course you'll be able to change at will. Magic isn't in the water. It's inside of Ciaran's soul and inside of yours. He didn't give you anything you didn't already have.

"And in the same way he can awaken power, I believe he can put it to sleep."

If Tristan hadn't already had our undivided attention, he certainly did now. "Are you trying to say a child can destroy the entire Sidhee race?" Tomas asked, doubt evident in his voice.

"No," Tristan explained patiently. "For years, the Dryma have been trying to unlock the key to how the Sidhee use water as portals from their world to ours. I think it has something to do with the Asrai."

I shook my head. "There weren't any there."

"But there were glittering crystals," Zain pointed out. "I'd never forget those. They were so bright I couldn't even see when we first got there."

"About the only thing that was," Tomas contended. "Their world was like being blind."

"Crystals?" Ciaran inquired quietly. "Like moonstones?"

"Moonstones? Could be," Zain offered. "I'll let you see later."

I focused on my friend. "You have one?"

"Yeah, I nicked it on our way out."

"You would." I rolled my eyes, noticing Tristan had started to pace as though in a trance. "Love, are you okay?"

"I wonder…." Tristan came to a dead halt. "If everything is connected, we could lure the Sidhee to the water and then use their portals against them."

"How exactly?" Micky asked, reminding us of his presence.

"By manipulating their power so instead of opening the portals, they are closing them," Tristan continued. "Think about it. If Ciaran is able to change their spells so every portal they enter becomes closed, we could lead them to the castle. Once they were here, you could transform into swans and—"

"We'd have a fighting chance," I finished. "Brilliant."

Tomas looked like he had a headache. "I don't follow, Kanji."

"Not only will you have the advantage of fighting in your true form," Tristan said, his words rushed, "but we'll have the castle as our defense. Beneath the castle, there are several rooms completely submerged. I have to do some research to make sure, but I'd bet those rooms are maintained with Asrai magic. Maybe we even have moonstones of our own."

"So… fighting a bunch of demons in your basement is the plan?" Tomas scoffed, reaching for his forgotten cigarette. "Great."

"Without sacrifices, they cannot possibly return. They must have come here with the intention of sacrificing whoever they came across." I shuddered at who they might have had to sacrifice in order to get here and realized the only ones left in the Sidhee world were the demons themselves. "But if they are all congregated within one entry portal, maybe Ciaran can send them back."

"Uh-huh," Zain said cautiously. "And Ciaran would alter their magic how?"

"The other Asrai didn't want me." Ciaran's voice was low. "But that doesn't mean I don't know how to use our magic."

"Sounds like absolutely ludicrous." Tomas tugged at the back of his hair. "But if Kanji's in, so am I."

As if I'd expect anything less.

"What do we tell the others?" Zain indicated the Kuro still resting.

Looking over, I realized there had been a change within my kind. There was no denying the power they'd accumulated from Zain and Tomas's difficult training, but what I saw now was strength of an entirely different caliber. Hesitation was at a minimum and self-esteem was at an all-time high. Out of respect for me, they maintained loyalty, but instead of standing at attention, they leisurely joked.

"Tell them we will start residing in the castle," I said, my voice ringing with authority I actually felt deserving of. "There are three known portals across Pasky, so we'll break into three groups to keep watch."

"What if the demons show up before the star things are ready?"

"Moonstones," Tristan corrected gently. "And they will be, won't they, Ciaran?"

Ciaran gave a fierce nod. "Absolutely."

With a grumble, Tomas turned to give orders to the Kuro who were instantly at attention. I saw a look of uneasiness spread out over their faces at the prospect of living in the castle, and I really couldn't blame them.

When they were dismissed in order to go pack, the easy chatter returned.

"The happiness on your face right now," Tristan whispered, only for my ears. "I wish I could see it all the time."

If we won, I was sure he would. If we lost... I couldn't even entertain the notion.

CHAPTER FIFTEEN

"CLOSE YOUR eyes, love."

I did without question, Tristan's hands coming to rest on my shoulders. Blindly, I let him guide me as my bare feet slid over the plush carpet of his master suite. He situated me on the edge of the mattress, the bed so tall my toes could only graze the floor. I felt the soft brush of silk as the strings tying back the canopy were undone and fell free.

A hand caressed my neck, moving to the tender spot behind my ear. Gone was my ponytail and then my shirt until Tristan let out a soft moan telling me he was pleased.

"Hold out your hands."

I did.

"Baby, you're shaking." His voice was cautious. "Are you afraid?"

"No," I breathed. "Excited."

He chuckled as he dropped something into my waiting palms. "I hope I do not disappoint."

"Can I open them?"

He pinched and gently twisted my nipple. "Not yet," Tristan whispered. "Do you feel good?"

"Yes," I gasped.

His fingers left my chest, working their way over the flat planes of my stomach to the throbbing bulge in my pajama pants. We had just showered and were locked away within his suite in the castle. I had wanted to explore, but all thoughts of adventure were erased when he touched me.

Even without him telling me, I had seen the look of utter lust hidden behind his eyes. The need he'd harbored ran far deeper than just a misguided want. He desired me with every fiber of his core, the same way I yearned for him.

"Shall I take you into my mouth?" Tristan's lips were pressed to my lower stomach, just above the opening of my pants where he'd already taken the liberty of easing them down. "Or shall I torture you?"

I wasn't sure what made me say it. Even in the darkest level of our intimacy, Tristan was always merciless, striving to deliver nothing less than mind-blowing pleasure. But this time, his kindness was not what I wanted.

"Torture," I replied, breathlessly.

"Hmm." He sounded surprised. "Are you sure, my sweet Kanji? I may be kind, but I assure you, making you cry with pleasure is something I have fantasized about."

"Very sure."

He immobilized me by grasping my throat. "Do not let go of what you're holding."

Speaking wasn't an option, so I did the best I could with a submissive duck of my head.

Then I was flipped onto my stomach, my pants yanked to my ankles but not removed entirely so they could serve as restraints.

"Lift your hips," he directed. "And put your arms behind you."

With my throat free, I could reply, "Like this?"

"No." My hair was grasped tightly, the side of my face pushed into an oversized pillow. "Clasp your elbows."

Maneuvering without letting go of what I possessed was difficult, but I managed. Instead of actually touching my elbows, I let my closed fist bump against the crook of my inner arm. He seemed pleased because he let out a low groan of satisfaction.

"On second thought," Tristan mused, "I want your arms on the bed, spread out on either side."

The comforter was cool against my skin. "Whatever you want."

"Really?"

"Do you doubt me?" I asked softly.

Tristan's knees hugged my waist as he hoisted himself onto the bed. I felt a soft touch of gold as his curls tickled the back of my neck. "Show me your wings, Kanji."

I could feel his arousal like a blade at the base of my spine and my own cock was leaking all over the sheets, but somehow, this request was more intimate than anything he could otherwise command.

My shoulders spread, bones and muscle contorting to adjust. The tingle in my toes caused my legs to shake and when I felt Tristan wrap his hand around my throbbing shaft, I nearly blacked out.

"Keep going," Tristan urged, his touch merciless. "Go as slowly as you can."

"Tristan," I whimpered, continuing to obey, even as I felt my entire being going limp with exhaustion and pleasure. There was no way something like this should be as intimate as it was, but I'd never felt more aroused than I did now. "Please, love, please."

"Not yet." Tristan dipped his pinky into my slit, allowing his other hand to softly caress the inside of my wing. "So stunning, my swan. I can see every color in existence hiding between the folds of your black wings. You're bucking your hips up into me so hard, I can only imagine how tight you would feel around my cock."

"Do it," I pleaded. "Enter me."

There was only a little bit left of my wingspan to release. I trembled violently, unable to find a solid grip on the sheets without releasing the object and my sanity.

A lubed finger easily slid past my tight ring of muscle. "You aren't prepared to accept me."

Tears as heavy as raindrops leaked from the corners of my eyes. I bit down on the nearest blanket, my entire frame convulsing in what had to be the most gratifying torture I'd ever been subjected to.

"Tristan." I felt as though my mind was bleeding. Promises, begging, conceding to anything he wanted, I whimpered the way I knew he liked. "Can't, can't, can't...."

His thick shaft replaced his fingers as he gave in. "My Kanji, how could I deny you anything?"

My wings released to their fullest potential, just as he sheathed himself inside of me.

"Your wings are a canvas of color," he remarked, rocking into me so the sheets created much-needed friction for my pulsing cock. "Your heart is beating so fast I can see your wings mimicking the rhythm."

"Make my pulse go even faster," I panted, drowning in his scent.

Dryma and Kuro had one thing in common: their ability to release pheromones. Meant to alert a mate to their interest, releasing pheromones was uncommon. For Tristan to do it now, he really did wish to drive me completely and utterly mad.

"Beg me and I might grant your wish."

Eyeing Tristan through the curtain of my dark hair, I forced my eyes to focus on the most glorious sight I'd ever witnessed. "My prince, my mate, my love…." I could hardly speak through the blinding pleasure. "I beg you to go harder. I'm so close I can't hold back."

He stopped, silencing both my senses and my mind. Gripping my hip hard, he thrust forward until my legs trembled and I wondered if I'd ever again be able to stand.

"Go ahead, baby," Tristan commanded, his hand heavy on my leaking cock. "Come for me."

I shot so hard I was momentarily blinded. The pleasure was so intense, I barely heard his loud moan as he pounded through his release, determined to make sure I was thoroughly milked of mine.

Slowly, like butterflies withdrawing, I allowed my wings to slide into the safety of my back. Rolling me so I was tucked into his side, Tristan pulled my face to his chest.

"Do you hear my heart, how fast it's racing?"

"Yes."

"Only for you, Kanji." He kissed the top of my head, as if marking me as his own. "Did I hurt you?"

"God no," I whimpered, too enraptured to fully focus. "Did I please you?"

His chuckle was possessive. "As if you even need to ask. Sleep, baby, you're barely holding on."

There was no way I could ever refuse his command, especially when it was something I needed desperately.

"LOVE, WAKE up."

I tried to do as he asked, but my eyelids were glued shut. The most I managed was a slight flexing of my fingers. "Must I?"

"I know you're tired, Kanji." I felt the bed dip and then Tristan stroking my hair. "But Aiden begged for me to put you on the phone."

Aiden? What could've happened to sweet Chiaki to make his mate desperate enough to beg for my audience?

"My prince." Aiden's voice was humble, but there was urgency in his words. "I am so sorry to disturb your rest, but I…. Chiaki."

I sat up so fast the room spun. Gathering my bearings, I felt Tristan holding me for support. "What's wrong?"

"Nothing physical," Aiden said cautiously. "But he's been sleeping much longer than usual and every time he sleeps, he has nightmares."

"Is he sleeping now?"

"Yes."

There was nothing unusual about having restless sleep, especially considering the amount of stress he was under. As fragile as Chiaki may have appeared, his loyalty ran deep and that quality was the true measure of his strength.

"Nightmares?" I repeated. "About what?"

Tristan was staring at our entwined fingers, but I could see lines of worry etched across his forehead.

"The Sidhee overpowering you," Aiden replied. "He's so fearful that he even asked me to come back to your side so I can protect you."

"What does he see?"

"The life we had led as prisoners to the Sidhee. Joel and I were so busy taking care of the Kuro, I hadn't even stopped to consider how much he was suffering at their hand."

I held my breath, my extreme tiredness coupled with my fear incapacitating me.

"Do you wish to come back?" I finally asked.

Aiden hesitated. "If my prince wishes it."

"Stay where you belong. Stay with Chiaki."

There weren't words to describe his relief. "Prince Kanji, be careful, please. Chiaki adores you, more than you'll ever know."

My mouth was dry at the admission. "Take care of him." I saw Tristan's tight expression. "And when Chiaki wakes up, have him call Tristan. I am sure he wants to know the status of his kind."

In the background, I heard a soft cry and knew it was Chiaki. "I have to wake him up."

"He'll appreciate your comfort."

"And Prince Kanji?"

"Yes?"

There was a pause. "Thank you for letting me stay…."

My tongue felt thick. "I may be your prince, but your mate must always come first. I understand that need better than anyone."

When Chiaki let out another bloodcurdling scream, Aiden said a hasty goodbye and the line went dead. For several moments, I was too tense to move.

"Are you all right, Kanji?"

I gave a shaky nod. "Just seems more real, you know?"

He narrowed his eyes. "You were taken by Christophe and kept as his prisoner. I am sure you can understand what Chiaki dreams as he too was a prisoner."

"Chiaki is a healer. A delicate Kuro. If anyone apart from him had had nightmares, maybe it wouldn't weigh on me so." I shrugged, dropping the phone onto the comforter. Everything in Tristan's palace suite was ornate and extravagant, down to the carpet. "But I'm worried because he's our only healer. We need him."

"Is there the possibility he is just overly concerned?"

I looked up at my mate. He had shifted so if anyone came into his room, they would have to go through him before even having a chance at seeing me. Combined with his terse expression and anxious words, I was sure he was protecting me on purpose. "He's very gifted."

Tristan's eyes flashed.

"Where are you going?"

Tristan had left my side, striding toward the door with newfound purpose. Because of the massive size of his lodgings, he still had a good ten feet to go, but I was amazed at how far he seemed.

"To talk to Zain and Tomas about the guard."

The only window was covered in a heavy curtain the color of chocolate. "Why? Won't they be sleeping?"

"If they are, I promise I won't disturb them. I just want to ensure their comfort."

"You mean tell them about Chiaki's vision," I threw back bitterly. "Simply say it."

Tristan's shoulders slumped. "Even thinking of our downfall, let alone saying it, is too painful. I only have the strength to say it once, so I'll tell those who need to know."

"I should tell them." I made to get out of the bed, but my legs were weak and I stumbled.

"Please," Tristan pleaded, closing his eyes. "Trust me. Just rest."

I grunted in frustration, but he was right. I was barely holding on to consciousness and knew the moment he left, I'd give in to sleep. "You will be back when I wake up."

His glittering teeth were a stark contrast to the dull paint on the walls. "Yes, always."

THINGS CHANGED more drastically than I could've imagined.

In the few days that followed, security became tighter than before, the Kuro training in the field behind the castle rather than the usual clearing beside the Crystal Lake. At all times, Zain or Tomas were there, their presence so close I felt as though I were suffocating.

Tristan and Ciaran worked fast. They first had to separate the tiny moonstones so there were enough pieces to scatter around the known entry portals. Then I collaborated with Zain and Tomas to ensure the moment we knew the Sidhee had arrived, our kind would be in position. Coordinating where certain Kuro would be in order to trick the Sidhee into entering the portal, thus coming back to the castle, proved difficult.

With so little to work with, the preparations fell to Ciaran. If he weren't ready to transform the swans, then everything would crumble. Once the Sidhee were locked within the portal, the only way to destroy them would be by keeping them locked in the water. As swans, we had the advantage of being able to hold our breath while maintaining our agility.

For once, Zain and Tomas weren't within sight. While stones were perfectly placed and everything in the armory shined and sharpened, I was left alone. Ciaran would be responsible for changing our kind's anatomy, but I had to find the best possible location where we could shift without leaving ourselves vulnerable.

Sighing, I'd given Tristan my ironclad promise I wouldn't leave the castle and had then gone in search of the underwater caverns. The entry had once been hidden from view, but because there were no Dryma to protect the lair, the concealing magic had faded.

My heart beat fiercely, a crescendo of sound so loud I wanted to cover my ears.

"Kanji, are you okay?" Micky's touch was gentle on my shoulder. "You were mumbling."

I forced a smile. "Remembering…."

"This is where you were before, isn't it?" Micky whispered. "We were frantically looking and couldn't find you. Christophe said we'd never see you again."

My heart ached. "Whatever he may be, he is persistent."

"But it must've been worse in the demon's world, right?"

Except it hadn't. There, I had expected everything, right down to Christophe's cruel grin and unwanted advances. Here, in a world of peace, I hadn't expected to feel so vulnerable.

"I felt more helpless when he kept me here," I admitted. Taking a breath, I pushed open the door and stepped inside.

The corridor was long and winding, minimizing how far down the hallway I could see. Where there were not doors of strong iron, there were glass panels exposing the contents of the lake. Because the water was still partially frozen, there were few fish and fewer currents.

"Was there a reason you needed me?" I asked, turning to Micky.

He took a sip of his drink guiltily. "I wanted to take a turn protecting you."

"Ciaran?"

"Is with Tristan. I think I was getting in their way."

When he was brutally honest, I couldn't even think of sending him away. "As planned, all of the Sidhee will be sent here from the other portals."

"And then?"

"If I can find a way to enter the lake without shattering the entire structure—" I poked my head into the first room and, realizing the library would be of little use, moved on to the next. "—then Ciaran can transform us and we will use the water to our advantage. Not only will the demons be caught off guard, they will not be expecting us."

"Is there any way to stay in here and just shoot them or something?"

I gave a small smile. "Unless we develop missiles that can kill Sidhee, not likely." The next room was empty, but so small, only a twin-size bed would be able to fit inside.

"Sounds complicated."

I inspected another room, this one slightly larger but not enough to accommodate the Kuro who would be waiting. "The idea is the Sidhee will be so angry with us for sending them here that we can fight them long enough for Ciaran to find a way of sending them back and sealing the portal."

"So they are being brought here by Ciaran forcefully and don't need sacrifices? Then how will they return?" Micky asked, confused.

I took a deep breath. "They are meant to be the sacrifices."

"Oh…." This made him more uncomfortable than I thought he could admit. "Should we practice?"

Stacked within the glass cabinets of the castle's kitchen were goblets and flutes made of the most exquisite stained glass. But rather than risk breaking the tableware, Micky opted for a plastic Solo cup.

"Practice what?"

"Shifting."

"Eager, huh?"

"Being a swan, I felt so free."

I started to respond but stopped when we entered the last of the rooms. Unlike the others, this one had six walls, all perfectly positioned with a large window in the center. Tables, chairs, and a platform were set up as if awaiting a concert that would never come.

Just as I was about to declare this the room of choice, I heard thundering footsteps and was pulled roughly against my mate's chest. Tristan was breathing heavily, beads of sweat dripping down his beautiful golden chest.

"Tristan, I—"

"The Sidhee have arrived."

Micky dropped his cup, making the white tile bleed red. "Already?"

I snapped out of my shock.

"Where's Ciaran?" Micky started toward the door, but I caught him by the back of his collar and held him still just as Zain arrived, tugging a nervous Ciaran behind him.

"Tristan, is there any way to get through these windows without waterlogging ourselves?" I asked, trusting in my friends to protect Ciaran.

His pulse thumped in his neck. "If we shut the door"—he indicated the one he'd burst into—"then this room is all we'll lose."

"Good, let's show these Sidhee bastards what we're made of." Zain released Ciaran's hand, the Asrai instantly racing to the platform with a small moonstone glowing in the palm of his hand. "Anything you need from me, Tristan?"

This was the absolute last place I should be getting emotional, but seeing my best friend and mate working together made me feel complete. "Tomas?"

"Coming," Zain called. "He's gathering the rest of the Kuro who didn't already leave to go to the portals."

"Are you sure the Sidhee will be at the portals?" Micky asked.

"They'd have to be or else how are they gonna get here?" Tomas entered the room like a prince at the forefront of a parade. His head was held high and his clothes clung to his lithe figure, but the enthusiastic grin was what showed his confidence. "Every portal is covered, Kanji. Even if the demon scum don't go through all of them, we've got it all planned."

My heart raced. "Ciaran, are you ready?"

The Kuro were silent as they waited.

"Put down your weapons," I instructed, unsheathing my weapon and allowing it to clatter. "Those of us who have stayed here will be fighting in our most instinctive, primal form. If we want to win, we need to trust in our ancestry."

Uproar swam around the room.

"But we trained with weapons?"

"How will we all be able to change?"

"The Sidhee will overrun us."

I held up a single hand. Tristan was within my grasp, but I knew I couldn't reach for him. Not now when I needed to stand on my own in order to convey hope to my kind. I would never think myself weak for relying on my mate, but I needed him to know he could in turn lean on me. I was strong enough to fight at his side, not behind him.

"Leave the weapons outside of this room. If for whatever reason we cannot hold our true form, then they will be there. But fighting with a sword was never the end goal."

Even Zain raised his eyebrow at my admission.

"Learning to wield these swords wasn't about learning how to use Dryma weapons. It was about exploring our own strength. We are strong. We are loyal. And we can win."

"Wish I had a camera right now," Zain said in annoyance.

"Um, why?"

"So I could take a picture of Tomas. He seriously looks so damn proud."

"What about you?" Tomas threw back. "You're all gaga over Kanji."

"What's wrong with being proud of your prince?" Tristan asked quietly, interrupting their debate. "It's okay, love. Connect your mind."

The moonstones were in place, the Kuro who had volunteered to be at the portals were on their way, and the rest of us were prepared to take the Sidhee on, swan or not. Everything was as perfectly placed as we could hope, so I needed to gain eyes and ears into the situation.

I took Tristan's face in my hands, not caring who saw. "You.... Before we open the window you need to get back into the hallway."

"Kanji." His voice was even. "Ciaran and I will be fine."

Then I couldn't hold back. My mind felt like a mirror being shattered into a million pieces. Interlocking images wove webs within my mind until my reality was distorted and blurred. Just as we had anticipated, the Sidhee had sent a legion of their kind to fight a war they were determined to win. Unlike in their world, they wore heavy layers of armor glittering in hues of black and silver. Their faces, made of material as heavy as their armor, concealed their expressions.

But I could feel the truth in their footsteps.

They were not here to take prisoners; they were here to annihilate.

Tristan and I had gone past each and every portal, over and over until my feet blistered and the images were committed to memory. I raced to the first one, the scattered images of the forest bleeding together until I couldn't tell what was alive.

Even though I was blinded, I knew Ciaran was at my side. I felt his soft presence as solidly as I felt the trunks graze my side in my haste to gain insight. Shinji and the other Kuro stood their ground, fighting the swarm of Sidhee exiting the water. When I saw how few Sidhee came from the portal, I knew they had carefully planned their attack.

Abandoning that portal, I moved on to the next and saw my speculations were correct. Sensing our presence in the woods, the Sidhee had separated so each and every portal was covered. I started to panic, going from one to the next until everywhere in Pasky was littered with streams of Sidhee bursting from the water like lilies in bloom.

I swung back around to Shinji and Kei, both of whom were desperately trying to maneuver the Sidhee back to the water. Their wings had been caught in the uproar, rooting them to the ground where the demons had the advantage. If something wasn't done, then the portals would be littered with dead Kuro.

Then something shifted I did not expect.

Shinji and Kei twisted, their bodies contorting violently as cloth was torn and skin disappeared beneath layers of soft fur and feather. Their faces elongated to form swooping beaks, and dark feathers burst from their backs. Their transformation complete, I caught sight of shocked expressions as the Sidhee stared in wonder.

I could hardly blame them considering I wasn't sure I believed it either.

Intrigued and entirely too cocky, the demons chased after the Kuro, probably thinking they would be easy prey. Once their rocklike feet stomped against the moist watery earth, they were swept up into Ciaran's magic.

"They're coming!" I shouted. "Be ready."

The hand on mine should've disappeared, but didn't. I tried to break through my fog, but I was riveted within my thoughts. As I entered the minds of my Kuro, I was mentally transported into the woods so I could survey the fight without ever having left the castle.

Shinji and Kei had flown into the air before they too were swallowed up in the Asrai magic. Wings beating as fiercely as their hearts, they changed directions as they hurried to the castle.

Flipping through my thought panels like images on a television, I was mesmerized at how the Kuro shifted and changed in order to meet the challenges set out before them.

I heard shouting and the breaking of glass, but Tristan's voice was the only one I could center on. Breaking from my mind, I saw the walls had begun to leak as the Sidhee slammed violently into them, over and over until I wondered how strong the magic must be to keep the seemingly thin walls intact.

I tried to break through my reverie so I would be able to visualize both the events directly in front of me as well as those farther, but I felt only disorientation.

Around me, Kuro were dropping to their knees as the shift began to commence.

Zain practically lifted me from the floor in a hug so intense, I worried he'd bruise my rib cage. "Thank you, Kanji, for leading us this far. Everything you've done is miraculous."

"Why are you—"

He pushed me roughly into Tristan's waiting arms and gave a single nod. "Take him."

"Wait." My eyes widened in disbelief. "What the hell. I have to stay and fight."

"Our plan didn't work," Tristan said sadly. "There are other Sidhee already breaking into the castle. In order to force them into the water, we have to go to the surface."

Anger instantly melted. In Tristan's face, I could only see adoration and love. Instead of trying to take me to safety and away from my kind, he offered a different chance at redemption, one I had not yet seen.

"Will you come with me?" Tristan murmured, his voice barely audible above the cawing of my Kuro and the rush of the water caving the walls. "Will you fight with me?"

"Yes."

Ciaran's eyes glowed a faint blue, but when I reached for him, he brushed my gesture aside. "You promised," he reminded me, "promised I could stay with you."

I blinked back tears. "I did."

"So I'll see you after."

No longer the same child I'd found weeks ago, he held a surge of power gathered within his slight frame I knew would put any Sidhee to shame. His magic was needed; he was needed, and so were Tristan and I.

The door slamming shut behind us was as deafening as a cannon. I didn't need to see past the concealed walls to know they had finally given in. Where there had been the sounds of shattered glass and caws, there was nothing.

Silence.

Disoriented and unsure where Tristan was, I started to wonder if I'd somehow lost my hearing. The crashes inside would've been enough to knock any human completely out. Fumbling for my mate, I was beyond relieved when I caught scent of his body and heard his voice.

"Your Kuro will be fine." He urged me down the hall and back through the lower level of the castle. "As swans, they'll be able to hold their breath longer and will make it to the surface. Don't worry."

My eyes adjusted. "Where are we going?"

"Did you see Christophe in your thoughts?"

"No."

"Or Calhoun?"

I felt my stomach sink. "No."

"That's how I know they came separately. While the rest of the Sidhee left every portal guarded by you Kuro, Calhoun would've been smarter and come directly here."

"How can you be sure?"

He gave me a look like he'd been forced to swallow acid. "Whether or not I want to, I know him. His intention was to come for me, and I won't endanger the rest of the fight."

"Noble."

Tristan shoved me backward until I was pressed to the wall, his stance protective in front of me. Gripping his blue jacket, I looked over his broad shoulders, already knowing who I would see.

"Calhoun." Never had I heard such venom in Tristan's voice. Even to those far beneath him, he was kind and understanding. To hear the anger now made his hatred tangible. "You are alone?"

"Did you think I'd need an army to get what I desire?"

In all the stories I'd heard of the mighty demon prince, nothing had prepared me. With eyes as red as the blood I tasted on my lips, he had the look of a dragon who would not be stopped. He was several feet taller than Tristan, making my muscular mate inconsequential. Despite my resentment, a part of me was awe-stricken.

His armor was different than his followers', made of something resembling human skin. The cloth was pulled taut over his chest, arms, and legs, seams popping where his muscles were heavily developed. What surprised me most of all was his skin. Unlike every other demon I'd seen, Calhoun's skin was absent of blemishes and scales. Dark hair swooped over one side of his face, the rest falling to his shoulders.

There was no denying he was attractive.

And even in my frightened state, I was slightly jealous.

"This room." Calhoun spun in a slow circle, his eyes to the ceiling as if enjoying the scenery. "Is where I should've declared our marriage to your kind."

Tristan shuddered. "But you didn't. Why go back to the past?"

"The past is where we look when realizing how we want to move forward." Calhoun rubbed his jaw. "Such a beautiful ballroom. I'll have one fashioned for you in my world so you will feel at home."

"I'm not going with you. Surely you know that."

"Why? Because of your mate?" Calhoun moved closer, a mere five feet. With his long arms, I didn't doubt he'd reach Tristan's throat before we had time to move. "What can he offer you?"

"He saved me from you," Tristan said flatly. "By coming here in your stead."

I thought Calhoun might be angry, but instead he laughed. "Yes, Christophe has informed me of the truth. To think, I actually believed the Dryma would refuse my offer. After all, you are insignificant, weak, and useless."

All of Tristan's strength wasn't enough to hold me back. Lifting myself from the ground, I tore at my shirt until the cloth lay in ribbons on the gleaming floor and my torso was bare. Feeling the familiar bite of my wings tearing through flesh, I realized there were bonds holding me back.

No, it was Tristan.

"Love, he's not someone you have to worry about."

Calhoun cackled so hard, tears sprung to his eyes. "I see why you enjoy this boy. He has spirit for a Kuro. Pity…. Had he learned his place, perhaps he could've served as your slave. I suppose the Kuro will have to appoint a new prince."

"The fuck they will," Tristan roared, leaping at Calhoun like a deranged creature.

The force with which he'd knocked me back sent me sprawling to the tiled floor. Rolling, I skidded to a stop when my body collided with the wall. Heaving myself up onto my elbows, I saw flashes of blinding light as Tristan unleashed a power I hadn't known existed.

His wings spanned the length of his body, inky black and as dangerous as death itself. Calhoun responded by darting around the room like a spider who knew it was trapped.

"I don't wish to hurt you," Calhoun spat, blood trickling from his chin and staining his cream-colored armor. "After all, what would be the point of beating up my prize before I even get him home?"

Tristan let out a cry as wild as I felt.

Over and over, their entangled bodies were thrown to the floor, the wall, the ceiling without any chance of failure. Despite his intention to leave Tristan in one piece, I knew he would resort to deadlier attacks if that was what it took to end the fight.

"Give in, my beautiful Tristan," Calhoun teased, grabbing my mate by the throat and spinning so they were enraptured in a macabre dance. When he pinned Tristan to the wall, my mate's wings crumpled underneath the sheer force Calhoun exerted. "Rest here while I take care of that boy."

"Even if you take me," Tristan choked, "the Kuro will destroy every Sidhee you've brought."

Calhoun shifted his position slightly, contemplating. Then with a flex of his wrist, there was a loud snapping sound and Tristan slid to the ground. With his back to the wall and his arms listless at his sides, he looked like a beautiful doll.

"No," I roared, grabbing Calhoun's arm with every ounce of force I harbored. "If you touch him again, I'll destroy you."

Tristan's breathing was faint, but the slight rise and fall of his chest calmed my nerves.

Calhoun was strong, possibly the strongest creature I'd ever encountered. Sheer muscle wasn't going to be how I won, if at all. Tucking my wings away, I flipped over his shoulders until I landed behind him.

"Giving up already." He looked over his shoulder. "About time you recognize your position."

But I would never give in. Not to him. Not to anyone.

His saunter was slow, purposeful, and meant to intimidate. When he extended his arm with the intention of gripping my throat, I fell to the floor and swooped his legs out from under him with one of mine. Caught off guard, Calhoun reached for something to steady himself. His mistake was trying to choose me as his brace.

I let him think he had me, but the moment his large back smashed into the floor, I twisted until I was sitting on top of his chest. Joel and Chiaki were battling to save the lives of the Dryma. And Zain, Tomas, and Micky were battling the Sidhee. Ciaran was occupied. Tristan was unconscious.

Calhoun's hands were wrapped securely around my throat, but I hardly felt the pressure. My eyesight grew hazy and I pretended to go limp, waiting, holding on until the precise moment where he thought he prevailed.

Then in a blast of willpower, I shifted. I let go of everything imprisoning me in a human form and released my true potential. With me as a human, Calhoun had perfectly positioned himself for the kill. But with me as a swan, he was left unsettled and unprepared.

Leaving no room for hesitation, I went straight for his throat. The taste was vile, and I resisted the urge to immediately vomit. Letting his dark, poisoned blood drip from my beak, I didn't stop biting until I heard an audible snap and the crimson color of his eyes bled to white.

There were many advantages to being in my form, but multitasking was not one of them.

I caught sight of shiny red hair the color of freshly picked strawberries and toned features better suited to marble statues. Christophe.

The former Dryma captain stared motionlessly at the carnage I'd left behind. Even after what he'd witnessed, I could see the desire in his eyes.

"Kanj—"

But his words were cut short. I had been frozen, Calhoun's corpse sickening beneath me as my breath grew shallow. I barely caught sight of my mate's golden curls as he zipped past me and ripped out Christophe's throat in a display of possession.

"He's mine, Christophe," Tristan whispered, his arm falling to his side as red droplets dripped from his fingertips like wax. "Only mine."

The last bit of light within Christophe's deranged mind faded and empty, he fell to the floor, a shadow of what he'd been. My body shuddered violently and I knew I'd shifted back, but the action had been involuntary. Almost as if my body knew what I needed even if my physical form didn't.

I hadn't realized I was still practically on top of Calhoun until Tristan wrapped an arm around my waist and pulled me away. "Tristan—"

He buried his face in the crook of my shoulder. "He was actually going to try and take you from me. Again. I couldn't let him. Just couldn't."

I stroked his head, remnants of blood from my hand staining his beautiful hair. "The Sidhee, do you think they know?"

Everything was far too quiet in the midst of war. A surreal moment where nothing existed.

"About Calhoun's death? Yes. Surely as your Kuro are connected to you, the demons were connected to him. And—"

I looked into Tristan's confused face. "What?"

"There's no way."

Without an explanation, I let my mate keep a firm grip on my wrist as we barreled through the rest of the castle. The door we'd chosen led directly to the garden and the largest of the lakes. My Kuro were fighting viciously, each and every one of them in their true form. I instantly recognized Micky because Ciaran was seated on his back like a true Asrai prince. Had the moment not been so dire, I would've taken a picture just to preserve the beauty that was our world.

The Sidhee were having a difficult time escaping the water because every time their heavy boots tread on the slippery ground, a Kuro would sweep down and force them back. Shattered bits of glass meshed with the Dryma weapons my kind did not need, swirling in the water like a kaleidoscope of wreckage.

But despite the odds being stacked against the demons, they had done their fair share of damage.

I knew many of my kind were wounded, could see the blood dripping from their feathers as they continued to fight with every ounce of energy they could muster.

"It's not enough." The truth was heavy on my tongue.

I thought Tristan might've lost his mind because he was grinning. "Love, look." His arm was firm around my waist, but he pointed upward into the billowing sky. "They came."

Because my eyesight was still hazy after the stress of killing Calhoun, I didn't see what he referred to. When I did, I nearly lost my breath at the dazzling sight.

Hundreds of winged creatures were raining down from the sky like bolts of lightning. Their wings, so much paler than ours, were a stark contrast once they joined the fight.

Fight with the Dryma, I urged, placating the confused minds of the Kuro. *Draw the Sidhee back to the water.*

Tristan and Seth did not speak often, but at some point my mate must've relayed the plan because the Dryma charged straight for the water. Using their wings as a way to maintain balance, they picked through the water to reclaim their beloved weapons. Holding them high over their heads, they joined the fight, and chaos ensued.

A clink of metal at my hip reminded me Tristan and I were not meant to be bystanders. With my form once again changing to serve as my weapon, he had a sword to serve as his. Our wings fluttered together madly, like the ring of our hearts, beating and joining until we could never be separated. Even our minds were now working as one, creating a silent bond in which the Dryma realized our plan just from our body language, although I was certain Tristan was communicating with them the same way I was with my kind.

Tristan had more stamina than me but remained close out of his desire to protect. When two other swans came to an unceremonious landing beside me, it took me a moment to realize Zain and Tomas had joined me. Another figure, still human, landed gracefully beside me.

"Joel," I breathed. "You're here."

He flashed me a shy smile. "Of course, Kanji. I have to protect you."

With my three friends and Tristan encircling me, they left little for me to do. The Sidhee knew they were defeated, having been outnumbered and knowing their prince had been slain. Knowing the truth weighed them down and with one final attempt, they were driven mercilessly back into the water.

"Now!" Tristan and I screamed in unison.

Every swan and Dryma sprouted from the water as Ciaran's magic began to take place. Like a cyclone, the Sidhee were forced into the spiraling holes he created in the portal. The moonstones we'd placed on the surrounding trees glowed blue and even in the madness, not seeing them was impossible.

Things moved quickly. Screaming ensued and I lost sight of every creature apart from Micky and Ciaran. Other Kuro who had been stationed at the portals came flying back, still in their swan form. Rushing down, the scouts joined the ranks and in a blinding surge of unrelenting power, the Sidhee were drowned in their own disarray and forced back through the portal.

Trying to catch their breath, the hordes of Dryma flew to the ground. Most of them wore little apart from the torn clothes they'd worn in the Sidhee world. With little time between their awakening and making it to the fight, I was glad their pride had taken a back seat to realizing what must be accomplished.

Seth landed on his feet and I expected him to speak, but he let another Dryma almost identical in features step in front of him. When he spoke, I could see the startling resemblance to my mate. "Tristan, brother, without your quick thinking and planning, we would've lost our home. And perhaps... not even have awoken."

Bastard, Zain growled, *Kanji, you—*

Tristan, as always, beat Zain even without hearing his thoughts. "Thank you, Sampson, but I fear you are wrong."

The princely Dryma gave a confused expression, holding fast to his sword as though afraid of the swans surrounding him. "The Kuro prince, Kanji, is the one who saved you."

I almost gagged. "No, I just helped."

"Without Kanji, you could very well be back in the Sidhee world. And it was his finding the Asrai boy, Ciaran, who made this possible."

Sampson rubbed his jaw thoughtfully, and it was then I saw the true signs of tiredness behind his eyes. The Dryma were exhausted, as we all were.

"No more fighting," I stated, brushing past Tomas who, like the others, had returned to his human form. "My kind are free and so are you."

Whatever fight was left in the Dryma wasn't about to be wasted on reinstating our enslavement. Houses needed to be reclaimed, trees needed to be healed, and more importantly, the Dryma had yet to learn how to live on their own. Without needing the trees to survive, they no long required protection and I could see that realization coming to life in Sampson's eyes.

"We have a lot to talk about, little brother." The elder Dryma finally resheathed his sword. "But after we've had time to rest."

"The Kuro have been staying here," Tristan pointed out. "And I expect we owe them that much until such a time when they choose to leave."

There were no arguments. "We must heal and recover. Who occupies the castle is the least of my worries. Not to mention—" Sampson leaned in so his words were concealed from the other Dryma. "Considering what you have done for us, I expect I have a lot to make up for."

Having said all he needed to, Sampson waved his hand and the fairies quickly set to work righting the wrong.

"Kanji." Chiaki burst into my arms like a bird running from a predator. "I can help heal too."

"But of course." I smiled. "We need your skills."

Tomas and Zain were speaking eagerly to Joel, but their eyes stopped when Ciaran and Micky approached. Even in their acceptance, I could see how Ciaran was a fearful presence. He had just managed to squash an entire army of Sidhee.

"Wait until you see what we've done inside," I said slowly. "In fact, we need to go clean up before any other Kuro or Dryma sees."

"Leave disposal to me." Zain wrung his hands. "I'm only sorry I didn't get to Christophe first."

"How did you know I was talking about him?"

"Please. The moment I didn't see him in the water, I knew he had some scheme to get you."

"But you let me go anyway?"

Zain closed his eyes. I wasn't sure if the hand on my shoulder was for my comfort or his. "Yes. I trust you, my prince. After all, I always knew you would save us."

His declaration took me back to a past time, an earlier time. Despite being enslaved and having no foreseeable future, we'd had each other and with nothing else to consider, our friendship had developed accordingly. No matter what I chose, the Kuro closest to me now were never going to leave my side.

Our lives may have been easier, but freedom was what made loyalty that much stronger.

Once Ciaran was in my arms, his face pressed against my thumping heart, I allowed my eyes to close as Tristan took possession of my lips.

"We're being watched."

Tristan simply shrugged and gathered Ciaran and me into his arms. "Let them. My kind needs to know how much things are going to change. I promised you your freedom and I plan to keep my word."

A giggle escaped my lips, causing Tristan to arch his eyebrow.

"Don't believe me?"

"No, I do. All that matters is that you keep me."

"Me too," Ciaran chimed, his pale hair fading back to a light blond.

My mate's green eyes flickered with intense pride and desire. "Forever."

EPILOGUE

Three Months Later

"IS THERE anything you need me to grab?"

I shoved Ciaran's pillow into the back seat before straightening and turning to face my mate. Tristan was wearing a pair of loose canvas pants and a tank top that made his arms look absolutely glorious. With skin as tanned as the sun and hair like gold, I wasn't surprised humans stared.

With fifty houses, our community was the largest of the gated communities in the area. In Florida, there wasn't a shortage of wealth or retirees, but considering we didn't completely isolate, humans got their fair share of staring at Tristan.

And the other Dryma when they came down too.

I wasn't exactly sure how much the Dryma had dished out to buy the gated community so my kind could migrate here during the winter, and I wasn't sure I wanted to see all those numbers. The best we did was reserve ten of the larger houses for the fairies if they ever wanted to visit in the future.

So far, only Seth and a few younger Dryma had taken me up on the offer.

After the complete and utter destruction of Pasky, there had been a month of work. Every night, Kuro and Dryma alike passed out, sometimes in the same room. Over time, pride had fallen to the wayside in order to make room for our world's survival.

We had a long way to go and the reality was we might never be friends, but as long as our survival was ensured, we had hundreds of years to work up to it.

Probably my influence as prince and Tristan's as the royal advisor helped too.

"Nope." I wiped my hands on my pants. "I think we've got enough to get back to Pasky. Probably need to stop and get food a couple times."

"The way Ciaran eats," Tristan joked, "try a million."

"Where is he anyway?"

"Saying goodbye to his friends."

I wrinkled my nose. Apart from Micky and Shinji, Ciaran was only interested in hanging out with the alligators that lived in the murky ponds. I had thought a month and a half of living here would've changed that, but apparently he was as content as ever.

"Speaking of dangerous animals." I sighed. "I totally forgot to pack the cooler with all our perishables."

Alligator meat was not one of them, but Tristan and I had considered buying some exotic jerky until Ciaran begged us not to. That was that.

"Be right back."

"I can—"

"Stay and talk to your friend."

Tomas had already taken off with the Kuro who would be flying and as far as I knew, Zain was leading the driving envoy with his precious Jeep.

Looking up, I saw Joel and a cautious Seth hanging back.

"Hey, what's up? Thought you left already?"

"Was going to, but I had something I wanted to ask first." Joel nervously ran a hand through his light brown hair.

"What?"

"I'm going to check on my brother," Seth mumbled, obviously trying to give us some privacy. "Don't leave until I get back, Joel."

"I won't." His expression was as soft as a marshmallow.

"So you two finally got together?" I teased.

"Don't even start."

"Oh, why not? Clearly he's protective of you."

Joel sighed. "I'm not coming back next winter."

My laughter died. "What?"

"I'm going to stay in Pasky."

"Even in the winter?"

"Even then."

"Why?" I finally asked.

"Some Kuro should be there. If it's our home too, then you should have eyes and ears on the place."

"Is this about Seth?"

Joel looked guilty as he leaned against my car. "He won't come out and say it, but I know he spends more time away from Pasky than he should. Seth is one of the elder princes, you know? It's hard on him."

"So you would sacrifice your health?"

He raised an eyebrow. "If Tristan said he couldn't come here every winter, what would you do?"

It had actually been Tristan's idea to come here every cold season, so I knew it would never happen. Still, I understood where Seth was coming from. "Being without him would make me sicker than any cold weather could."

"Exactly."

"So... was that all you had to ask?"

"No. It's about Ciaran."

I blinked. "What about him?"

"Seth and I are going to buy a really big house in Pasky. Actually, he's going to have one made for me." Joel blushed until he looked like one of Tristan's scarlet flowers. "That way I can continue to take care of orphaned Kuro and I was wondering, do you want Ciaran to stay with me?"

Tristan and I had never come out and said we were keeping the Asrai. We'd just assumed everyone knew because the two of us did. "We're going to adopt him, Joel. Just as soon as we can figure out how to do that without birth certificates and stuff."

"Are you sure that's a good idea? He was thrown away for being male, but one day, the Asrai might come back for him. Do you want to have to deal with that?"

"I've dealt with everything that's come from Tristan and his problems. What kind of person would I be if I ran from those I loved?"

The corner of Joel's lips ever so slowly turned upward. "I'm glad to hear it."

"You were testing me, weren't you?"

"I love you, man," Joel teased back, "but I will always look out for kids' best interests. Just who I am."

"Must be why Seth adores you."

"I wouldn't go that far."

"He's building you a house."

"Fair point."

"Think I grabbed everything. Do we have room?" Tristan asked, placing a large blue cooler at my feet. I'd sensed his presence several minutes ago but he'd given me privacy.

"Give it here." Seth easily swung the cooler around like a mere pebble. "We have room in ours."

"Every Kuro already leave?" I asked, mentally saying goodbye to our overly cheery yellow house. "Except for us, of course?"

"Yes, we're the last."

"Say goodbye to your friends?" I asked Ciaran.

He gave me a look that made me want to cry. "Yes."

"See you guys there." Seth somehow balanced the cooler and managed to pull a continuously blushing Joel into his arms.

Without the constant laughter and frequent visits from Chiaki, Aiden, Micky, Shinji, Zain, Tomas, and Joel, the silence was all-consuming.

"Worried about something, love?" Tristan pressed his nose into my temple, inhaling softly.

I shook my head. "They'll be there waiting. Forever."

"And always."

Ciaran held one of my hands tight, Tristan the other. My heart had been tested and nearly broken, but the two very different beings who held me now were the reason I had managed to piece myself back together.

Without my mate or our child, happiness would be nonexistent.

This feeling... this is what true freedom was.

And I would never let it go.

ANA RAINE writes because she loves to believe in magic, dragons, and that there is more to life than what human eyes can see. Ana lives in Michigan where, when it's not snowy and wet, there are beautiful state parks and lakes to visit. When she was eighteen, she married her best friend and they live with their two cats, Mason and Misaki. Ana has celiac disease, but that hasn't stopped her from learning how to cook and bake so she can eat tasty treats. Fudge, enchiladas, and anything involving yucca/cassava are her absolute favorite.

Ana has studied in Osaka, Japan where she learned about theater and drama. She would love to go back after she is sure her Japanese is efficient enough. Ana loves anything to do with foxes, especially Arctic foxes. One day, Ana will find a way to incorporate her love of foxes into a novel, but until then, she'll stay focused on fairies, shape shifters, and mythology.

Feel free to stop by her blog for tasty recipes, freebies, and more.

Blog: anarainebooks.blogspot.com
Twitter: @AuthorAnaRaine
Email: anaraine@rocketmail.com

Anima: Book One

Kanji is the last royal Kuro swan, an ancient race who once served the demonic Sidhee. The Kuro were betrayed and given as slaves to the Dryma fairies. When a Dryma is born, his soul attaches to a tree, and to sustain their lives, the Dryma conscript the Kuro to protect their woods. In their servitude, the Kuro are languishing and dying off. Kanji is desperate to reunite his people with their stolen wings, but the task seems impossible.

When Kanji discovers a plan to unite the Sidhee and the Dryma, he tricks the Sidhee prince and attends a masked ball in disguise. There he meets Prince Tristan, who is nothing like the other fairies. Kind and compassionate, Tristan has a plan to free the Dryma from their dependence on the trees—and their need of the Kuro's protection. It could mean freedom for Kanji's people, but it might also mean choosing between them and the life of the fairy who is—impossibly—his mate.

When Tristan is wounded in battle and left for dead, his survival depends on the success of his experiments. Can Kanji dare to believe, or must he come to terms with the loss of his mate?

www.dreamspinnerpress.com

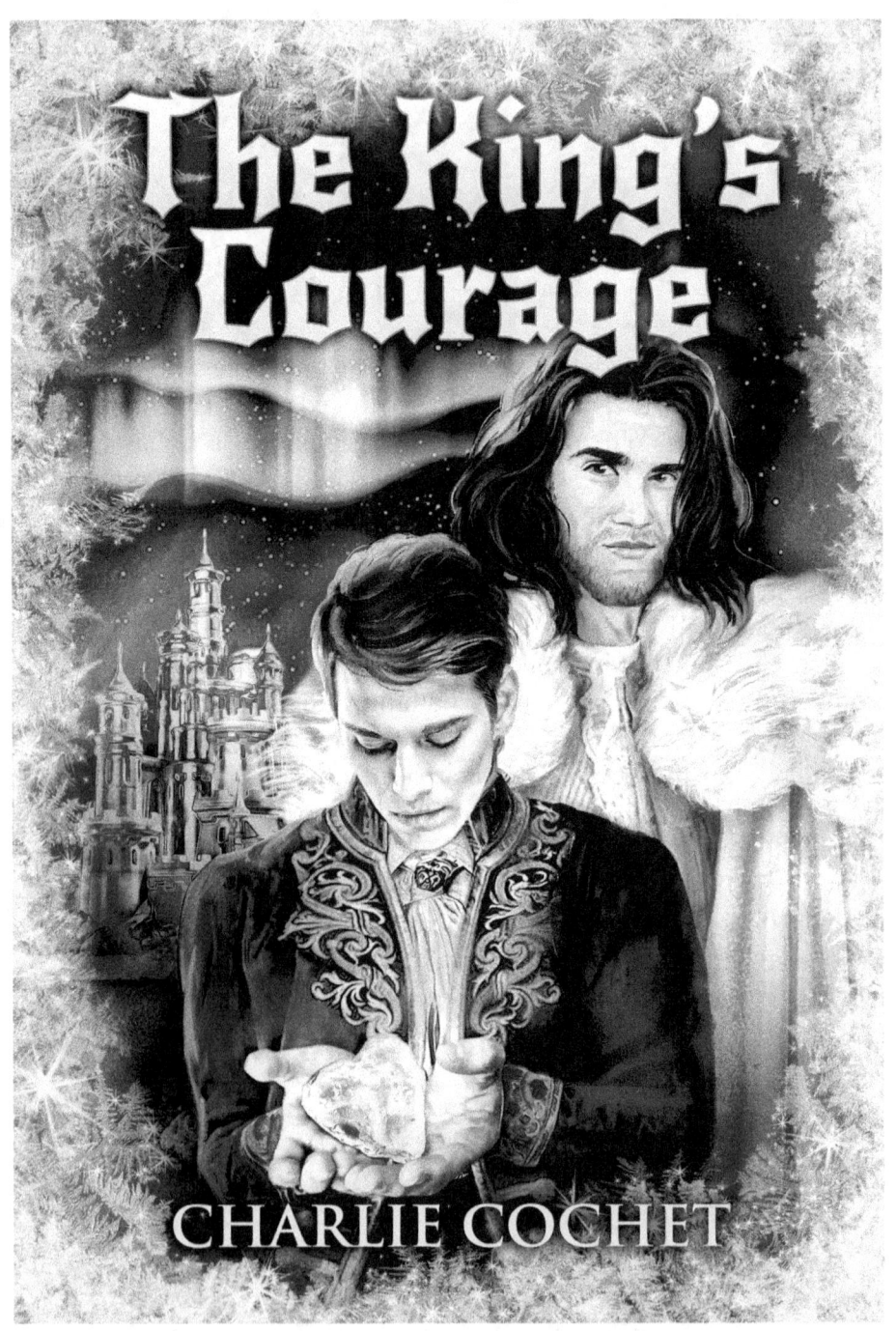

The King's Courage

CHARLIE COCHET

www.dreamspinnerpress.com

Also from Dreamspinner Press

DREAMSPUN BEYOND

MAGE OF INCONVENIENCE

Parker Foye

Can they find the magic in a practical union?

FOR **MORE** OF THE **BEST GAY ROMANCE**

dreamspinnerpress.com

www.ingramcontent.com/pod-product-compliance
Lightning Source LLC
Chambersburg PA
CBHW070119260626
47160CB00004B/1537